TREVOR DOUGLAS

Cold Trail

Bridgette Cash Mystery Thriller Series (Book 2)

Version 1.6

First edition

This book was professionally typeset on Reedsy.
Find out more at reedsy.com

I am occasionally asked if the character, Bridgette Cash, is based on a real-life person.

While Bridgette is a fictitious character (except perhaps in my mind), many of her character traits, principles and ethics are drawn from three women who I admire and respect greatly. This book is dedicated to Annette, Pam, and Clare, for the wonderful example they continue to display in their day-to-day lives.

Contents

Chapter 1

Bridgette slowed her Honda Civic down to little more than a crawl as she saw the warning sign for black ice ahead. Tired from the two-and-a-half-hour drive from her home city of Hartbourne, she was determined not to become another accident statistic as she started the steep descent down the winding road. She saw the first glimpses of the town through the fir trees as she came around a bend and guessed it would take another ten minutes of careful driving to reach the township. She thought about the week ahead — it was an unusual assignment for a rookie detective, but one she was looking forward to.

Spotting a lookout about halfway down the mountain, she decided to stop for a moment to take in the view of the town she would call home for the next two weeks. After parking in a tiny gravel parking lot, the bitter chill of the wind had her reaching for her coat as she stepped out of the car. She buttoned the garment as she walked across to the edge of the lookout to admire the view of the mountain range and valley below. She leaned on the wooden railing as she surveyed the long wide valley below, most of which had been cleared of trees for housing and small farms. In the overcast conditions, the lengthening shadows of the day drained the color out of her view, leaving the town of Sanbury coated in a somber, blue-gray hue. The township was spread out and the number of houses that had smoke spiraling out of their chimneys surprised her. It reminded her of simpler times, and she imagined many of the residents must still use local timber from the surrounding forests to keep them warm.

The official start of winter was still a week away, but she could already see a light dusting of snow forming in pockets of the valley just outside the township. Bridgette knew Sanbury had the coldest state winter temperatures and tried to imagine what it would look like in coming weeks when covered in snow. She felt her phone vibrating in her pocket and checked the name of the caller. She frowned when she realized it was her boss. Chief Inspector Felix Delray wouldn't be ringing this late on a Sunday unless it was important.

"Hi, Chief."

"How are you, Bridgette?"

Bridgette stuck her free hand in one of her coat pockets as she replied, "Cold."

"I take it you've arrived then?"

"Almost. I'm currently stopped at a lookout about ten minutes east of town and taking in the view."

"And freezing?"

Bridgette laughed and replied, "Pretty much."

"I won't keep you long then. I just got a call from Corey Payne, the Sanbury Chief of Police. He's moved your morning meeting forward to eight o'clock and insists you see him before you do anything else."

"Okay. That shouldn't be a problem."

"I know Payne's not exactly enthusiastic about Hartbourne Metro conducting an investigation on his turf, but since getting a personal call from our Commissioner, he's agreed to cooperate. If he gives you grief, you let me know."

"I'll try to keep a low-profile Chief. I'll read the reports and get as much background information as I can before I do anything else. That should keep me busy for a couple of days without ruffling any feathers."

It was Delray's turn to laugh.

She frowned and asked, "What's so funny?"

"If you don't mind me saying, you seem to have a knack for ruffling feathers whether you mean to or not."

Bridgette rolled her eyes as the corners of her mouth threatened to turn into a smile. Only just out of her probationary period as a detective with the Homicide Unit, her start at Hartbourne Metro had been far more dramatic than she would have liked. Within days of joining the force she had broken open a murder case. Following Delray's lead of not strictly following the procedural manual, she had earned the wrath of Assistant Commissioner Cunningham despite catching a killer who had murdered seven women.

Now, about as popular with Cunningham as Delray was, she realized her boss's attempt at humor and declared, "Chief, I am hoping for a quiet two weeks."

"Aren't we all? Remember I'm here if you need me Bridgette and the Commissioner is more than happy to pick up the phone if you get any grief."

Bridgette replied vaguely, "Good to know Chief," as she stared down into the valley.

Sensing her distraction, Delray asked, "Are you okay Bridgette?"

"I'm just taking in the view. The Sacred Mountains are much larger than I expected."

"Close to five thousand acres of uninhabited forest if memory serves."

As she surveyed the mountains in the distance, Bridgette

responded, "I'm not sure what I was expecting Chief..."

"No one's expecting you to find him, Bridgette — you know that's not what this is about."

"I know Chief."

"The Commissioner has every confidence in you and so do I. Rookie or not, anyone who can catch a serial killer on their first assignment has what it takes for this investigation."

"I appreciate your confidence Chief."

"You must be frozen, so I won't keep you. Let me know if you get any grief from Payne."

"Thanks, Chief, but I'm sure it will be fine."

They said their goodbyes and Delray disconnected.

Bridgette leaned on the railing again and stared out across the valley as she thought about John Tyson. As a recovering alcoholic, the detective had taken a twelve-month temporary transfer from Hartbourne Metro to Sanbury Police to help get his life back on track. By all reports, he had settled well into the small community and was happy in his new role. It had been almost four months since he had failed to show up for work one Monday morning. He'd made no contact with relatives or friends and his bank accounts remained untouched. The extensive search by the local Sanbury Police hadn't turned up any clue to his whereabouts. Nobody now expected he would be found alive, but the Commissioner wasn't prepared to process the final paperwork on one of his officers without a formal investigation by his own team.

Bridgette wondered what the week ahead would bring. As she stared out across the valley at the mountain range beyond, she wondered if he was out there somewhere? She'd heard of hikers who had gone missing in the Sacred Mountains for months and sometimes years before their bodies were discovered. Bridgette knew the chances of finding John Tyson, dead or alive, were slim, but she would leave no stone unturned. She'd never met Tyson, but from all reports, he was a good cop who deserved the best investigation she could muster.

* * *

Bridgette was relieved when she finally pulled up out front of the timber cottage that would be her home for the next two weeks. Her car was close to twenty years old and had developed several new rattles during the journey. She decided this was the last trip she would risk in the vehicle outside the city limits and made a mental note to start searching for a replacement car as soon as she returned home. She sat in the car studying the house for a moment listening to the tick of the engine as it cooled down. The structure was set back from the road on a large block that made it look small. The white exterior needed a coat of paint and the carport that butted up to the right-hand side of the structure had three wooden packing crates stacked on top of one another as if waiting for removal. The house was part of a cluster of three set in a row on an unsealed laneway several minutes out of the township in a rural setting. She didn't need to consult her map again to know this was the house she had rented. Bridgette looked around as she got out of the car but saw no sign of life in any of the other houses. Pulling a key from her pocket that she had picked up from a real estate agent on the way through town, she walked up a cement pathway and onto the house's tiny front porch. After inserting the key in the front door, she turned the key to her right and raised her eyebrows as she heard the soft metallic click of the door unlocking.

She whispered, "Home sweet home," with no enthusiasm

as she stepped into a small living room with worn carpet and furniture that looked like it had come straight out of the nineteen-seventies. The air smelt musty and stale, but she figured leaving the front door open for a while would fix that. She walked up the small hallway and counted off three small bedrooms and a bathroom — more than adequate for her needs. She returned and explored a tired kitchen which linked to the main living area. The refrigerator (empty) seemed to work, but she wasn't sure anyone had cooked on the stove in this century. Relieved to see a microwave built into one of the cupboard areas, she resigned herself to surviving on frozen meals if she couldn't get the stove to work.

Bridgette sighed as she took one last look around the kitchen. She didn't plan to do much more than eat and sleep here and it would suffice for the two-week period.

She had seen enough and decided it was time to retrieve her bags from the car. As she stepped back into the living room, she was confronted by a man standing in the doorway of the house. She gasped as she looked up into his face. He was huge — close to six foot five and overweight. He had a receding light brown hairline and an impassive look which she found difficult to read. She guessed he was around thirty-five and felt a rush of adrenaline flood through her body as he raised a shotgun and pointed it at her chest. She silently admonished herself not to panic and slowly raised her hands and waited for him to make the next move.

Chapter 2

Bridgette found breathing impossible and the shock of being confronted by the man caused an instant throbbing sensation in her ears in time with her heartbeat. The man held the shotgun perfectly still — the twin barrels remaining fixed on the center of her chest. She estimated he was about fifteen feet from her and knew trying to run or dive for cover was futile. If he had been holding a pistol, it might have been possible to avoid being hit by a single bullet, but shotguns were different. The load of small steel or lead pellets was designed to spread out quickly to disable their intended target. She had seen photographs of how shotgun wounds left their victims in enormous pain, slowly dying from organ shutdown, shock and blood loss.

Bridgette braced for the gun's discharge and wondered how much pain she would experience before it was all over? As she imagined being cut to pieces by hundreds of tiny projectiles, she debated screaming for help, but decided that would only hasten the inevitable. Seconds seemed like minutes as she looked up into the face of the silhouetted man as he stood in the doorway. She tried to stay calm and conveyed no aggression as she kept her hands high above her head.

The man cocked his head and in a high-pitch, almost child-like voice asked, "What you doin' here?"

Barely able to breathe, Bridgette kept her hands high and responded as calmly as she could, "I'm supposed to be living here for the next two weeks."

The man frowned as if trying to process her answer.

Not wanting to start an argument, Bridgette added, "I'm a police officer. I'm here to look for John Tyson."

The man nodded but made no move to lower the gun. "They ain't gonna find him."

Bridgette sensed there was something unusual about the man and asked, "Did you know John?"

The man shook his head but offered no further explanation as he kept the gun pointed at her chest.

Bridgette waited a moment for him to say something else, but when he stayed silent, she tried to steer the conversation. "I never met John, but the people I work with say he's a good man. We're all worried about him because he's been missing so long."

"He was gone before I got back. I've only been out for two weeks."

Bridgette nodded as if she knew what he was talking about. Although unable to relax, she suspected the man was more curious than aggressive and asked, "Do you live around here?"

The man nodded and said, "Next door."

"My name's Bridgette."

"You're not from around here."

"No, I'm from Hartbourne."

"You a Hartbourne cop then."

Bridgette wondered if the man had an impaired intellect but didn't think lying would help and answered honestly. "Yes, I'm from Hartbourne Metropolitan Police. I've been asked to come and help find him."

"Everyone says he's dead."

Bridgette nodded as she replied, "They may be right, but I'm here to find out for sure."

"Jack Sutton said he got lost in the mountains, but I wasn't here, so I don't know."

Bridgette sensed the man's tone was changing to be more conversational.

As casually as she could, she asked, "Can I lower my hands?"

The man nodded and said, "I never known anyone called Bridgette before."

Bridgette breathed a small sigh of relief as she lowered her hands. The man still had the weapon pointed at her and she knew she couldn't afford to relax. She didn't feel like they had connected enough for her to ask him to point the weapon somewhere else.

Instead, she asked, "What's your name?"

"Hughey Warren, but my real name's Hugh."

Bridgette forced a smile and said, "Well, I've never met anyone called Hughey before."

The man beamed and seemed to stick his chest out with pride. Bridgette saw the gun move slightly and was concerned it might accidentally discharge.

Now or never she thought. "Hughey, now that we know each other, can you put the gun down?"

To her surprise, Hughey mumbled an apology and gently leaned the shotgun up against the inside wall of the living room next to the door. Bridgette tried to hide her relief as she racked her brain for what to say next.

She needn't have bothered as Hughey asked, "You got any bags you want bringing in?"

Bridgette's instant reaction was to say no to get the man and his gun out of the house as soon as possible. But now convinced he was intellectually disabled, she found herself saying, "I've got two bags and a small box of groceries."

Hughey was gone before he had finished saying, "I'll get them," leaving Bridgette standing alone in the living room trying to make sense of what had just happened.

He appeared a moment later with the two bags and gently placed them in the middle of the living room. Before she could thank him, he announced he would get the groceries and disappeared again. She stood shaking her head in disbelief as she watched the man lumber back out to her car and gently retrieve her grocery box from the back seat. Bridgette stiffened slightly as Hughey walked back into the house.

As he walked past her towards the kitchen, he said, "I'll just put this in the kitchen for you."

Bridgette watched as Hughey put the grocery box down on the kitchen bench before returning to the living room. She wondered what would happen next as he stopped three feet from her. She studied his face for a moment. He seemed anything but aggressive and it almost felt as though Hughey was seeking her approval.

She thanked Hughey for his help and then added, "I think I'll be okay for now Hughey."

Hughey nodded, and to Bridgette's relief, headed for the door.

He paused in the doorway and looked back. "I live next door. If you need anything, just come over. Okay?"

Bridgette pointed at the shotgun that was still leaning up against the wall. "Have you forgotten something?"

Hughey looked down and mumbled a sorry as he picked up the weapon.

Bridgette's curiosity got the better of her. "Hughey, is the gun loaded?"

Hughey shrugged and said, "I don't know. Mom used to use it a long time ago to keep the foxes away from our chickens."

Bridgette nodded and asked, "Do you always point guns at total strangers?"

Hughey looked embarrassed as he replied quietly, "No."

"Then why did you point it at me?"

Hughey swallowed and wouldn't look at Bridgette.

When he didn't answer, Bridgette pressed him, "Hughey, why did you point the gun at me?"

"I was scared."

Bridgette was taken aback by the answer. "Scared?"

Hughey nodded. "I thought you might have been robbing the place..."

Bridgette wondered if Hughey had other issues apart from just a low IQ. She was tired and didn't want to continue the conversation any longer, but neither did she want to be rude.

She thought for a moment and then said, "Hughey, if you ever suspect someone is breaking in, just call the police — okay?"

Hughey wouldn't look her in the eye but nodded as if he understood. Even though he could barely squeeze through her doorway, Bridgette felt like she was lecturing a small child.

Hughey mumbled, "I'm going now," and disappeared leaving Bridgette standing alone in the middle of the living room. She shook her head and then closed the front door, taking care to make sure it was locked. She didn't think Hughey would be a problem, but she wasn't about to take unnecessary risks either.

* * *

Bridgette spent the next half hour unpacking and then settled in on a slightly lumpy sofa in the living room with a peppermint tea. She would have preferred something a little stronger but didn't feel inclined to drive back into the township after her encounter with her new neighbor. As she relaxed, she noticed it was getting dark and got up to close the front curtains. She walked to the window and peered out into the gloom as evening closed in and noticed a white police car driving up the road. It stopped at the house next to hers and she watched as two grim looking uniformed police officers got out of the car and drew their guns.

Bridgette frowned and thought of Hughey. She remembered how he had said he'd only been 'out for two weeks' and had wondered whether that meant prison or something else. Curious, she opened the front door and stepped out onto the porch. She was partially camouflaged from Hughey's front door by a large bush set in a garden bed between the two properties. She could see the two officers rapping on Hughey's front door, demanding he open up. A moment later, a porch light came on and she saw Hughey's enormous frame step out onto the landing.

Bridgette was left puzzled as the two officers pushed Hughey up against the front wall of the house to handcuff him. She could hear Hughey howling as the officers holstered their guns and pushed him down the pathway towards the car. She frowned as one officer pulled a baton from his service belt and struck Hughey hard across his back and demanded he move quicker. Hughey howled again and pleaded with the officer to stop as he was roughly pushed towards the car. From her position, she could not see any reason for the force. Hughey was doing his best to hurry, but his lumbering gait and the handcuffs seemed to make it difficult for him to keep up with the two officers. As they reached the car, one officer stepped forward and opened the rear door of the vehicle. The other officer pushed Hughey forward and demanded he get in.

She watched as Hughey tried to comply, but the large man was clumsy and had difficulty lowering his head sufficiently to get in the car. Bridgette watched in horror as the officer standing behind Hughey raised his baton again and struck her new neighbor across the left ear with a sickening blow. Dazed and disorientated, Hughey groaned and collapsed as the officer pushed him roughly into the car.

Bridgette had seen enough and yelled "Hey," as she stepped off the porch.

The two officers spun around and looked in her direction, at first surprised and then angry they had been observed.

Bridgette stopped a few feet short of their car and glared at both men before saying, "That force was totally unnecessary — he was fully cooperating."

The shorter and slightly older of the two officers took two steps towards her and then stopped again.

He was slightly shorter than Bridgette and pointed a pudgy finger at Hughey who was now sprawled out on the backseat of the car. "You know who this is?"

Bridgette replied evenly, "His name is Hugh Warren and as of today, he's my neighbor."

The officer shook his head and said, "Up until two weeks ago he was locked up in maximum security where he belongs. His scumbag lawyer got him out on a technicality, but he'll be going back inside very soon. He broke parole today by not checking in with Sanbury Police, so we've done the community a big favor by getting him off the streets."

The other officer barked at Hughey to sit up straight as he slammed the rear door. Bridgette could see blood streaming from a gash on Hughey's left ear as the frightened man sat up and looked at her with pleading eyes.

The first officer fixed the baton back to his service belt and rested his hands on his hips as he slowly looked Bridgette up and down.

"This doesn't concern you. Go back to your house and leave us to do our job."

"Your job doesn't include beating someone who clearly wasn't resisting arrest."

The officer took one more step toward her and in a slightly more aggressive tone said, "You're not from around here are you?"

"No."

"Then let me tell you how it works. We decide who's resisting arrest and we decide how it's dealt with."

Trying to control her anger as the cop leered at her, Bridgette replied, "It's guys like you who give cops a bad name."

The cop's mood darkened as he snapped, "No, it's people like you who meddle that give us a bad name."

"I'm not sure you'd be saying that if you'd been caught on video."

The stocky cop lunged forward and grabbed Bridgette by the shoulders. The move was slow and clumsy and could have been easily deflected but she decided it was unwise to escalate the situation any further. Stocky cop shoved her hard up against the rear of the squad car and kicked her legs apart.

After twisting her left arm up behind her back, she felt the cops free hand frisk her as he leaned forward and whispered, "You didn't film us, did you? Because if you did that would be a mistake..."

The cop spent a few moments searching her pockets and then groped her breasts before backing away.

He called out to his partner, "No phone."

Bridgette spun around and did her best to keep her composure. She wasn't about to give him the satisfaction of seeing her angry or upset.

With a satisfied grin, he said, "Around here, a police officer's word is highly regarded and without video, you've got squat."

The cop didn't wait for a reply and left Bridgette standing at the side of the road as he and his partner got into the squad car. She could hear Hughey crying as the vehicle's flashing lights were switched on and the car pulled slowly away from the curb. She walked into the middle of the road and watched as the car picked up speed before it disappeared around a bend in the road.

Bridgette stared into the darkness, barely believing what had happened. She breathed in slowly until she got her anger back under control. The cop's abuse of power and his juvenile attempt at groping her were unacceptable, but she was more worried about Hughey. Convicted criminal or not, vigilante justice was never the answer, and she wondered whether the cops would continue beating him or just lock him up when they got back to the station.

She whispered to herself, "Well there goes your early night," as she turned and walked back to her house to retrieve her car keys.

Chapter 3

The man stood looking out of the window of his office. It was almost dark, and he still hadn't heard a thing. He massaged his temple as he stared out into the gloom. It was becoming increasingly difficult to hold it all together, and he wasn't sure how much more he could take. He closed his eyes and breathed in deeply as he tried to calm his nerves, but nothing was working. He knew what he needed and walked back to his desk and sat down again. Now an almost reflex action, he opened the bottom drawer and pulled out a bottle of whiskey. Long gone were the days of savoring a quality single malt in the quiet of an evening — this was all about survival.

He pulled a blister pack of tiny pink pills from his top drawer. Two left — they would barely get him through until tomorrow, but they would have to do. He would see a doctor in the morning who he knew, for a premium fee would write him a script for anything he wanted. He poured the remaining whiskey into a dirty shot glass and after popping the last two pills into his mouth; he drained the glass in one gulp. He closed his eyes as the liquid fired up his throat and then swallowed. It would be at least ten minutes before the pills started to work, and he planned to sit quietly until then — nobody would see him until he was back in control.

His smartphone buzzed on his desk.

He checked the number as he picked up the phone and said, "You should have called hours ago."

The voice on the phone was as calm.

"Some things can't be rushed."

"Did you get it done?"

"Yes, contracts will be signed on Friday."

The man massaged his temple again. "Friday is too long — we need to get this done tomorrow or Tuesday at the latest."

"We've been over this before. I can't be seen to be taking shortcuts or people will get suspicious."

The man declared, "I can't take much more of this."

The voice continued in a soothing, but firm tone, "We both know what's riding on this, and we don't want to attract any unwarranted attention."

Their conversation stalled while the man thought about the week ahead. He wished he had more pink pills.

The voice on the phone said, "I'll be back in town tomorrow. We'll discuss what happens once the contract is signed, and the transfer goes through. Friday will be my last day in Sanbury. After this, I'll be disappearing for good."

The man stopped massaging his temple for a moment. "I just want this finished."

The voice said, "You need to hold it together for five more days."

The line went dead. The man got up from his chair again and walked over to the window. He could feel the pills working and took another deep breath as he felt his body start to relax.

He looked down at the street one floor below. It was a Sunday evening and the town center was almost deserted. Tomorrow would be different and he would need to be ready to go through the whole charade again. He closed his eyes again and wondered if he could do it for another week.

He whispered, "You have no choice," and consoled himself with the prospect of being wealthy beyond his wildest dreams before the week was out.

Feeling energized by the pills, he returned to his desk and locked the whiskey bottle and shot glass in the bottom drawer. He scanned his desk as he did every night to make sure he'd left nothing incriminating behind before pulling his coat off the back of his desk chair. He walked out to the general office and turned all the lights off and set the alarm before heading for the exit. He paused at the front door and looked back through the office he had called home for over fifteen years. On Friday, he would walk away from everything he had ever known. He admonished himself — now was not the time to be sentimental. He had chosen this path, and nothing could change that now. He wondered how long it would be before they all knew. He figured he would be gone one or two days at the most before their secret was out.

Chapter 4

Bridgette pulled up across the road from the Sanbury Police Station and sat for a moment with the engine running as she studied the low set single story building. Apart from the small, blue police neon sign out front and a few lights on in the main reception area, the rest of the building looked dark and deserted. She could see only one patrol car out front, but it was a newer model Ford than the squad car that had picked up Hughey. Bridgette twisted her head and stared down the long double wide driveway that ran down the side of the building. She could see no sign of any other cars parked in the shadows and hoped there was a parking area around the back — her worst fear was the cops had taken Hughey somewhere else to continue the beating.

She switched the engine off and checked her watch as she opened the door. It was almost six p.m. and she knew they would likely only have a skeleton crew on duty on a Sunday evening. She wondered if this would work against her as she pushed through the front glass doors to the building. Bridgette entered a small foyer area replete with white plastic waiting chairs, linoleum floor, and signage that declared the Sanbury Police Force was a caring part of the local community. She scanned the office area beyond the service counter but couldn't see anyone and tapped once on a bell that was taped to the countertop. She thought about how different this was from the city police stations in Hartbourne. At this time on a Sunday evening, they would still be bustling with life. Finally, a young uniformed police officer with a bad case of facial acne appeared through a rear door and called out, "Can I help you?"

Bridgette suppressed an urge to be rude and replied, "Yes you can."

The young officer waited for Bridgette to say something, but when she remained quiet, he picked up on the cue and made his way through the office to the front counter.

"What can I do for you?"

"Did two officers bring in a man by the name of Hughey Warren a few minutes ago?"

"I'm sorry Ma'am, but we don't discuss police matters with members of the public."

"I witnessed the arrest and I'd like to make a statement."

With a wary look, the officer asked, "And what is the nature of your statement?"

Bridgette twisted her mouth into a grimace and responded, "Well that depends."

The young officer frowned and replied, "Depends on what?"

Bridgette leaned forward and said, "On whether I get to speak to the arresting officers."

Bridgette let the sentence hang in the air as she held the officer's stare.

The officer frowned again and growled, "Wait here," and then walked back through the main office.

Bridgette waited for close to two minutes before the rear door opened again. The young officer reappeared, followed by the stocky cop who'd beaten Hughey and groped her. Bridgette watched the two men as they walked through the office — the young officer wouldn't make eye contact with Bridgette, while the stocky cop glared at her with a look of contempt.

The stocky cop took the lead when they reached the counter and said, "What's this about a statement?"

"I want to see Hughey Warren for five minutes. He's intellectually disabled and someone needs to apprise him of his rights, particularly that he's entitled to phone his lawyer."

The stocky cop stuck his hands on his hips and let out a short laugh.

"There is absolutely no chance you'll be getting anywhere near Hughey Warren tonight or any other time soon for that matter. I told you before, this is none of your business."

Bridgette kept calm. "Then I want to make a formal statement."

The stocky cop shook his head and with a look of amusement replied, "You don't listen, do you? I told you before, a cop's word carries a lot of weight around here. Without video or a witness, nobody will believe you."

Bridgette held up her Hartbourne Metro police badge. "Maybe this changes things?"

The stocky cop features darkened as he locked eyes on Bridgette's badge.

He glared at Bridgette and said, "You're way out of line lady — you should have told us you were a cop when we made the arrest."

"Was that before or after you groped me?"

Stocky cop stepped up to the counter and through gritted teeth responded, "You've got no proof. It's your word against mine."

"I'll make this easy for you. You allow me five minutes with Hughey and provided he hasn't been beaten to a pulp already, I won't make any statements or press any charges."

Stocky cop fumed and then turned to Pimply cop. "Take her through to the holding cells. Five minutes with Warren and then get her out of here."

Without another word, stocky cop turned and walked out of the office.

* * *

Bridgette followed Pimply cop down a long, dimly lit corridor past a series of holding cells that were all empty. He stopped just short of the last cell and said, "I'll be back in five minutes," before turning and walking back down the corridor again.

She could hear a soft whimpering sound coming from the last cell and wondered what condition she would find Hughey in as she walked the last few steps. She stood looking at Hughey's enormous frame sprawled out on a narrow bed and was relieved to see he didn't appear to have been beaten any further.

"Hughey."

Hughey turned his head and looked up. He stared for a moment and then rubbed his eyes as he twisted his body and lowered his feet to the ground.

"What're you doing here Bridgette?"

"I came to make sure you're okay."

"They haven't fed me yet. Do you think I'll get dinner?"

Bridgette smiled to herself as she replied, "I'll make sure of it."

"They said I didn't come to the station today like I'm supposed to, but I did. I remember."

Bridgette squatted down close to the cell bars and said, "Maybe you only thought you came today? Sometimes we can forget to do things."

Hughey shook his head. "I got a calendar at home and cross off every day after I get home. Today, they made me wait for two hours before the policeman said I could go."

Bridgette thought for a moment. "So, tell me what happens Hughey."

Hughey explained in his own childlike English that he would arrive most mornings around nine a.m. and sit in one of the plastic chairs in the waiting room until a Sanbury Police officer came and registered his visit to the police station. It sounded to her like he often had to wait for hours as he explained how he had been buying a bag of chocolate chip cookies each day to keep him company while he waited.

Bridgette asked, "So Hughey, who did you see today?"

Hughey frowned and thought for a moment and then said, "I don't remember his name, but he had red hair. He made me wait until lunch time and then came up to the counter and told me I could go.

"Did he write anything down in a book?"

Hughey frowned again. "I didn't see him write anything."

"Do they normally write something down?"

Hughey nodded.

Bridgette wondered if the policeman had been sloppy and had forgotten to register the visit. With shift changes, she knew it was vital that everything was written down to avoid mistakes. She knew there was nothing more that she could do about his situation tonight but decided she would follow up on it tomorrow.

"Hughey, I'm only allowed five minutes with you tonight and my time's almost up. Have they allowed you to call your lawyer yet?"

Hughey shook his head and said, "Dan's coming on Tuesday to see me."

Bridgette nodded and said, "Would you mind if I called him and let him know you're here."

Hughey nodded and said, "Do you think he'll be mad at me? He told me I had to stay out of trouble and do everything the police said."

"I don't think he'll be mad at you. Do you have his phone number?"

Hughey shook his head, "I got his card stuck next to the phone at home. It's blue — I always ring him from there."

Bridgette thought for a moment. She didn't remember the police officers locking Hughey's front door but couldn't be sure.

"Hughey, do you have a spare key to your house?"

"Mom made me put one under the flower pot at the front door, just in case I lost mine. There are no flowers in the pot, but the key's still there."

"Would you mind if I go into your house and get your lawyer's phone number. I'd like to ring him if that's okay and let him know what happened."

Hughey frowned and looked at her with alarm and said, "Can you feed Molly for me as well? Her food is in the laundry."

Bridgette was about to ask who Molly was but heard the footsteps of Pimply cop as he walked back up the corridor. Her five minutes were up, and she didn't think it wise to ask for more time.

"Hughey, I have to go now. I'll make sure you get fed and I'll look after Molly okay?"

Hughey nodded.

Bridgette stood up again and looked down at Hughey, who was on the verge of tears again.

"I'll call Dan when I get home. You should hear from him tomorrow, okay?"

Hughey nodded and mumbled thanks before laying down on the bed again.

Pimply cop stopped short of Bridgette and said, “Time’s up.”

Bridgette looked down at Hughey and whispered, “Sleep tight Hughey,” and then followed Pimply cop back down the hallway.

Chapter 5

Bridgette pulled up in her driveway and switched the engine off. She sat in the car for a moment and thought about her first two hours in Sanbury. Having a shotgun pointed at her had been bad enough but being assaulted by a police officer and witnessing their brutal treatment of her new neighbor caused her to shake her head.

She whispered, "Surely it can't get any worse," as she got out of her car. She braced herself for what she would find next door. Even though Hughey had mentioned his mother, she was almost certain he was living alone. As she walked up the path to his front door, she took a deep breath as she thought about what she would find inside. Her expectations for a man with a low IQ and only just out of prison weren't high. She paused at the front door which was still ajar and knocked twice. When no one answered, she pushed the door open. The door opened straight onto a living room, which was similar in size to the one she had just moved into next door.

Everything was quiet. Bridgette called out into the shadows, "Hello, is anybody home?"

When no one answered, she stepped inside and switched on the light. She stared in disbelief as she looked around the living room. She had pictured a room strewn with dirty laundry, empty pizza boxes, cockroaches and other trappings that accompany unkempt males. Instead, she stared at a room that was impeccably neat and tidy. The furniture wasn't modern, but it was all neatly arranged. Against one wall was a single bookshelf full of titles all lined up in perfect rows she felt sure Hughey had never read. She walked over to a wall full of photos and stood looking at pictures of a childhood version of her neighbor, standing with two people she assumed were his mother and father. Bridgette moved to the adjoining kitchen and flicked on the light switch. Apart from one empty glass on a wooden drainage rack, the kitchen was also spotless.

Bridgette raised her eyebrows as she looked around at the cleanliness and order and whispered, "You surprise me Hughey."

She cocked her head to one side as she heard a soft whining sound coming from behind a door that lead off the kitchen. She knew the doorway would probably lead to the laundry if the layout was similar to her house and walked over and stopped to listen again. The whining noise continued, but it was now slightly louder.

Bridgette opened the door and looked in. The laundry was long and narrow and spotlessly clean like every other room in the house. At the end of the laundry, she could see a dog sitting on a blanket in a shallow cane basket. The dog stopped whining as soon as the door opened but made no move to get out of its bed. They stared at one another for a few seconds. Bridgette didn't know much about dogs but knew they could be quite territorial. She decided not to go in until she'd worked out whether the dog was aggressive or not.

She remembered Hughey asking her to feed Molly and called out the dog's name. The dog shifted in its basket but made no move to get out. She noticed Molly had a stocky build and was dark brown in color with white markings on its chest and front feet like it was wearing socks. The dog appeared to be shy and Bridgette called the dog's name again.

The dog shifted again, and this time wagged its tail but remained in the basket. Encouraged, Bridgette took one step inside the laundry and squatted down.

She held a hand out in front of her and called out a third time, "Molly."

This time the dog responded and nimbly jumped from its basket and walked towards her. The dog's tail continued to wag as it approached with its head slightly down. Bridgette wondered if the dog was shy or bashful as it stopped and sat in front of Bridgette, thumping its tail lightly on the floor.

Bridgette smiled and gently patted it on the head. "Hello Molly, I'm Bridgette."

The dog licked her fingers in response and Bridgette was sure she'd made a new friend. She scratched the dog behind its ears as she studied its features. She was fairly sure it was a Staffordshire Terrier as the dog closed its eyes to soak up the attention.

Bridgette whispered, "We better find you something to eat," and stood up to search for dog food. She opened a broom cupboard door but found nothing but neatly arranged mops, brooms and other cleaning equipment. Undeterred, Bridgette searched in a cupboard under the laundry sink and found what she was looking for.

She pulled out a bag of dog food and held it up in front of Molly, who wagged her tail vigorously.

Bridgette laughed at the dog's enthusiasm and poured a generous serving of the pellets into a dog bowl next to the dog's bed. Bridgette wondered about Molly's future if Hughey went back to prison as she watched the dog devour its food. The meal was finished in under a minute and Molly looked up at Bridgette eager for more.

Bridgette shook her head and said, "I think you've had enough," as she put the bag back in the cupboard.

Bridgette found it strange at first to be talking to a dog, but she seemed to sense her voice had a calming effect on the animal.

She stood with her hands on her hips wondering what she should do next. The laundry, like the rest of the house was immaculately clean. There was no litter box like cats had, so she knew Molly would need to be let out at some stage for a bathroom break. She wondered if Molly would bark if left alone in the house all night.

Bridgette needed a good night's sleep and didn't fancy the prospect of being woken by a dog barking next door. "How would you like to have a sleepover at my house Molly?"

Molly cocked her head slightly to one side and let out a little whining sound.

Bridgette smiled and said, "I'll take that as a yes," as she picked up the dog's cane bed.

They walked back through the house to the front door, Molly staying close to the side of her new best friend. Bridgette remembered she needed to get the phone number for Hughey's lawyer and paused at a small wooden side table near the front door to memorize the number on a blue business card next to the phone. She switched the lights off and found the house key under the flower pot just as Hughey had described. After checking the front door was locked, she turned around only to discover Molly had disappeared.

Bridgette anxiously scanned the front yard and was relieved to see Molly had only wandered off to the edge of a garden bed. Bridgette smiled to herself as the dog finished its bathroom break and then trotted back to her side. Picking up Molly's bed seemed to be all the encouragement the dog needed to follow Bridgette back to her house. Once inside, the dog seemed a little timid and Bridgette wasn't exactly sure what to do next. She had planned to cook a simple meal and then do some online research into Hughey's case before she called his lawyer. She placed Molly's bed in the living room near the entrance to the kitchen and said to Molly, "Sit."

To her surprise the dog hopped into its bed and looked up at her expectantly.

Bridgette laughed again and said, "Molly — you're a bright spot in an otherwise dark day."

* * *

After finishing a simple meal of fish and steamed vegetables, Bridgette spent an hour on her laptop doing some online research into Hughey's case. It didn't take her long to find information dating back to when he had been first arrested seventeen years ago following the disappearance of a local girl. While a major search effort had been mounted by Sanbury Police and the local community to find the senior high school student, Olivia Hodder, Hughey Warren had been arrested on suspicion that he was involved in her disappearance.

Bridgette continued to scan more articles, which detailed how the charges against Hughey had been upgraded from kidnapping to murder when the search efforts recovered no sign of her. The newspaper articles were all very emotive and she could understand the people of Sanbury wanting justice. Bridgette knew she would need a lot more information before she could form her own opinion and decided she would keep an open mind until she knew more. She pushed back from the dining table she had been working at and checked her watch as she massaged her neck. It was close to nine p.m. but still early enough to call Hughey's lawyer. She picked up her smartphone and dialed the lawyer's phone number from memory.

The call went through to voice mail and Bridgette left a short message explaining who she was and that she had witnessed Hughey being arrested earlier that evening. She asked the lawyer to call her back as soon as possible and then tiptoed past Molly who was snoring softly in her bed to the kitchen. She had just finished making a cup of peppermint tea when her phone rang.

"Hello this is Bridgette."

"I got a call from this number, something about Hughey Warren being arrested?"

"I take it you're his lawyer?"

"Sorry, yes I'm Dan Strickland and I'm Hughey's lawyer. Can you tell me what happened?"

Bridgette gave the lawyer a quick summary of Hughey's arrest and how he had been assaulted. Strickland made no comment as Bridgette went on to explain how she had followed the police into Sanbury to make sure the assault didn't continue.

When she had finished, Strickland said, "It's Bridgette right?"

"Yes."

"And you're a cop too?"

"Hartbourne Metro. I'm a detective with the Homicide Unit."

"If you don't mind me saying so, it's unusual for a cop to be giving up this sort of information to a defense lawyer?"

"I'm not privy to all the information about Hughey's case but assaulting someone who is fully cooperating during an arrest helps no one."

They were quiet for a moment before the lawyer said, "I've got a bail hearing first thing tomorrow morning that I can't miss. I can rearrange the rest of my schedule, but the drive down from Rochford will take me about two hours. I can't see myself getting there before noon."

"I'll get a message to Hughey tomorrow morning so that he knows you're coming."

"Thanks, although I'm not sure it will do any good. The judge is looking for any excuse to put him back inside."

"How well do you know Hughey?"

Strickland thought for a moment and said, "I think I know him pretty well. Why do you ask?"

"When I visited him in the holding cell, he described in detail his daily routine for checking in at the police station."

Bridgette went on to explain the calendar that she'd found in his house with the police visits crossed off and how neat and tidy everything was.

She then added, "His behavior is very methodical — I'm wondering if the police were sloppy in their record keeping and forgot to record his visit?"

"It's possible. I'll call them first thing in the morning and ask them to provide evidence."

Bridgette hesitated and then asked, "You don't have to answer this, but do you think he murdered Olivia Hodder?"

Strickland shot back, "I see you've done some research."

Bridgette persisted, "I know you're a defense lawyer, but hypothetically, if you were on the original jury for Hughey's case, would you have found him guilty of Olivia's murder?"

To her surprise, Strickland was forthcoming with an answer.

"They found an empty school bag of hers in the back of a cupboard in Hughey's bedroom just days after she disappeared. It had been wiped clean — not a fingerprint on it. Hughey doesn't strike me as the kind of guy who would be smart enough to think of that and he denies ever seeing the bag except when Olivia had it in school. The jury badly wanted to blame someone for what happened and Hughey was probably set up to take the fall. The fact his original lawyer panicked and tried to pass off the bag as something Hughey had found and had not turned over to the police was a huge mistake. If Olivia had been a middle-aged man and not a seventeen-year-old girl, I don't think the jury would've been as quick to find Hughey guilty based on the evidence."

They talked for several more minutes about what would happen tomorrow before Strickland said he had to go. After disconnecting, Bridgette took a sip of her peppermint tea as she replayed their conversation over in her mind. She reminded herself that she was here to find out what happened to John Tyson, not to figure out if her neighbor was innocent or guilty of a murder charge. The image of Hughey Warren lying on a cot in a holding cell kept returning, and she found it hard to get it out of her mind. She felt a nudge at her leg and looked down to see Molly standing beside her. The dog wagged its tail and gave a soft whine.

Bridgette smiled and asked, "Do we need another bathroom break?" as she followed the dog to the front door.

Bridgette opened the front door and stood in the doorway sipping her tea as Molly disappeared out into the darkness. She looked up at the moon and wondered what tomorrow would bring? She was fairly certain stocky cop would be working overtime circulating his own version of events about their confrontation. She sighed as she realized her formal start tomorrow was likely to be hostile. She'd been hoping for a trouble-free couple of weeks working cooperatively with the local police on the Tyson Report, but that was now looking increasingly unlikely.

Chapter 6

Bridgette parked her car across the road from the Sanbury Police Station. She was fifteen minutes early and decided it wise to wait until eight o'clock before she walked in. The station looked quiet, but the bakery and small suburban supermarket across the road had a steady stream of customers walking in and out. She wondered how Hughey was coping with life behind bars again as she watched the street coming to life. Bridgette frowned as she studied the supermarket and got out of her car. After walking down a short concrete ramp, Bridgette entered the supermarket and spotted a man in his late thirties standing behind a service counter with his head down, studying a stock sheet.

He heard her approach and looked up with a practiced smile and said, "Can I help you?"

Bridgette wasn't sure what she wanted to say and replied, "I'm not sure. Do you ever get a big guy come in here? Goes by the name of Hughey."

The man's smile disappeared. "He's been coming in here every day since he got out of prison. I've asked the police if there's anything I can do about it because he scares my customers, but they said no."

"What time does he normally come in?"

The man frowned. "Why do you want to know?"

Bridgette pulled out her Hartbourne Metro police badge. Even though it carried no jurisdictional power, she hoped it would be enough to persuade the man to keep talking.

The man studied the badge for a moment. "He usually comes in just before nine each day to buy a bag of cookies."

"Did he come in yesterday?"

The man turned towards a rear service door and yelled, "Joe, I need you out front for a minute," before turning back to Bridgette. "I don't work Sundays, but Joe was here, and he'll know for sure."

A skinny man in his early twenties pushed his way through the service door and said, "What's up?" to his boss.

"Did Hughey come in yesterday?"

Joe looked from his boss to Bridgette and back again with a slightly confused look. "Yeah, just like always."

Bridgette asked, "And he bought his chocolate chip cookies like normal?"

Joe looked warily at his boss who nodded and said, "It's okay, she's a police officer."

Joe looked back at Bridgette and said, "We were out of choc-chip, so I sold him vanilla."

Bridgette nodded and then asked, "Is there any chance it was Saturday and not Sunday?"

Joe shook his head, "I don't work Saturday's, so no chance."

The other man asked, "So what's this all about?"

"The local police are claiming Hughey didn't check in at the station yesterday."

The man responded, "We've got stray dogs in this town who are smarter than Hughey. But even so, Hughey's bright enough to find his way across the road and into that police station."

The man explained how the police would often make Hughey

sit for hours on end before they would let him go.

Bridgette thanked them for their time and walked out of the supermarket. Buying cookies across the road was no proof that Hughey had actually entered the police station, but it showed he was following his regular daily pattern. She was eager to avoid being seen to be interfering any further in Hughey's case and wondered whether she should tell the police what she now knew or simply pass the information on to his lawyer?

* * *

Bridgette looked up at the clock in the main reception area of the Sanbury Police Station. She'd been sitting patiently on one of the white plastic chairs for almost forty minutes after announcing to the duty desk officer that she was here to see Police Chief Payne. She felt like a zoo exhibit as several uniformed cops walked up to the front counter to take a look at her before disappearing without acknowledging her presence. She figured stocky cop had circulated his version of the truth from last night's events and judging by the looks she was receiving, they had all bought his story.

She was fairly sure the extended wait was payback for last night and she resisted the urge to ask what was taking so long. Instead, she contented herself with catching up with news on her smartphone and tried not to look put out by the delay.

At nine-thirty, a man in his mid-forties, with a shaved head appeared at the counter and called her name. The man was large, Bridgette guessed at least six foot three, and his loose business shirt did little to hide his bulky frame. The man glared at her and drummed the fingers of his right hand on the countertop as Bridgette walked across the reception area. His body language was less than welcoming as he opened a door next to the counter and grunted, "Follow me."

The man turned and headed back through the open office without waiting for Bridgette. She quickened her pace just slightly to keep up with him and pretended not to notice the stares and glares she was receiving from police officers as she followed. The man walked into the first of three glass offices at the rear of the open office area and instructed Bridgette to close the door behind her as he sat down at his desk. Bridgette complied and sat across from him in the only other chair in the office. The man put his elbows up on his desk and stared at her over his steepled, interlocked fingers.

Bridgette had been in this position before — men, and even some women, with too much power trying to intimidate her with stares and body language. She kept her expressions neutral and easily held the man's stare while she waited for him to speak.

The man seemed to realize he would not win the contest and folded his arms across his chest. "My name is Chief Payne and I run this police force. My sergeant tells me you interfered with one of our arrests last night."

"I'm not sure I've met your sergeant?"

"Sergeant Mitch Conden was the senior officer in charge of last night's arrest of Hughey Warren."

"Then, yes I have met him."

"You're here to file a report on John Tyson's disappearance, not to interfere with local police matters."

Bridgette debated whether it was worthwhile getting into an argument or not. She knew she was already unlikely to get much support from the local force and making Payne angry would only make matters worse.

She decided she would leave it to Hughey's lawyer to fight his battles and replied coolly, "I saw what I thought was more force than was required to arrest someone."

Payne scratched at his full beard as he assessed her answer.

"I'm going to cut you some slack on this one. You stay out of local police matters and I'll let you stay. Any more stunts like you pulled last night and I'll be calling your boss. Are we clear?"

Bridgette managed a nod in response.

Payne could see she was struggling to control her anger and said, "I read about you. A rookie detective who somehow managed to catch a serial killer on her first case."

The sentence was tinged with sarcasm. Bridgette kept her anger in check as she replied, "Yeah, I must have got lucky."

Payne's features darkened a little. He picked up a pen off his desk and started twirling it between his fingers as he studied Bridgette.

"I read your partner wasn't so lucky. What was it — two rounds in the chest trying to save you?"

The horror of seeing her partner gun downed by the killer was still raw for Bridgette. She had taken Lance Hoffman's death hard and part of the reason for the Sanbury assignment was to get her away from Hartbourne Metro to give her time to heal.

She wasn't in the mood to debate the case any further and said unequivocally, "No, it was one round, but it's true, I wouldn't be alive if it wasn't for his bravery and sacrifice."

Payne shifted in his chair and said, "I'm surprised they sent you alone. I thought city cops always worked in pairs? I wonder what makes you so different that they don't bother sending a second cop?"

Bridgette ignored the inference that cops didn't want to work with her and in a measured tone, replied, "You'd have to take that one up with my boss."

Payne seemed to grow bored. "I have far more important things to do than babysit a rookie cop from the city."

He got up from his chair and pointed through his glass window to a small desk without a computer in the far corner of the open office area and said, "You see that desk next to the photocopier?"

Bridgette turned in the general direction that Payne was pointing to and answered, "Yes."

"That's your desk. We've decided you don't need computer access, so I've asked Chivers to assemble a paper file for you. Everything that we have on the Tyson case will be in there. We mounted an extensive search and rescue complete with tracking dogs and helicopters but found nothing. His body will turn up eventually, but apparently your Commissioner can't wait. You read the file and notify me of anyone you want to interview. After the stunt you pulled last night, I don't want you damaging our good reputation any further, so you'll need my approval before you talk to anyone outside this station. Is that clear?"

Bridgette knew she would not win an argument and replied, "Perfectly."

Payne sat down and said, "We're done for now, so you can see yourself out."

Bridgette opened the door but stood in the doorway for a moment studying Payne who now had his head down reading a file.

"What do I call you?"

Without looking up, Payne replied, "Chief Payne, just like everybody else."

Bridgette nodded and then asked, "How important is the reputation of the Sanbury police to you."

Payne looked up and glared at Bridgette as if she was an idiot. "It's very important."

Bridgette nodded again and said, "Then here's a piece of advice. Hughey Warren's lawyer will be here around lunchtime. If he's half as smart as I think he is, it won't take him long to figure out that Hughey didn't violate his bail conditions and was wrongfully arrested."

Payne snarled and replied, "And how do you figure that?"

"Hughey claims the duty officer with the red hair didn't register his visit when he finally told Hughey he could leave yesterday. I suspect that information wasn't passed on to your sergeant because it wasn't written down."

Payne's facial expressions darkened. "I'm not interested in any testimony from that Neanderthal."

"I'm just trying to protect your reputation."

Payne let out a short laugh and said, "I don't need you to protect our reputation."

"You don't have cleaners come in on Sunday nights, do you?"

Payne frowned. "What do cleaners have to do with this?"

"At Hartbourne Metro the cleaning contractors only come on week nights to keep costs down."

Payne nodded and said, "Everybody is cost cutting, but how is that relevant?"

"Hughey is a creature of habit. He buys cookies from the supermarket across the road every day before he comes in here to sit and wait. I found an empty vanilla cookie bag in the bin in your waiting area this morning. My guess is it's Hughey's bag from yesterday."

"You're wrong. He eats chocolate chip not vanilla."

"Not yesterday. I spoke to the supermarket employee who sold Hughey the cookies. They were out of choc-chip, so he bought vanilla."

Payne shot back, "I'm not interested in your B grade detective work."

Bridgette held her ground and said, "Maybe not, but it won't play out very well in front of a judge or the media if Hughey's lawyer can produce a witness and a client statement that strongly suggest Hughey was here yesterday like he claimed."

Bridgette turned to leave and then added, "You might also want to make sure Hughey's head wound is properly dressed. Your sergeant hit him pretty hard and split his ear wide open. I'm sure his lawyer will have a camera on his phone."

Chapter 7

Bridgette spent the next two hours reading the John Tyson file at her desk next to the photocopier. It was by far the noisiest place in the office with a steady stream of staff making use of the device throughout the morning. Almost everyone ignored her, and she wondered if Payne had issued specific instructions or whether it was just stocky cop's version of last night's events that was having a lasting impression.

When she had finished, she pushed back from her desk, satisfied with her four pages of notes and pleased that she had blocked out the distractions. She massaged her neck for a moment and then stared up at the ceiling as she thought about what she had learnt. She already knew John Tyson was separated, desperately missed his eight-year-old son and was a recovering alcoholic when he had volunteered for the posting at Sanbury. The report provided no further background on Tyson, other than he had been engaged by Sanbury Police for twelve months while one of their senior detectives was on leave recovering from a serious car accident. The report focused on Tyson's last known movements and the search itself. Bridgette debated rereading the report but decided she should learn more from interviewing local people who had made statements to the police.

She got up from the desk and headed towards Corey Payne's office. It was empty, but a young non-uniformed assistant was sitting at a desk just outside his office reading a magazine.

She looked up when she saw Bridgette approaching and said, "He's not here at present," as if trying to stop Bridgette getting too close.

To her horror, Bridgette didn't stop until she was at her desk.

Bridgette pasted on a pleasant face. "When will he be back?"

The assistant shrugged and with a smug look replied, "He didn't say."

Bridgette knew she was wasting her time pursuing the conversation any further and placed her business card on the assistant's desk. "Could you please tell him I'm out interviewing witnesses? My number is on the card, if he needs to contact me."

Bridgette didn't wait for a reply and headed back through the office to the front door. Most of the desk staff ignored her as she walked through the office, which she took to be a good sign.

Once outside, she put on sunglasses and headed for her car. There were about ten witnesses on her list she wanted to interview. She would start with several interviews in town before heading out of town to interview a man by the name of Jack Sutton. According to the report, Sutton and Tyson had become good friends and it was Sutton who had raised the alarm when his friend went missing. She figured if anyone was going to know the inside story, it would be him.

Chapter 8

Roman Quinn closed the file he had been working on when he heard the knock on his office door. He took his time clearing his desk of confidential documents. When he was satisfied that everything was in order, he said, "Enter," in a loud voice and waited for the door to open.

It had been several months since he had seen Ellie Pearce. He was disappointed that she wasn't wearing a tight-fitting dress like he insisted she wear every day when she'd worked for him. Making no attempt to hide what he was doing, he looked her up and down as she walked across his carpeted floor towards his desk. For someone in her early thirties with two children, he was still amazed at how good her figure was.

Without getting up, Quinn looked up at his former employee and said, "So good to see you again Ellie. Please sit down."

Pearce glared at Quinn for a moment and said, "Why am I here?"

Quinn steepled his fingers and said, "I hear your husband John has been laid off... I thought you might like your old job back."

Pearce did little to hide her hostility as she shot back, "I know you interfered and had John sacked."

Feigning surprise, Quinn replied, "And why would I do a thing like that Ellie?"

"Don't insult me..."

Ignoring her response, Quinn leaned forward on his elbows and stared at her breasts for a moment before looking up and making eye contact again.

"You know Ellie, I'm prepared to forget all about our little... misunderstanding. I'll happily take you back and even give you a raise. I can't be fairer than that..."

Quinn watched as Pearce shifted in her chair as she thought about his offer. He found her perfume distracting but ignored it as he added, "You know Ellie, the office ran so much more efficiently when you were in charge. You can start back tomorrow if you like?"

Pearce responded, "Just to manage your office?"

Quinn nodded. "Office manager, just like before, but with a raise."

"And no out-of-town trips or conferences."

Quinn let out a short laugh. "You know my business takes me interstate sometimes and I still need to attend conferences..."

Pearce declared, "I want no part of that. You almost cost me my marriage when my husband found out."

"Nobody needs to know Ellie. It can be our little secret."

Pearce shook her head. "No trips, no conferences and definitely no sex Roman. I'm happily married and want to stay that way."

Quinn tilted his head to one side and shook his head as he feigned disappointment. "Ellie, you disappoint me. You should know what I want by now."

"The first time was a mistake, Roman. The second time was rape."

Quinn's features darkened. "I'd be very careful throwing that word around Ellie. Your husband losing his job will be the least of your worries. I can make life very difficult for—"

Pearce stood up. "I don't have to listen to this. You're not my boss anymore."

Quinn watched with amusement as she walked to his office door. With her hand resting on the handle, she turned back and said, "I made two mistakes. Sleeping with you in the first place and then not reporting you after you raped me."

Quinn laughed and said, "You were drunk and begging for it."

"No. I'd had one drink and repeatedly told you to stop, but you didn't."

No longer amused, Quinn leaned forward and said, "This job was the best thing that ever happened to you. Look at you now. No job, your husband is out of work and you're running up debts around town that you've got no hope of paying back. You disgust me."

Pearce looked back at him through tears and said, "I'm going to do something I should have done a long time ago."

"And what's that?"

"See my lawyer. I know this is not the first time you've done this, and somebody needs to stand up to you."

Quinn held her stare and said in a quiet voice, "Be careful Ellie. You think your life is miserable now... just wait and see how bad I can make it."

"I've got nothing to lose..."

Quinn laughed as Pearce slammed the door for effect as she left his office. It wasn't the first time someone had made a dramatic exit and he doubted it would be the last. He sat back in his chair and thought about how he would respond. Finally, he picked up his phone and dialed a number.

When the call was answered, Quinn said in a pleasant voice, "Hello Robert, it's been a long time."

There was silence for a moment before a wary voice responded, "Hello Roman. What can I do for you?'

Quinn studied his fingernails as he responded, "Nothing really, I just called to say hello..."

Another moment's silence before Robert responded, "I see..."

Quinn said casually, "There is one thing. Ellie Pearce might come and see you. She's just left my office and appeared quite upset."

"Can I ask what it's in relation to?"

"Of course. She's threatening to have me charged with rape."

"I see. Well, that's not something I'm prepared to make a comment on."

Quinn made a mental note to get a manicure as he responded, "Spoken like a true lawyer Robert. By the way, I saw your wife Valerie the other day over at Mossman Accountancy. She seems to be doing well there."

Robert cautiously replied, "Two promotions in two years, so she's happy."

"It's a shame about the business isn't it?"

"I'm not sure I'm following you?"

"You haven't heard? Mossman is retiring and I have an option to buy. I've looked over the books, but there are too many overheads. I'm going to have to cut about half the staff..."

There was more silence on the phone before Robert came back in a frustrated voice and said, "What do you want Roman?"

Quinn dropped the pleasantries. "It's very simple Robert. You convince that silly little bitch that attempting to have me charged with rape is a bad idea for everyone. I don't care how you do it, but make it happen and make sure no other lawyer in Sanbury touches the case either. In return, I'll make sure your wife gets to keep her job."

Quinn disconnected. He'd made his point and saw no need to continue the conversation. He sat back in his chair and thought about Ellie again. It was a shame she had said no. With his wife away, she would have made for very pleasant evening company.

Chapter 9

Bridgette drove at a steady pace down Sanbury's main street on the way to her first interview. Lined with one and two story buildings, she was surprised at how busy the town was as people went about their daily routines. She cruised past the town's courthouse, library and fire station before parking out front of a two-story brick building signposted as the Sanbury Community Bank. She had no appointment but decided to stop in on the off chance she could speak to the bank manager — Richard Griffin. The bank manager had been mentioned in Tyson's missing person's report. There were several anomalies with his statement she thought worth pursuing. She had learned that catching people off guard and unprepared often gave her the edge in interviews. Bridgette hoped her unannounced visit would have that effect on Griffin as she pushed through the front door.

Bridgette walked into the reception area and stood on plush maroon carpet scanning the office space. The bank was fitted out in heavy oak paneling and covered with placards and signs imploring customers to save, invest and borrow with Sanbury Community. Two bank clerks stood behind a large service counter that ran down the right-hand side of the office space. Bridgette walked past a line of customers waiting to be served over to an information counter and was greeted by a slim, young woman in a maroon uniform. "Hello, how can I help you?"

"My name is Detective Bridgette Cash and I'd like to speak with Richard Griffin if he's in?"

The smile disappeared from the woman's face. "I'm sorry, I wasn't aware Sanbury Police employed any female detectives."

Bridgette flashed her badge, "I'm actually a police detective with Hartbourne Metro."

The woman said, "Wait here," and then turned and walked into a back office.

A moment later a balding man in his late forties with a pasty complexion emerged. He looked irritated as he approached the counter and pointed to a meeting room to Bridgette's left which had a small sign above the door that read Customer Conferences.

Bridgette followed the man into the room and waited for Griffin's cue to sit in one of the four chairs neatly arranged around a small conference table.

Instead, Griffin closed the door and stood with his hands on his hips glaring at her. "You've got a lot to learn about country towns Detective. Around here, you don't go around flashing your badge and demanding to speak to people. That's the way gossip starts, and hard-earned reputations are damaged. "

Bridgette decided there was little to be gained by pointing out Griffin's clerk had challenged her credentials first and responded, "I'm sorry, I meant no offense."

Griffin stayed standing and said, "I'm very busy, so what's this about?"

"I was hoping to speak with you about John Tyson's disappearance."

"I've already told the Sanbury Police everything I know."

"I'm here to write a final report on John's disappearance for Hartbourne Metro. There are formalities we need to go through before we can provide financial support to his family."

Griffin replied, "I don't see what that has to do with me. I barely knew the man."

Still standing, Bridgette responded, "I was curious when I read the statement you provided to police when they questioned you about John's disappearance."

"As far as I'm concerned, nothing has changed, and I have nothing to add."

"I've been reading other witness statements and several of them report observing a heated argument between you and John here at the bank just days before his disappearance?"

Griffin's features hardened. "Tyson was a customer in our bank and got upset over a couple of fees that were incorrectly charged to his account. We had words here at the bank one morning, but I'd hardly call it a heated argument."

"According to the statements, you argued with John Tyson in full view of everyone in the bank for several minutes?"

Griffin put his hand on the door handle and said, "This meeting is over. I've been over this with the police and I'm not interested in going over it again. He's not the first person to get upset over bank fees, nor will he be the last. If you want to interview me further, you'll need to make an appointment with my lawyer."

Griffin paused as he opened the door. "Feel free to see yourself out."

Without another word, Griffin turned his back and walked out. Bridgette raised her eyebrows slightly as she watched Griffin head back to his office and close the door.

She found his reaction surprising since he had never been under serious consideration as a suspect by Sanbury Police. She wasn't sure she had learned much from the interview other than the people she'd met in Sanbury so far, were less than friendly. Her next stop was Roman Quinn's office. As President of the local Chamber of Commerce, he had lodged an official complaint with Corey Payne within days of John Tyson starting his investigation into Olivia Hodder's disappearance. She wasn't sure what to expect, but she had a feeling his reaction would be similar to that of Richard Griffin.

* * *

Bridgette walked half a block to a modern two-story stone and glass building that was trimmed with pressed-steel. A sign above a revolving door at the building's entry informed her she had arrived at the Sanbury Professional Center. She walked into a tiled lobby before stopping to read the building's tenant directory. There were six tenants in total; two doctors, a firm of accountants, an architect, a dentist and an investment company. It was the last tenant which occupied the entire upper floor that she was interested in. Bridgette took the stairs to the upper level and paused long enough on the landing to read the list of company names stenciled in gold lettering on the glass front doors. The Quinn Group had been busy and had a string of companies involved in everything from retail to venture capital.

She walked into a modern, almost sterile, reception area furnished in glass, chrome and white leather. The receptionist, a young woman in her early twenties with peroxide blonde hair and heavy makeup was on the phone.

When the receptionist ended her call, Bridgette introduced herself and asked if it would be possible to speak to Roman Quinn.

The receptionist became wary the moment Bridgette mentioned she was a police officer and asked, "Do you have an appointment?"

Bridgette shook her head. "No, I don't, but I only need a few minutes of his time if he's free."

The receptionist replied, "Please have a seat while I check."

Bridgette sat down and expected the receptionist to pick up the phone. Instead, she got up from her chair and walked across the foyer and knocked softly on a door before entering. The door closed behind her and Bridgette waited another thirty seconds before it opened again.

The receptionist reappeared and said, "Mr. Quinn can give you five minutes," as she walked back to her desk.

Bridgette thanked her and walked to the open doorway. She peered into a large office that had been fitted out with the same chrome, glass and white leather office furniture.

Roman Quinn sat behind his desk and looked at Bridgette with a confident smile as his eyes scanned up and down her body. Bridgette guessed he was in his mid-thirties. Dressed in a tailored white business shirt and silk tie, he had a confident, almost smug demeanor. His curly, brown hair was slightly too long and at odds with what he was wearing. Bridgette thought he looked more like a university professor than a business executive.

Quinn nodded once and said, "Come in Detective."

Bridgette ignored Quinn's stare and responded, "Thank you," as she walked in. The office reeked of cigarette smoke which she did her best to ignore as she sat in a visitor's chair opposite him.

Quinn rested his elbows on his glass desktop and clasped his hands together. He seemed relaxed, as he said, "I heard you were coming Detective. You're here to investigate the unfortunate disappearance of John Tyson if I'm not mistaken."

"News travels fast."

Quinn allowed himself a grin, which exposed a gold front tooth. "Sanbury is my town. I make it a point to know everything that happens here..."

"I won't take up much of your time Mr. Quinn, but—"

"Call me Roman, Detective."

Bridgette decided she wasn't about to return the favor, and responded, "Okay, Roman, I won't take up much of your time, but I've read the police report compiled on John's disappearance and have a couple of questions to ask you?"

"Fire away."

"The report says you had an argument in the street with John not long after he started investigating Olivia Hodder's disappearance. Several witnesses reported you shouting at him quote, 'I'll sue your ass,' unquote."

To Bridgette's surprise, Quinn chuckled and shot back, "Yes, I do recall that encounter with Tyson. I told him in no uncertain terms that his investigation was pointless and that I would sue him if he made a media spectacle of it. The town has a lot riding on the Snowbridge development, which I'm sure you've heard about. We don't need some out-of-town cop coming in here and stirring up trouble and giving the town a bad name."

"I see."

Quinn's smile disappeared. "I'm not sure you do Detective. Sanbury's future is in tourism and as president of the local chamber of commerce, it's my job to protect us from any potential bad publicity."

Bridgette nodded. "The report implied you'd made a formal request to Chief Payne to stop Tyson investigating further?"

"No. Corey Payne is a friend of mine, so we talk. I'm not privy to what's in any police report and frankly, I don't care."

"Why don't you care?"

Quinn crossed his arms and leaned back in his chair. "It wouldn't surprise me if Tyson turns up alive somewhere. For all we know he's back on the bottle and living the life of a homeless drunk."

"You knew about his alcoholism?"

Quinn laughed. "Detective, Sanbury's population is just over ten thousand people. You can barely sneeze here without it making the front page of the local newspaper."

"The report says you had a second argument with him at the police station."

"Possibly, I don't recall."

"You don't recall an argument with a police officer at the police station?"

Quinn scratched his chin as he stared at Bridgette. "You really are quite attractive for a police detective."

Bridgette resisted the urge to roll her eyes and said, "Please just answer the question."

Quinn sighed as if he was getting bored with the conversation. "The truth is Detective; in my position I get involved in lots of arguments. I'm trying to put Sanbury on the map so to speak. Not everyone likes me. Half the town loves what I'm doing, the other half doesn't want change and would be happy to stick a knife in my back. So don't be surprised if I say I don't recall an argument — they're an everyday occurrence for me."

Quinn looked at his watch and said, "I must be going Detective, I have an important meeting I need to get to. If you need more information, can I suggest a drink this evening? I'm free from about six p.m. and there's no one better to show you the Sanbury nightlife than me..."

"That won't be necessary Roman. I think I have everything I need for now."

Quinn nodded and slid a business card across the table. "You strike me as a woman of some intelligence and that's a commodity in short supply here. I can promise you an evening of stimulating conversation, so call me if you change your mind."

Quinn stood and smiled as he reached a hand across his desk. "It was a pleasure meeting you Detective. Let's hope our paths cross again before you leave Sanbury."

Bridgette stood and said, "If I need anything else I'll be in touch," and reluctantly shook Quinn's hand.

She turned and walked out of Quinn's office and decided to head straight for a bathroom. Bridgette didn't have any phobias that she was aware of, but she had a sudden urge to wash her hands before she did anything else.

Chapter 10

Bridgette pulled up at the top of a long steep driveway and looked down at Jack Sutton's house. The house was set on acreage and hidden behind trees that encroached from the surrounding forest. The property was only a five-minute drive out of town, but it felt like she was on the verge of wilderness. Her phone rang as she debated whether to park the car or risk driving down the long steep driveway.

She recognized the number as Hughey's lawyer and pressed answer.

"Hello, Dan."

"Hi Bridgette, I'm just calling to say thanks for what you did for Hughey this morning."

Bridgette frowned. "Sorry Dan, I'm not following?"

"I got a message while I was in court from someone at Sanbury Police. When I called back, I got put through to Corey Payne. Hughey has been released and the charge of failing to comply with bail restrictions has been dropped."

Bridgette was taken aback and said, "Well that's news to me."

"Payne admitted there had been some sort of clerical oversight."

Bridgette couldn't help herself and said, "I'm guessing that must have been hard for him."

Strickland laughed and said, "He wasn't happy. When I asked

him if he'd been speaking to you, he got a little hot under the collar, so I figured you must have had something to do with it."

Bridgette smiled as she thought back to her confrontation with Payne. She was pleased she hadn't been completely ignored. "Well, I'm glad Hughey's out. So where are you now?"

"I'm still in Rochford. I saw no need to come down today now that he's out. But I was wondering if you wouldn't mind checking on him for me — just to make sure he's okay?"

Bridgette thought back to her conversation with Corey Payne. She didn't want to get involved in local police matters, but she saw no harm in checking on a neighbor.

"I'll swing by and say hi on my way home tonight. If I think he's not coping, I'll call you."

"Thanks, I appreciate it. I'll be down there tomorrow for the court hearing anyway, but he's fragile at the moment and it's something I want to keep on top of."

They made arrangements to meet up the following evening for a quick drink before Strickland drove back to Rochford. After finishing the call, Bridgette sat in the car and thought about Hughey again. She was happy she had helped but wondered if there would be any payback from Payne for showing his staff up as incompetent. She decided she would stay out of the office and continue with interviews for the rest of the day. If Payne wanted payback he would have to wait until tomorrow.

* * *

Bridgette stood on the front deck of Sutton's house wondering what she would do next as she took in the view of the surrounding forest. She had knocked twice and patiently waited for a couple of minutes before deciding no one was home. As she contemplated which witness she would approach next, she heard a sound coming from the rear of the house. It sounded like metal striking metal — a human sound and worth investigating.

She stepped off the deck and headed around the side of the timber house towards the rear. As she rounded the corner, she slowed her step for a moment. She had expected to see a typical backyard with lawn and maybe a garage but instead found herself staring at three large steel and timber buildings connected by a circular driveway. The door to the largest of the structures was open and she could see a man in his early sixties bent over the engine bay of an old rusted blue motor car.

The man looked up as she approached and scratched his head. He looked a little wary and made no move to greet Bridgette as she stopped a few feet short of him.

Not wanting to get into a staring contest, Bridgette broke the ice. "Good afternoon, I'm looking for Jack Sutton."

The man, who had thinning gray hair and a wrinkled complexion from spending a lifetime outdoors, replied guardedly, "You've found him."

Bridgette reached into her jacket pocket and pulled out her Hartbourne Metro police badge and held it up. "My name is Bridgette Cash. I'm a detective from Hartbourne Metro and—"

The man took the badge from Bridgette and studied it. As he returned it, he said, "I heard you were coming. You're here to find out what happened to John Tyson."

Bridgette nodded and said, "Yes."

The man put down his spanner and said, "I've been over everything I know with the local police. I'm not sure there is anything else I can tell you."

He pulled out a yellow packet of roll-your-own tobacco and began to rub the tobacco between his fingers.

Bridgette could see by the man's posture that he was defensive. She hoped the interview would be more pleasant than the last two and decided to try a different approach to break the ice. She pointed at the car he was working on and said, "Sixty-six or sixty-seven?"

The man raised his eyebrows slightly and he responded, "It's a sixty-six. I'm surprised someone as young as you would know anything about classic Mustangs?"

Bridgette smiled and said, "My father owned a sixty-seven. It was his pride and joy."

Sutton nodded, "I prefer the sixty-six. The sixty-seven Mustang was a little too boxy in the rear for my liking."

Bridgette ran her fingers across the rusting chrome front bumper. "It's a dream of mine to own one of these one day."

"I'm hoping to have this one fully restored in about three months. Does your father still have his?"

Bridgette grimaced slightly. "No, he's not with us anymore."

Sutton mumbled an, "I'm sorry to hear that," and pointed at a steel drum next to the car. "You can sit if you want."

Bridgette sat on the drum and watched Sutton make his cigarette. She could see his features relaxing a little and said, "I'm not sure what you know, but John Tyson was here relieving for twelve months — he was one of ours."

Sutton nodded as he lit his cigarette. After taking a long draw and exhaling a plume of blue smoke he said, "John and I met up at a meeting in town not long after he arrived."

"I only arrived yesterday. I read the police file this morning and from what I can gather, you probably knew him better than anyone else in Sanbury?"

Sutton nodded, "We hit it off, so I got to know him fairly well."

"I'm hoping you might be able to tell me in your own words

what happened. The police report doesn't really say a lot."

Sutton seemed to mellow a little as he responded. "To be fair to the police, the search they mounted was comprehensive. Helicopters, ground crew, local TV coverage — the works. The only problem is, I don't think he got lost out in the mountains."

"Why do you say that?"

Sutton took a long draw on his cigarette and blew another plume of smoke as he pondered the question. "Did you ever meet John Tyson?"

Bridgette shook her head, "I've only been with Hartbourne Metro for about six weeks, so he was long gone before I arrived."

Sutton came and sat on a drum next to Bridgette. "John Tyson came here to get his life back together and from my take on things, he was doing a pretty good job."

Bridgette sensed Sutton was opening up. She wanted to encourage him to tell the story his way without a cop's interruption and said, "I'd be interested to hear your take on it, Mr. Sutton. The report didn't really go much beyond his last known whereabouts and the search itself."

"Call me Jack."

"Thank you, Jack."

Sutton scratched his head for a moment and then said, "I'm guessing you know he was a recovering alcoholic?"

Bridgette nodded. "I got a briefing from my boss before I came. He said John was looking for a fresh start after his marriage broke down. He took this assignment to get out of the city for a while."

Sutton nodded, "That about sums it up."

Sutton paused for another draw on his cigarette. "There was a lot of wild ass talk about what happened to John. Most of it was just small-town gossip — people with too much time on their hands. Some think he got lost in the mountains, some think he disappeared to start a new life and some even think he slipped away to where no one would find him to kill himself."

"What do you think happened?"

Abruptly, Sutton got to his feet. "This is going to take some time to explain and I need a brew..."

Bridgette wondered what he meant by 'brew' as she followed Sutton out of his workshop, across the driveway and up onto a large rustic back porch at the back of his house. He nodded for her to sit at a large wooden table and said, "Enjoy the view," as he disappeared inside the house.

Bridgette pulled her coat tight to keep out the cold as she sat down. She marveled at the forest backdrop that surrounded the house as she heard Sutton moving around inside in what she assumed was his kitchen.

He called out through a slightly open window, "You drink tea?"

"Thank you, but no milk if that's okay?"

"Got it. You drink normal tea or fancy tea?"

"What kind of fancy tea do you have Jack?"

"Lemon or Peppermint. And some tea made from flowers — it tastes like jungle juice but helps with indigestion."

Bridgette smiled at Sutton's turn of phrase as she responded, "Peppermint would be great."

A few moments later, Sutton appeared carrying two non-matching mugs of steaming tea. His hands shook a little as he placed the mugs on the table.

Bridgette thanked Sutton and waited for him to sit down. As she took her first sip, she said, "You have an amazing view here Jack."

Sutton looked out at the view. "I've lived here most of my life. You never get tired of it."

She watched as Sutton picked up his mug in both hands and

took a long sip.

When he had set his cup down, he said, "My wife died thirteen years ago. I took it pretty hard and lived out of a bottle for almost three years. I had a few friends here that stuck by me, one of whom convinced me to try Alcoholics Anonymous. I've barely missed a week in ten years — that's where I met John Tyson."

Sutton paused a moment and fixed Bridgette with his sharp blue eyes and said, "After ten years of seeing all sorts of misery walk in and out of AA, I know a little about people's state of mind. John Tyson never missed a week and was in a good place. I don't know what's in that police report, but he didn't kill himself."

Bridgette decided there was nothing in the report that was confidential. "The report was open in its finding. It concluded that while suicide or disappearing to start a new life were both possibilities neither scenario was likely. They focused mainly on John getting lost in the mountains somewhere. Apparently, it was common knowledge that he went hiking regularly."

Sutton raised his eyebrows as he replied, "Hiking is an interesting term."

"So, what do you think happened Jack?"

Sutton took another sip of his tea as he thought about the question. "There's a few things you need to know that probably aren't in that report. John came here to relieve for a local detective by the name of Bishop who broke his leg in six places in a car accident. Bishop is one of three detectives here, and frankly, they all have a pretty easy ride. We don't get many murders out here and apart from the odd meth lab and stolen car, it's mostly petty crime which the patrol officers handle."

Bridgette nodded, "So John Tyson was bored?"

"You got it. Chief Quinn brought him on to make sure he wouldn't lose his funding for his third detective, but there simply isn't enough work for all of them. It didn't help that he wasn't a local either. According to John, they froze him out of the few good cases that came up and just gave him scraps."

Bridgette nodded. After the reception she had received that morning, she could well imagine the challenges John Tyson would have faced trying to integrate.

Sutton continued, "He began to look for things to do and that's when he met Della Warren."

Bridgette raised her eyebrows. "Any relation to Hughey?"

"Della is Hughey's mother. I'm not sure what you know about the Olivia Hodder case, but Hughey was charged with the girl's murder. Della has claimed all along that Hughey was innocent and when Tyson came to town, she hounded him until he promised to look into it."

"So, does Della still live in Sanbury?"

Sutton nodded. "Kind of. She's been in the Community Hospital for almost two months awaiting a heart transplant."

"I'm sure you know Hughey's out of jail at the moment and living back at home?"

Sutton nodded again. "Della and I are friends. I took care of her dog until Hughey came home."

"I met Hughey yesterday, shortly after I arrived. I inadvertently rented the house next door."

Sutton's face broke into a wrinkly grin. "So I've heard." He took another sip of tea and continued, "For what it's worth, I think Hughey's harmless. The local community was rightfully upset when young Olivia went missing, but they arrested Hughey for the wrong reasons and beat a confession out of him. It broke his father and mother and as far as I'm concerned, whoever killed Olivia is still walking around a free man."

They were quiet for a moment while Bridgette processed the

information.

She took another sip of tea and said, "The report said John didn't show up for work on a Monday morning and that's when the alarm was officially raised?"

"I was worried about him on the Saturday evening. He was supposed to come up here for a card game, but when he didn't show, I rang but got no answer. It was out of character for him not to contact me, but I let it go."

Sutton paused for another sip of tea. "He spent a lot of time studying the Olivia Hodder case. Even though Hughey was in jail for the murder, there's still an active file on account of Olivia's body never being discovered. He interviewed a lot of locals to find out what happened when she disappeared and then suddenly switched his focus to searching in the mountains."

"Did he tell you why?"

Sutton shook his head. "He wouldn't tell me. He said I was a local and it was better I didn't know anything until he was sure, whatever that means."

Bridgette frowned. None of this was in the report and she wondered if it was connected.

Sutton drained the last of his tea in one long gulp and then wiped his mouth. He pulled out his yellow packet of tobacco and rolled another cigarette as he gazed at the mountains in the distance. "I tried calling him again on the Sunday morning after he failed to show for the card game but got no answer, so I drove down to his house. His car was in the driveway, but his house was locked up. I had a good look around to make sure he hadn't fallen or passed out somewhere. When I couldn't find any sign of him, I raised the alarm."

Sutton paused for a moment to light his cigarette and then continued. "John did hike a lot searching for Olivia, but he knew the danger of the mountains and always had an emergency GPS tracker with him when he went exploring. When I saw it on the front seat of his car, I was pretty sure this wasn't going to end well."

"So, what do you think happened?"

Sutton exhaled a plume of smoke and answered, "I think he was murdered."

Chapter 11

Bridgette looked in her rear-view mirror at the figure of Jack Sutton standing at the top of his driveway watching her as she drove away from his house. She had respected his openness for revealing he was a reformed alcoholic and had no reason to doubt any of the information he had shared with her about John Tyson. She glanced at her car's clock — it was well after two p.m. and she had spent far more time with Sutton than she intended to. She decided to head straight home and enter everything she had learned into her laptop and organize interviews for the following day.

Bridgette frowned as she changed gears and recalled Sutton's words, "I think he was murdered."

She didn't have enough information yet to make her own decisions, but the circumstances Sutton had described surrounding Tyson's disappearance troubled her. She began to formulate a plan for the following day as she wound down the mountain and entered the northern end of the township. She would check in with Payne but planned to spend most of the day out interviewing witnesses. Bridgette pulled up at a stop sign and glanced at the sign on the cross street which read, 'Tilbrook Street (through to Hobson Lane)'.

Bridgette remembered reading in the missing person's report that John Tyson had lived in Hobson Lane and put her left indicator on as she decided on a detour. She drove up Tilbrook in a low gear getting a feel for the neighborhood before turning into Hobson Lane. There were only 9 houses in the laneway and Tyson's house was at the far end. With its carport out front and large pine tree overhanging the house, the small, single story timber cottage looked the same as it had in the photos she had seen in the police report. After switching the engine off, Bridgette sat for a moment taking in the surroundings. The driveway of the house next to Tyson's house was empty and everything looked quiet. Bridgette wondered if the neighbors were at work as she got out and walked down the footpath towards Tyson's front door. She was reminded how quickly life moved on to establish its new normality as she passed a 'for rent' sign in the front yard.

She walked up two concrete steps and knocked softly on the front door. She didn't think the house was occupied but never made assumptions. After waiting a few seconds, she peered in through a window next to the front door. The curtains were open just enough to give her a partial view of a living room which looked dark and empty.

Bridgette decided to investigate the rear of the property and walked through the carport and a side wooden gate that creaked as it swung open. There was little to see. The garden beds that followed the fence line were framed by old railway sleepers and had long since yielded to a motley collection of weeds and undergrowth.

Bridgette stared at the rack and ruin. She lived in a small one-bedroom apartment in inner city Hartbourne but hoped to be able to afford to buy a house one day. She couldn't imagine ever letting something she owned fall into this much disrepair. Stepping up onto a rickety wooden back deck, Bridgette peered through a rear window into what looked like a sunroom. The room was almost bare of furniture and apart from a couple of dead cockroaches on the floor, showed little sign of being inhabited. She tried turning the knob on the wooden door, but it was locked.

She moved to her left and peered through another window into the kitchen. The layout was similar to the kitchen in the house she was renting, even down to the Lino floor. The benches were clear and there were no tell-tale signs anyone was living there. Bridgette was positive the house was empty and had probably not been rented since John Tyson's disappearance. She turned to leave and noticed the window above the kitchen sink had the same flimsy metal latch that was on the house she was renting. The gap between the window and the frame was large enough to fit a screwdriver blade between and she knew the window could be opened easily with the right implement. She looked around for something suitable to use as she debated whether breaking into the house was worth the risk of getting caught. She'd asked Payne earlier if she could visit the house to look around and received an emphatic 'No'. Payne who seemed to take great delight in telling her it was now back in the hands of its owners and would require a search warrant.

After stepping down off the deck, she walked into the middle of the backyard. She saw nothing that could help her break in and walked over to the neighbor's fence. She peered into their backyard — it was much neater and tidier than Tyson's place and looked to be well cared for. The curtains at the rear of the house were closed, and she suspected the owners were out. She made a mental note to come back later and interview them. As she went to move away, her coat caught on a rusting metal strap that was nailed to the fence post she was standing next to. Bridgette thought about the kitchen window again and tried to pull the strap free, but the nail held firm. She looked around to make sure she was still alone as she bent the strap up and down against the nail. Her effort was quickly rewarded as the metal fatigued and snapped.

After spending a moment to straighten the strap, Bridgette held it up and nodded. The strap was about the size of a butter knife and perfect for what she had in mind. She walked back and up onto the rear deck and looked over her shoulder again as she approached the kitchen window. Confident that she was still alone, she slid the metal strap between the window and its frame. She knew she was breaking the law and if Payne or one of his officers caught her, she would have a lot of explaining to do when she returned to Hartbourne Metro but decided to risk it.

She whispered, "Let's make this quick," as she worked the metal strap against the latch until it sprung free. Within sixty seconds she was standing in the kitchen dusting off a few cobwebs she had picked up as she had crawled through the window opening.

Bridgette started by opening the kitchen cupboards and drawers. Apart from half a packet of plastic forks and an old plastic cup they were empty. She moved quickly into the sunroom and scanned the contents. An empty wooden bookcase, an old wooden table, and two rickety stools were the sum total of the furnishings. Bridgette moved across to the bookcase and tilted it forward. She expected the local police would have been thorough in their search, but it paid to check. Finding nothing, she moved through into the main lounge area, which apart from one sofa, was also devoid of furniture. Bridgette slid her hand down into the cracks between the cushions of the sofa and was rewarded with an old wooden peg and a few unidentifiable food crumbs that years ago may have been pizza. After a quick check under the sofa and behind the room's gas heater, she moved through the rest of the house checking each of the bedrooms, the bathroom, and the laundry. In each case, the rooms had been cleared of all belongings and cleaned ready for property rental.

She returned to the kitchen and as she stood contemplating what she would do next, she whispered, "It's as if you have never been here John."

Looking up, Bridgette noticed a small access panel for the ceiling cavity. Apart from the small crawl space underneath the house, the ceiling cavity was the only other area she hadn't explored. She knew she should check it and wondered how she could gain access without a ladder?

She thought of the two wooden stools in the sunroom and retrieved the least rickety of the two and positioned it on the kitchen bench beneath the panel. Nimbly, she climbed up onto the kitchen bench and then onto the stool. Doing her best to keep her balance, Bridgette half stood and pushed the ceiling panel to one side. Slowly, she rose to her full height, easing her head and shoulders up through the opening. After grabbing hold of the frame with one hand to keep her balance, she raised her smartphone and shone it around the interior of the roof space. She found it difficult to see anything through the layers of undisturbed dust and cobwebs and was confident no one had been in the roof space recently.

Bridgette eased down out of the roof space and replaced the access panel. After climbing down off the stool and the bench, she checked to make sure she had left everything as she found it. Satisfied, she re-locked the latch on the kitchen window and noticed two rusted chrome bolts on the window ledge as she turned to head toward the back door. Bridgette picked one up to examine it in more detail. As she held it between her thumb and forefinger, she noticed the thread was very fine. Bridgette frowned and looked around the kitchen wondering what they belonged to? She knew little about woodworking or home repair, but the fine thread suggested the bolts had come out of something metal rather than wood. She stood for a moment thinking of possible alternatives, but nothing immediately came to mind and she decided with her car parked on the street, she needed to get out of the house before anyone noticed. After carefully replacing the bolt where she had found it, Bridgette headed for the rear door but stiffened as she saw the silhouetted figure of someone walking around the side of the house through the dining room curtains. Instinctively, she retreated into the shadows of the small hallway that joined the main living room to the sunroom. She watched through the sunroom window as a police officer walked up onto the deck and tried opening the door. Bridgette's heart raced as the door rattled in its frame. It would be impossible for her to explain her presence inside the house without lying if she was caught. She instinctively took a step back further into the hallway as the familiar squat face of Chief Payne pressed up against the window to look inside. She held her breath not daring to move as Payne cupped a hand over his eyes on the glass to shield his eyes from the glare of the late afternoon sun. Bridgette knew he was looking for her. She cursed herself for leaving her car parked so visibly on the street as she watched Payne looking for any sign that someone was in the house. After about a minute, Payne stepped back and scanned the backyard. She watched as he stepped down off the deck and walked across to the side fence to check the neighbor's back yard. Instinctively, Bridgette checked that her smartphone was set to silent. The last thing she needed was for Payne to try calling her mobile number and hear it ring inside the house.

Payne spent another two minutes scanning the backyard before disappearing up the opposite side of the house. Bridgette waited in the hallway scanning both the windows at the front and back of the house until she saw Payne emerge at the front of the house again. She watched as he walked back to his car talking on his mobile phone.

Bridgette held her position and waited for several minutes after he had driven off before deciding it was safe to leave.

She left by the rear door, making sure to lock it behind her. After stepping off the back deck, she paused at the rear corner of the house and to make sure she was still alone. Confident that it was safe to leave, she took one last look at the back yard before moving off again. Her eye was drawn to the house's air conditioning unit that stood on a concrete slab at the side of the deck. The unit was housed in a large off-white metal box that was scarred and rusted from years of exposure to the elements. There was nothing remarkable about the appliance, but Bridgette found herself drawn towards the unit as she stared at the service plate on top of the unit. The plate was hinged on one side and originally held in place by three bolts, but two of them were missing. Bridgette leaned forward to examine the panel and gripped the remaining bolt and tried turning it. She expected it to be stuck fast through years of rust but to her surprise, the bolt turned easily in her fingers. She worked quickly and, in a few seconds, had the bolt out. She held it up and examined it for a moment — it was a match for the two bolts she had seen on the kitchen window ledge.

Conscious that she needed to move quickly, Bridgette pulled back the hinged panel. At first, she saw nothing more than an air conditioning motor and some metal hoses as she looked inside the box. She moved in closer and then spotted what looked like cardboard wedged against the rear wall. Reaching in with her left hand, she gently withdrew the cardboard and realized it was an office file as she held it up. It was typical of hundreds of portable files she had seen at Hartbourne Metro except there was no filename written on the cover.

Bridgette knew she should head back to her car but was curious about what was inside. After unwinding the string that held the flap down, she pulled out a wad of documents and quickly flipped through the stack. Most of them appeared to be printouts from geology websites along with photographs of forest areas and clearings. Bridgette stopped when she found several handwritten pages of notes. She recognized the neat cursive script immediately and wondered why John Tyson would have gone to the trouble of hiding a file in his air conditioner?

Chapter 12

Bridgette relaxed as she pulled up in the driveway of her rental house. She had skipped lunch and contemplated early dinner options as her phone rang. She glanced at the number and pressed answer as she recognized it was her boss.

"Hi, Chief."

"Just called to see how your first day was going?"

"Let's just say it's been interesting..."

"Well, I'm all ears, so fill me in."

Bridgette started by giving Delray an overview of the morning. She glossed over the confrontation with Payne and focused on the open findings in the police report.

Delray listened without interrupting and then said, "So the police think he just went on a hiking trip and never came back?"

"Pretty much."

"It doesn't sound like the John Tyson I knew. He never liked doing much of anything other than sitting in a sports bar and playing cards?"

Bridgette explained to her boss how Tyson had been shut out of investigation work in Sanbury and had started looking into the disappearance of Olivia Hodder to cope with the boredom.

"I think I remember reading about her, but that was a long time ago."

"Seventeen years."

"So what does Olivia Hodder's disappearance have to do with John Tyson hiking. Surely he wasn't expecting to find her remains after all this time?"

"I'm not sure yet Chief. I've just finished interviewing a man by the name of Jack Sutton. He had become good friends with Tyson. According to Sutton, John Tyson started out re-interviewing witnesses around town that were here seventeen years ago. All of a sudden he started taking lots of hikes in the forest, but Sutton doesn't know why."

"Is there anything in the police report about this?"

"No, it really just focused on the search after he disappeared. The local police seem convinced he's just another hiker who got into trouble."

"If he really got lost hiking, he could be anywhere. It might be years before they find him."

"I'm not sure he went hiking."

"Why do you say that?"

"When I was talking to Sutton, he was insistent that John Tyson was aware of the dangers of hiking alone and even went as far as buying an emergency GPS tracking device. The device was discovered locked in his car in his driveway when he was reported missing."

"Maybe he just forgot it?

"Perhaps, but according to Sutton, you normally drive out of town to a place called Saddleback Ridge to hike in the Sacred Mountains. That's a good half hour walk from the house Tyson was renting and adds an hour on a round trip. He's positive John wouldn't have left his car at home if he had been planning another hiking trip."

"So is any of this in the local report?"

"Not really. The local police focused on him being a lost hiker. But they did investigate the possibility he simply disappeared to start a new life or committed suicide."

"I'm not buying the disappeared to start a new life angle. We know his bank accounts haven't been touched and no large amounts were withdrawn beforehand. I'd say that's highly unlikely."

"Sutton knew him better than anyone else here and doesn't believe he disappeared intentionally or that he killed himself."

As she wound her window a little to let in some fresh air, Bridgette continued, "Jack Sutton is a reformed alcoholic himself and he said John was going to AA every week and appeared to be happy and getting on with his life."

"There is one other possibility..."

Bridgette nodded. She knew where her boss was heading and said, "Just before I left Sutton's house, I asked him what he thought happened. He was adamant John Tyson was murdered."

They were both silent again. Bridgette could hear Delray letting out a long breath on the other end of the phone line as he muttered, "Well that complicates things..."

Bridgette had already worked through some of the complications in her mind but waited for Delray to provide his view.

"As a Hartbourne Metro detective, you have no jurisdiction to conduct any formal murder investigation Bridgette. You're simply there to review the local findings and write a report for the Commissioner."

"Jack Sutton told me the police weren't interested in his theories. If I'm discreet over the next couple of days I may learn more about what really happened without getting offside with the local police?"

More silence followed and Bridgette waited while Delray

thought. He normally made good decisions and she had never found it helpful to rush him.

Finally, he said, "I have a meeting with the Commissioner tomorrow. I'll let him know where we're at and the potential complications. We'll let him decide what we do next. In the meantime, like you said, keep it discreet and see what else you can learn."

Bridgette looked at the file on the front seat of her car that she had recovered from the air-conditioner at Tyson's rental property. She hadn't looked at the contents and didn't want to get into any awkward conversations with her boss about breaking into Tyson's house unless she had to.

She decided she would read the file first before she mentioned anything and said, "I'm going to use tonight to review everything I've learned today. If anything important comes up, I'll ring you tomorrow before you go to your meeting."

"I'd appreciate that Bridgette."

They said their goodbyes and Bridgette sat in the car thinking about what she should do next. She would examine the file first and figure out if it was important. It bothered her that Tyson had gone to the trouble of hiding the file in an air-conditioner. There had to be a reason and until she found out what it was, she would need to tread carefully — Payne would look for any excuse to get rid of her and send her back to Hartbourne. As she formulated a plan of attack, she was startled by a knock on her window.

She gasped a little as she looked up at the enormous frame of Hughey Warren standing next to her car.

* * *

Bridgette barely made it out of the car before Hughey stepped forward and thrust a casserole dish covered in a white tea towel toward her.

"I made you this. It's Mom's shepherd's pie recipe — it's my favorite."

Bridgette was a little taken aback. She didn't think it was wise to accept gifts from a convicted murderer or encouraging a friendship and politely said, "Thank you, Hughey, that's very nice, but I don't eat red meat."

Hughey looked disappointed and dropped his eyes to the ground. "I talked with Dan and he said you're the reason I'm not in jail... so thanks."

An awkward silence followed. Bridgette felt guilty she hadn't accepted the gift but was sure it was the right decision. "Hughey, this is really nice, but you didn't need to do this. I was just doing my job."

Hughey nodded and pretended to understand.

As he turned to walk away, Bridgette asked, "When did they let you out?"

Hughey turned back but wouldn't make eye contact. "About ten o'clock. They took me to a room, and I talked to Dan on the phone. And then I got told I could leave."

Bridgette managed half a smile and said, "Well I'm glad you're home Hughey.

Still with his head down, Hughey responded, "Chief Payne was really angry. I thought he was going to hit me again, but he didn't."

Bridgette studied Hughey for a moment. There didn't appear to be any more injuries for which she was thankful.

Hughey looked up and added softly, "Thanks for looking after Molly. I know you fed her because she wasn't hungry when I got home."

"She had a sleepover at my house last night. We hung out, and it was fun. I locked her in your backyard this morning before I went to work. I think she likes me."

Hughey seemed lost for words again.

Bridgette was keen to study the file she had found in John Tyson's air-conditioner and decided it was time to end the conversation. "Well, I've got some police work I need to do Hughey, so I'm going inside now..."

Hughey nodded and mumbled a goodbye and then walked back toward his house holding the casserole dish.

As she pulled the key to her front door from her coat pocket, she wondered again if Jack Sutton had been right about Hughey being setup as the fall guy for Olivia Hodder's murder. She watched Hughey open his front door and disappear inside. Innocent or not, she still felt uncomfortable sleeping in a house next to a convicted murderer. She decided she would visit the rental agency tomorrow to get another place to stay, even if it was just a dingy motel room.

Chapter 13

Bridgette got up from the dining table and stretched as she walked to the front window. She had lost track of time reviewing the information she had found in the file hidden by John Tyson in the air conditioner and it was now almost dark. Peering out into the front yard, she turned to her left and looked across into Hughey's front yard. She felt the pangs of guilt again as she thought back to their brief encounter earlier and how she had rejected the casserole he had cooked for her.

She wondered if there were romantic overtones in his gesture or if he was just grateful for the help she had given him?

She whispered, "He's lonely Bridgette, just like…", but didn't finish as she closed the curtain.

Bridgette sat back down at the table again but found it hard to concentrate as she sorted through the pile of photographs she had found in the Tyson file. Although she would never be interested in a relationship with someone like Hughey, she thought about her neighbor again. Sutton had referred to him as a gentle giant even though he was a convicted murderer. She wondered how many murderers cooked pies for their neighbors as a sign of gratitude. Not many, she thought, unless they were looking for their next victim. She pushed back from the table. There was only one thing she could do to ease her conscience.

She decided now was as good a time as any.

Bridgette unlocked her front door and walked across the front yard and into her neighbor's place. As she stood on the porch and knocked, she wondered if Hughey would open the door after what happened to him the previous evening.

She only had to wait a moment for an answer as the door was opened by her neighbor. His hair was still wet from a shower and he smelled like soap.

Hughey looked down at her with a confused look. "Have I done something wrong?"

Bridgette shook her head. "No Hughey, you've done nothing wrong. It's me that's in the wrong. The way I dismissed you earlier when you came over to give me the pie was rude... I'm sorry."

Bridgette could tell that Hughey was a little stunned by her apology as he stood holding the door with his mouth partially open.

After recovering slightly, he said, "That's okay," but Bridgette could tell he wasn't used to people apologizing to him.

Before she could respond, she felt a nudge on her leg and looked down to see Molly wagging her tail and looking up at her.

Bridgette smiled as she bent down to pat the dog.

She looked up at Hughey as Molly licked her fingers and said, "I think she remembers me."

Hughey nodded. "Molly likes you," as he continued to stand awkwardly in the middle of his doorway.

Bridgette wondered whether Hughey's awkwardness was because he was shy or if his time in prison had taken its toll as well as he stammered, "Do you want to come in?"

Bridgette was about to politely decline but found herself saying, "Okay," instead.

As Hughey stepped back to allow her to enter, Bridgette hoped she wouldn't regret the decision as she walked into the living room which was still neat and tidy. She looked across at Hughey's dining room table and noticed a large slab of the pie he had offered her earlier on a plate complete with knife, fork, and napkin.

Realizing she had intruded on Hughey as he was about to start his evening meal, she turned and said, "I'm really sorry Hughey, I didn't know you were about to eat."

"It's okay, I can always put it in the oven and warm it up later."

Bridgette salivated a little as she smelt the pie wafting through the air.

She half smiled and said, "Hughey that smells amazing."

In a quiet voice, he replied, "I know you don't really like red meat, but you can have some if you like?"

Bridgette murmured, "I haven't had red meat in years," as she realized she had skipped lunch.

Hughey frowned. "Are you one of those vegetarians?"

Bridgette suppressed an urge to laugh as she felt like she was being compared to an alien.

"I used to compete in a lot of martial arts tournaments and was on a fairly strict diet — lots of fruit and vegetables and mainly fish and chicken for protein. I don't compete anymore, but I've kept up a lot of the habits."

She found the smell irresistible and turned to Hughey and said, "One slice isn't going to hurt me, Hughey."

Hughey smiled and said, "I'll go get you a plate."

Bridgette waited a moment for Hughey to return with another plate. She watched as he carefully laid out a place setting for her and then got her a napkin from a draw.

When they were seated, she watched as he carefully cut another slice of pie and served it on her plate.

Before they began to eat, Hughey bowed his head and said a silent prayer.

When he had finished, he raised his head and said, "Sorry, Mom said I should pray before every meal. It wouldn't seem right if I didn't."

"That's fine Hughey, no need to apologize."

They were quiet for a moment as they both started their meals.

Bridgette swallowed a mouthful of the pie. It brought back pleasant memories of her childhood. She said, "Hughey, this is really quite delicious."

Hughey paused between slow and delicate mouthfuls of pie and said, "Thank you."

Bridgette watched Hughey eat. His movements were very deliberate as he forked tiny portions of pie into his mouth. He took his time chewing thoroughly before he swallowed.

Realizing the meal would take a while, Bridgette put her fork down and dabbed her mouth with a napkin. She was interested to know more about his case and the likelihood of him returning to prison. She wasn't sure whether Hughey would talk about it and decided to start with a general question.

"So did your mother teach you that recipe, Hughey?"

Hughey nodded. "She taught me a lot of things."

"I was up visiting Jack Sutton today. He told me your Mom is in the hospital?"

Hughey nodded again and stopped eating for a moment.

Bridgette could see the distress on his face and said, "We don't have to talk about it if you don't want to Hughey?"

"The doctors won't tell me what's happening."

"Why is that Hughey?"

Hughey shrugged and spooned another small fork of pie into

his mouth. After chewing and swallowing he replied, "They think I'm a murderer. They don't say anything, but I can tell when they look at me. They think I don't know 'cause I'm not smart, but I do..."

Bridgette ate some more pie as she contemplated Hughey's answer.

She decided not to patronize him and replied, "I guess that makes it hard when you visit your Mom?"

Hughey nodded again. "Nobody says anything to me much here in town. They all think I murdered Olivia and hate me. Except for Jack Sutton. He doesn't hate me."

Bridgette found herself feeling sorry for Hughey. "Jack doesn't think you're a murderer either — he told me so today."

Hughey frowned and asked, "Do you think I'm a murderer?"

Bridgette was a little taken aback by the question. She decided he needed to hear the truth and replied, "When you had a shotgun pointed at me yesterday, I would have said yes. When you were taken away in the police car, I wasn't so sure. But, after talking to Jack and to your lawyer... I don't think so."

Hughey nodded and started eating his pie again.

Bridgette realized he had been looking for a positive answer and was disappointed he didn't get one.

She continued gently, "Hughey, if I thought you had killed Olivia, we wouldn't be sitting here sharing a meal — okay?"

Hughey nodded. He didn't appear angry or offended and she decided to ask another question. "I did a little research into your case last night. It looks like the only evidence the police had was a bag they found in your cupboard?"

Hughey stopped eating and nodded. He looked down at the table again and replied, "It was behind my cupboard. Olivia used to carry all her books to school in it."

"Do you know how it got there?"

Hughey shook his head and said, "It didn't have any fingerprints on it. We never used to lock the back door of our house and Mom said someone must have come in and hidden it."

"Did your lawyer mention this at the trial?"

Hughey shrugged. "I didn't listen much to what he said. I was worried about my Dad."

"Why were you worried about your father?"

Hughey looked up and replied, "He had a heart attack on the courthouse steps and went to the hospital. They wouldn't let me see him and I didn't know how sick he was."

"I'm sorry to hear that Hughey."

Hughey looked down at his food. "He was in the hospital for about a month and then he died. I wasn't allowed to go to his funeral..."

Bridgette nodded. She could see her questions were making Hughey sad and decided to lighten the mood a little by changing the subject. She looked across at Molly who was sitting just inside the open kitchen door. Resting her head between her front paws on the Lino floor, she looked to be sleeping, but Bridgette could see her charcoal eyes were slightly open watching them.

"I've never had much to do with animals. When you asked me to look after Molly, I wasn't sure what I was signing up for. Are all dogs as easy to look after as her?"

Hughey shook his head. "We had a dog when I was young — his name was Bruiser. He used to bark a lot and Dad had to give him away. We never had a dog after that. But Mom got lonely when I was in jail and got Molly."

"How old is she?"

Hughey frowned and said, "I think about seven years old — Mom got her as a puppy."

"It was nice that Jack could look after her when your Mom went into the hospital."

Hughey nodded. "I don't think he wanted me to take Molly back when I got out of prison. But I wanted to look after her for Mom."

Bridgette smiled as Molly slowly wagged her tail at the mention of her name.

"You know Hughey, I don't know much about animals, but she looks very happy and content. You're doing a good job looking after her."

Hughey nodded and mumbled, "She's my friend."

Bridgette realized Molly was probably the only friend Hughey had and understood why it had been so important for him to get his mother's dog back.

As she cut off another piece of the pie, she said, "It's nice to have friends Hughey."

Hughey held her gaze and with pleading eyes, asked, "Are you, my friend?"

Bridgette was surprised by the question. She wasn't sure what answer Hughey was expecting but decided she needed to be as honest as she could be without hurting his feelings. "Hughey, I don't know you very well and for me, friendships take a long time to develop."

Hughey nodded.

Bridgette added, "But I am enjoying our meal together and that's always a good start."

Deciding she needed to steer the conversation a little more, Bridgette asked, "Did you always live here before you went to prison?"

Hughey nodded as he swallowed another tiny mouthful of pie. "I lived in this house all my life except when I went to jail."

He went quiet for a moment and stared at the table, before asking Bridgette, "Do you think they'll send me back to jail?"

Chapter 14

Bridgette parked her car in the usual spot across the road from the Sanbury Police station. It was eight-fifteen a.m. and she was waiting for a call back from Chief Delray. What she needed to discuss with Delray was not something she could discuss inside the police station and she decided to review the Tyson file while she waited. She only got halfway through the first page before her phone rang — it was Delray.

"Hi Chief, thanks for calling back."

Delray sounded cheery as he said, "No problem Bridgette, what's up?"

Bridgette wasn't sure he would be so cheery after the phone call and started by saying, "Something's come up and I need your advice."

"I take it things are getting complicated?"

"You could say that?"

"I've got five minutes until my next meeting, so fire away."

Bridgette wasn't sure where to start. She thought for a moment and then said, "On my way home yesterday I called into the house that John Tyson used to live in. It's empty right now and about to be rented, so I decided to have a look around. I found a file hidden in the air conditioning unit at the back of the property."

"What kind of file?"

"A paper file like we use at Hartbourne Metro Chief. I had

a look at it last night and it's full of information that I think relates to the Olivia Hodder murder. There are lots of photos of forest locations around here and some geological reports off the internet. I'm not sure what it all means yet, but the fact that John Tyson had it hidden worries me."

"Are you sure it's John Tyson's file?"

"There were a few pages of handwritten notes. I recognized John's handwriting from some samples that were in the police report I read yesterday — it's definitely him."

Delray was silent for a moment before responding, "Well this gets more interesting every time we speak."

"I've told no one here about the file Chief. I wanted to talk to you first. Also, because you're talking to the Commissioner this morning, I thought this may need to be included in your briefing?"

"Just so we're clear, you found the file outside the house?"

"Yes, the air conditioner is located outside on the back deck."

"Well, I'm glad about that, because if someone had, let's say hypothetically broken into the house and found it inside we would have had a lot of explaining to do."

Bridgette breathed a sigh of relief. Delray was no fool and knew better than to ask her a direct question that would put him in a difficult position. She responded confidently, "I definitely found it outside the house Chief."

"Good. So, if I've got this right, its geological reports, photos and some handwritten notes about Olivia Hodder?"

"The notes are cryptic and relate to the locations, not specifically to Olivia Hodder."

"What in the world was John Tyson up to?"

"I'm not sure what it all means yet, but I plan to spend most of today on it. I figure, if I can find out what he was up to, we might get a lead on what happened to him.

More silence followed before Delray said, "If I say anything to the Commissioner, this all becomes official and we'll have to talk to Sanbury Police."

Bridgette knew Delray was thinking and waited.

"This is getting messy Bridgette. If Tyson was murdered this file could be very important."

"I can make a copy of everything and send to you if you like Chief?"

"No, that also makes it official. I'm thinking, for now, spend your day looking into it and see what you can find out. If anything breaks, call me straight away, but for now I think it's wise if we don't say anything to anybody until we know more. We can make it official late this evening if we need to."

Bridgette liked the plan and said, "Okay," as she thought about her conversation with Hughey last night. She knew the Chief was pressed for time but decided it couldn't wait. "There's one other thing you should know Chief."

"And what's that?"

Bridgette winced, as she tried to think of a diplomatic way to say what needed to be said. "My living situation here has become a little complicated as well..."

Delray replied, "How so?"

"The man who was convicted of Olivia Hodder's murder is living next door."

More silence followed. Bridgette could imagine Delray sitting in his chair with his mouth open trying to process what she'd just told him.

"I'm going to ask a really stupid question here, but how did that happen?"

"He was released from prison two weeks ago. When I looked

on the internet for somewhere to stay, I decided a little cottage just out-of-town might be nice. This one was far cheaper than anything else on the market... now I know why."

"Bridgette, we need to get you out of there and fast."

"Yesterday I would have agreed with you. But now I'm not so sure."

Bridgette could hear rising alarm in Delray's voice. "And how do you figure that?"

Bridgette decided to skip the part about having dinner with Hughey and said, "He's simple and I think he was set up for Olivia's murder and I'm not the only one who thinks so. Before he went to prison, he'd lived there all his life. I showed him some of the photos in the Tyson file. He recognized one location, which I'd like to visit today."

"Are you planning on taking him with you?"

Bridgette breathed in a little and said, "That's the plan if you agree to it."

"I gotta say, Bridgette, I'm not very comfortable with this."

Bridgette decided it was wise to give her boss options and said, "I can go back to just interviewing witnesses around town if you would prefer?"

"I'm concerned about who you're hanging out with there and what Sanbury Police will say about it."

"I can be discreet Chief."

"You're sure this guy's not a threat? The last thing we need is for you to be his next victim?"

"My gut feeling says he's okay Chief, and it's hardly ever wrong."

"Bridgette I gotta go or I'll be late to see the Commissioner. For now, go with the plan but be careful. I'll call you again later in the day to get an update."

The phone line went dead. Bridgette was relieved that Delray hadn't forbidden her from getting help from Hughey. She slid the file under the front seat before getting out of the car. As she walked across the street towards the front of the Sanbury Police station she wondered what kind of reception she would get from Chief Payne? The best-case scenario was he was out of the office and she would just leave the list of witnesses she planned to interview with his secretary. She wasn't sure what the worst-case scenario was, but she knew the subject of her car being parked out the front of John Tyson's house was likely to come up.

* * *

Bridgette pushed through the front glass door and walked into the reception area. The police officer with the pimples and the red hair was on duty again. Bridgette nodded a good morning to him as he hit an electronic switch to allow her access to the main office area.

She pretended not to notice him pick up the phone and dial an internal number, but she knew who he was calling as he muttered the words, "She's just arrived."

Bridgette sat at her desk and pretended to be planning her day. She figured if Payne wanted to speak to her about yesterday, he could come to her.

No sooner had she opened her laptop than she heard Payne's voice behind her, "I need to speak with you in my office now, Detective Cash."

Bridgette did her best not to roll her eyes as she stood up and followed Payne back to his office.

As she walked in, Payne said, "Close the door behind you."

Bridgette complied but didn't get to sit down before Payne bellowed, "What the hell were you doing at John Tyson's house yesterday?"

Bridgette took her time sitting down opposite Payne before she answered. "I'm getting background on the town and where he lived for my report."

Payne pointed a pen at her and said, "I told you yesterday I wanted to approve all witnesses and locations before you went anywhere. What part of that don't you understand?"

"I was aware of the witness list, but I don't recall any mention of places I could or couldn't visit?"

"From now on you don't go anywhere or interview anyone without my approval. Are we clear?"

Bridgette held Payne's glare. She showed no outward reaction as she thought about how best to respond. She didn't want to make matters worse but answering to Payne for every step she made in Sanbury would make the investigation unworkable.

She knew whoever was asking the questions controlled the discussion and calmly replied, "What are you afraid of?"

Payne held her with an intense stare and said, "I'm not afraid of you if that's what you're asking."

"Then why do you need to know my every movement? You'll get a copy of the report when it's completed and have your chance to provide input as agreed with the Hartbourne Metro Commissioner."

Pointing the pen at her again, Payne responded, "Because I don't trust you. That little stunt you pulled on Sunday night showed me you're prepared to interfere with local police work, and I won't have that. For now, I want you to prepare a timetable of who you want to interview and why, and then I'll think about giving you permission."

Payne picked up the phone. As he dialed a number he added, "Right now, I have more important things to do than argue with you, so you can get out of my office."

Bridgette didn't want to play hardball with Payne. She could threaten to complain about what happened on Sunday night, but she knew that would only make matters worse.

Instead, she shot back, "I'll give you the list of witnesses I want to interview as agreed. But I'm not giving you a detailed itinerary of my movements."

Payne stopped dialing and put the phone down. He grinned to himself and then looked up and said, "What did you just say?"

Bridgette wanted to say, 'Are you deaf?' but decided that was unwise. Instead, she leaned forward and said, "Just so we're clear, I'm not giving you a detailed itinerary for my movements. You have a problem with that, you can ring my Commissioner."

Payne placed his hands on the table face down and stared at Bridgette for a moment before he said, "I don't know what arrangements you've made with your boss, but I'm not letting you run around my town interviewing people without my knowledge."

Bridgette calmly replied, "Like I said, I'll provide you with a list."

"Not good enough. I want your timetable."

"Were you following me yesterday?"

Payne's eyes widened, but he regained his composure quickly and shot back, "This is my town and I go where I want."

"I watched you leaving John Tyson's house and wondered why you or any other police officer would be patrolling such an out of the way area of Sanbury, particularly at that time of the day..."

Bridgette waited for Payne to respond and when he didn't, she continued, "At first I thought it was just a coincidence, but the more I thought about it, the more I realized I was being followed. I was at the house long enough for someone to have radioed my location in and for you to drive out to see—"

Payne rose to his feet and pointed to the door as he said, "Get out of my office."

He paused for a moment and then with satisfied look added, "And pack up your desk as well. As of now, Sanbury is no longer cooperating with Hartbourne Metro. I'll be calling your boss momentarily to let him know."

Bridgette decided now wasn't the time to back down. As she rose to her feet she said, "No problem. I'll leave you with my interview list on my way out."

Through gritted teeth, he responded, "You don't seem to get it, do you? There will be no more investigation — you're out."

Bridgette replied calmly as she went to head for the door, "As soon as I get formal advice from my superiors, I'll leave town. Until then I intend to carry on my work."

Payne quickly came around from behind his desk and put an arm out to stop her walking out the door. "You set foot outside this building and even look like you're continuing this investigation and I'll have you arrested."

"For what?"

"Whatever I god-damn like. You can sit in a cell until someone comes to collect you."

Bridgette looked up into Payne's eyes and decided she'd had enough. In a voice barely above a whisper, she said, "Listen carefully Payne, I will only say this once. If I'm arrested, I'll be making a formal complaint of sexual harassment against Mitch Conden as well as a formal complaint of unprovoked police brutality in your bungled arrest of Hughey Warren. The fact that you let him go without charge and that he's got a cut to his ear that should have been stitched doesn't bode well for you or your officer in an official inquiry... because that's where this is headed."

Bridgette pushed past Payne's arm and opened the door. Turning back, she said, "Make the call Payne. As soon as I'm told to leave, I will but not a moment before."

Bridgette walked out of the office and back to her desk. She ignored the stares of local Sanbury police officers as she packed up and walked towards the front exit. She had no idea what Payne would do next and didn't overly care.

Pimply cop with red hair watched her as she walked towards the entrance but said nothing. She smiled and handed him a piece of paper and said, "This is the list of witnesses I plan to interview. Make sure Chief Payne gets it."

Bridgette walked out into the early morning sunshine and thought about the day ahead. She had no idea whether she would be in jail, on her way back to Hartbourne or still investigating by lunchtime. She decided not to ring Delray straight away. The next move was Payne's, and she was happy to wait and see what he did next.

Chapter 15

Delray walked out of the elevator and into the plush surroundings of the Hartbourne Metro executive level. The modern timber furnishings, artwork, plush carpets and large open spaces made level four a far cry from the conditions he and his officers put up with on level two. He was glad they rarely got to see this part of the building and did his best to ignore the opulence as he walked over to the reception area.

The Commissioner's personal assistant saw him approach and dialed a number. He usually had to wait, sometimes for an hour or more, but this time he was waved straight through. Delray nodded a thank you as he walked further down the hallway before stopping in an open doorway. Delray could see the stocky Commissioner sitting behind a large wooden desk that looked close to the size of Delray's office. He had heard of several colleagues who had just barged into the office without waiting for an invitation and had earned the wrath of Commissioner Underwood in the process.

Delray had no intention of being the next victim and waited after knocking lightly on the open door.

Underwood looked up from a file he was studying and said, "Come on in Felix."

Although he didn't have an imposing presence, Underwood

was an intellectual giant. He had a capacity for rapidly absorbing and managing large amounts of information and made decisions quickly and decisively. Delray knew most of the police force respected his firm but fair management style. He was one of the few senior officers Delray genuinely trusted and the only one he would take a bullet for.

Delray greeted Underwood with a "Good morning Sir," as he walked in. He sat down in one of Underwood's three visitors' chairs and waited while the Commissioner closed up all but one of four open files on his desk. Delray declined the Commissioner's offer of tea or coffee as he always did and waited for the Commissioner to set the tone for the meeting.

"Before we start Felix, how's Detective Cash getting on in Sanbury?"

"She's making good progress Sir. She's read the official file on John Tyson and is now out conducting interviews."

Underwood nodded. "I'd appreciate being kept in the loop on this one Felix. We need to be as sure as we can be, before we make any pronouncement about John Tyson's death."

"Sir, as soon as I have anything concrete, I'll let you know."

Underwood nodded and fixed Delray with a stare. Delray had been in this situation often enough to know a hard question was coming.

"Part of the reason I gave this assignment to Detective Cash was to get her away from here for a while to help her clear her head... But it's not the only reason."

Delray nodded and waited.

"With an IQ of one-fifty-two, Detective Cash has already shown us how capable she is, and I expect she will get results..."

"I'm sure you're right, Sir."

Underwood continued. "So, what's her take on this so far

Felix?"

Delray responded, "In what way, Sir?"

Underwood gave a knowing nod and said, "You know as well as I do, this was never about just writing a report."

Delray grimaced. "Sir, there's nothing formal that I can report... not yet, anyway. All I can say is Detective Cash suspects John Tyson didn't perish in the mountains like Sanbury's report says."

"Just so we're clear here Felix, as soon as you have anything solid, I want to know. There's a lot of politics in play on this and Sanbury Police can put up a lot of roadblocks if we're not careful. Right now, they think we've just assigned a rookie detective to this to write a simple report. But if she can give me any evidence that contradicts their findings, I'll have what I need to send in a full team to investigate."

"Sir, as soon as I know anything solid, I'll be on the phone."

Underwood nodded and then looked down at the only remaining open file on his desk.

He studied in silence for close to a minute before he looked up. "Internal Investigations are getting nowhere with this investigation Felix."

Delray nodded. He knew Underwood was referring to the shooting incident in the basement that happened a few weeks earlier. Delray's star recruit had been reading through her mother's murder file late one evening on her own time when she had been shot at as she sat alone in the small records management office. In the ensuing struggle that followed, Bridgette had escaped serious injury, but the microfilm she had been reading had been stolen and her masked attacker had never been captured. Unsure of how he should respond, he waited for Underwood to continue. To his surprise, Underwood flipped the file around so that Delray could see it as he got up from his chair.

As he walked across to his office door Underwood said, "There are forty-six names on that suspect list Felix. These are the officers who were still in the building at nine p.m. on the night the shooting occurred."

Delray quickly scanned the list — his eyes widened as he read his own name.

As if reading Delray's mind, Underwood added, "Your names on the list Felix because you were here at that time."

Delray looked up at Underwood and asked, "Do you think I'm a suspect, Sir?"

Underwood shook his head and said flatly, "You rescued Detective Cash from a car fire in the forest several days after this incident. That hardly seems like the actions of someone who days earlier tried to shoot her in the back."

After closing the door, Underwood walked across to a large picture window that afforded him a partial view of the Hartbourne River.

With his back to Delray, he continued, "I've been a police officer for over thirty years and this basement thing... I've never seen anything like it."

Delray replied, "I don't think any of us have, Sir."

"Internal Investigations have been investigating this for weeks and have come up empty. Other than stealing the last known copy we have of a murder file, we have no clear motive, no prime suspect — not even a fingerprint. Frankly, I find this all very unacceptable."

Underwood turned around to face Delray.

"I've called you up here for a reason Felix. I don't believe anyone without a security clearance could get into our basement and out again without being noticed." Underwood paused and then said, "This is an inside job Felix, no question."

Delray nodded. "I agree."

Underwood frowned and walked back to his desk. "This whole incident that Detective Cash was investigating happened twenty years ago. I've only been Commissioner here for a short time. When this happened, I was still a base grade detective in Rochford. I need someone here who I can trust to bring me up to speed on who was here at the time and how everything worked."

Underwood locked eyes on Delray and didn't blink. Delray knew this might be his only chance and pulled out a folded piece of paper from his top pocket. He'd been carrying it around for a month and wasn't sure he would ever show it to anyone, let alone the Commissioner.

"Sir, given this is one of my team who was shot at, it goes without saying that I've been giving this a lot of thought. When someone is prepared to go to this extent to keep information hidden, it usually means they have a lot to lose."

As Delray unfolded the paper he added, "So with your permission, I would like to show you a list I've been working on. I haven't been privy to the investigation carried out by Internal Investigations, but this is the list of suspects that I think are worth investigating."

Delray took a deep breath. There was one name on the list that could end his career, but he decided he needed to be completely open as he slid the paper across the desk.

"I started with the names of police officers who were here at the time that Bridgette's mother was murdered. I'm not sure what's in your report, but there were rumors floating around back then that her father had discovered high-level police corruption while he was working undercover. It's my belief that Bridgette's father disappeared, not so much because he was framed for murdering his wife, but because he knew he would be the next victim if he went public with what he knew but couldn't prove."

Underwood picked up the piece of paper and studied the names. He raised his eyebrows slightly. "Having spent most of my policing career in Rochford, I don't recognize most of these names Felix."

Delray nodded, "Sir, there were nine names on the list when I started. You can see I've already struck off four names. I've learned that three of them now are dead and the fourth is in a nursing home and can't remember his name."

"So, we're down to just five names?"

Delray leaned forward and answered, "Technically, but there are a further two names on the list that I think we can also discount. Russ Pollard has been retired for close to fifteen years and now runs a homeless shelter for men. Paul Chappell got out and moved to New Zealand about nine years ago to run a bed-and-breakfast with his wife. Neither of them strikes me as having much interest in what's happening here anymore."

Underwood studied the remaining names for a moment and then looked up at Delray with raised eyebrows and said, "John Cotton used to be a police officer?"

Delray nodded. "Senator John Cotton worked in Vice for four years, before resigning to enter politics. He wasn't particularly well liked when he was here and was always looking for a fast way to the top. If he was involved in any form of corruption, he would have a lot to lose now if anything was made public."

"And Paul Ferringa?"

Delray frowned. "Paul Ferringa used to be the partner of Bridgette's father. He left the force about six months after the murder saying he couldn't cope with the job anymore."

Underwood nodded. "You hear the name Ferringa around town

a lot — mostly linked to security and investments."

"Paul Ferringa never looked back. He got involved in all sorts of businesses and is now reputedly worth over forty million."

Underwood looked up from the list. "A politician and a businessman — both with a lot to lose if they've been hiding something."

Delray shifted in his chair. "Of course, neither man would have risked breaching our security to carry out the attack personally if they were involved. But they're both rich enough and resourceful enough—"

Underwood nodded and added, "To recruit someone inside this police force to do the dirty work for them."

"The thing that bothers me about this is that Bridgette was very discreet. She was investigating her mother's murder case on her own time. Only a handful of people knew what she was doing."

Underwood looked down at the list again and without looking up said, "Tell me about the last name Chief Inspector."

Delray swallowed. He knew he needed to be careful with how he handled his answer, knowing his whole career could be over before he left the office. "Sir, Assistant Commissioner Leo Cunningham ran Internal Investigations back when Bridgette's mother was murdered. Because her father was a cop who went into hiding after the murder, he became the prime suspect. A lot of officers came forward and told Cunningham they believed the real murder target was Bridgette's father and not her mother, but he refused to listen. The murder investigation focused solely on finding Peter Casseldhorf in spite of evidence which suggested there were other suspects."

Underwood handed Delray back his list and leaned back in his chair. Delray could feel sweat forming on his brow as he realized he'd just accused a senior police officer of major corruption with no real evidence.

Underwood studied Delray for a moment and raised his eyebrows just slightly as Delray put the list back in his coat pocket. "If I were you Felix, I wouldn't be showing that list to anyone else. Are we clear?"

Delray nodded and relaxed slightly as he responded, "Perfectly clear, Sir."

Underwood continued, "I appreciate your candor Felix, but you have no evidence against any of these suspects and a lot of people might think you have Cunningham on your list simply because you have a grudge against him."

Delray nodded, but decided not to comment.

"For what it's worth, in the six months I've been here, I've found Assistant Commissioner Cunningham competent in the performance of his duties, but that's all I'm prepared to say for now..."

Delray replied, "Understood sir," as he realized the Commissioner was yet to make up his mind on Cunningham.

They were both silent until Underwood closed the file and said, "We agree on one thing Felix. Whoever is really behind this was unlikely to have been in the basement that night. You only survive this long by getting other people to do your dirty work."

Delray nodded as Underwood continued, "We need to look closely at people within our organization who worked with Detective Cash and knew what she was investigating..."

Delray sighed. "It's hard for me to accept that one of my team could be involved in this Sir, but it's something we can't ignore."

"I've worked with a lot of cops in my time Felix. Ninety-nine per cent of them are as honest as the day is long, but there's always one who can be turned for the right price. We just need to find out who that is."

Chapter 16

Bridgette pulled the Honda to a halt into her driveway and switched off the engine. She sat for a moment thinking about the meeting she'd just had with Payne and what she would do next. She decided pursuing interviews without having spoken to Delray was probably unwise. She didn't think Payne would follow through with his threat to put her in jail, but she wasn't about to test him either. She pulled the Tyson file out from under the front seat and started reviewing its contents while she waited for Delray's call. As she flipped through the file again, she frowned as she scanned the web pages on geological surveys of the region that John Tyson had printed off. Puzzled that there was no mention of the surveys in any of Tyson's notes, she wondered again whether visiting some of the sites Tyson had photographed would help her understand more.

Bridgette glanced up at Hughey's house as she started reviewing the photos again and thought back to her meal with Hughey the previous evening. She had learned a lot about her neighbor including that he was a great cook. She had shown Hughey the Tyson photographs without mentioning any detail of how they came to be in her possession. Before going to jail, Hughey had lived in Sanbury all his life and recognized several of the locations. He had offered to show her where they were, and she decided now was as good a time as any.

As she walked across to his front door, she realized her trust in the gentle giant was growing. Hughey had been both polite and shy during their dinner. Conversation had been awkward at first, but as he relaxed and grew in confidence, he shared with her some of the ordeals he had suffered in jail at the hands of other men. Fighting back tears as he recounted his story, Bridgette realized Hughey was on the brink of a breakdown and probably had been for a long time. Bridgette knocked on his front door and waited. She no longer felt scared or threatened by her neighbor and was positive Sanbury had jailed the wrong man for Olivia Hodder's murder.

Seconds later, Hughey opened the front door.

He looked confused and frowned as he said, "Hello Bridgette."

Bridgette sensed something was slightly off. "Are you okay, Hughey?"

"I've got to get down to the police station for my check-in or they'll put me back in jail again. I get nervous..."

"Would you like me to drive you?"

Hughey brightened a little and said, "Okay."

"I'm just wondering if I do you a favor, maybe you would do me a favor afterward?"

Hughey looked confused again and replied, "Okay."

"You know those photographs I showed you last night?"

Hughey nodded.

"You think you could show me where they are?"

With a concerned look, Hughey replied, "I only know where some of them were taken, not all of them."

"Well, how about you show me the ones you know? We can take Molly if you like?"

"I gotta go to the police station first. Molly's not allowed in there."

"I tell you what Hughey, Molly can stay in the car with me. We can wait together."

Hughey thought for a moment. "I guess that would be all right. I just have to be back to meet Dan at one o'clock."

Bridgette recalled how anxious Hughey had been last night as he told her about his court appearance today. His reaction was understandable, but before she had a chance to respond, Hughey disappeared back into his house. A moment later Bridgette felt a nudge on her leg and looked down to see Molly looking up at her and wagging her tail.

Hughey appeared a moment later with a dog lead and said, "We can go now."

After getting settled into Bridgette's car, Hughey seemed to calm down. As they wound their way down the tree lined road towards the town center, Hughey looked at Molly sitting in the middle of the back seat taking in the view.

"Molly likes to go in cars, but she doesn't get to very often."

Bridgette stole a quick look in the rear-view mirror at the dog. Molly was panting lightly as she sat on the back seat seemingly enjoying the view out the window.

She smiled and returned her focus to the driving and said, "You don't drive Hughey?"

Hughey shook his head. "I went to jail before I got a chance to learn."

"Well, hopefully, that's something you can set your mind to doing once you're cleared as a free man."

Hughey looked out the window. "I don't know..."

Bridgette changed down gears as she approached the first major intersection that led into the township.

"You're not sure about driving?"

Still looking out the window, Hughey replied, "I'm not very

smart."

"Hughey, you don't need to be smart to drive. It's more about practice than anything else. I'm sure you'd make a very good driver once you get the hang of it."

Hughey responded again, "I don't know."

Bridgette decided not to push it for now and looked across at her neighbor who was growing increasingly restless the closer they got to the police station.

She could understand his nervousness and in a soothing voice said, "Hughey, you've got nothing to be afraid of. You're reporting to the police station just like they've asked you to, so there's no need to be nervous. Okay?"

Hughey nodded but didn't look convinced as they pulled up in a car park across the road from the police station.

Bridgette said in a reassuring tone, "Molly and I will wait here for you."

Hughey replied, "Okay," as he got out of the car.

Bridgette watched as he walked into the police station and then turned to face Molly who had been watching Hughey as well.

"Hopefully he'll be back soon Molly."

* * *

Hughey's check-in with the police didn't take very long and the further they got away from the police station, the more he relaxed. Hughey had directed Bridgette to take a road that led up towards Saddleback Ridge.

As they passed Jack Sutton's house, Molly put her nose to the car window and gave a small whine.

Bridgette looked at the dog in the rear-view mirror and said, "Looks like she remembers staying there Hughey."

Hughey nodded and replied, "She's very smart."

In a quieter voice, he added, "Jack said she could come and stay with him again if I have to go back to jail."

Bridgette knew little about Hughey's appeal case and decided it was unwise to give him false hope by being too optimistic.

She decided to tactfully change the subject and asked, "So how far is it now Hughey."

Hughey frowned as he looked up the road as it began to twist and turn as they drove deeper into the forest. "I haven't been up here in a long while — maybe two miles?"

Bridgette hoped the road conditions wouldn't deteriorate too much further as her car bounced across the increasingly narrow and uneven road surface.

They climbed steadily through the forest for almost ten minutes before the car emerged into a clearing.

Hughey looked around. "This is it — we need to stop here."

Bridgette was relieved to bring her car to a halt. The road had turned into a rocky, single lane track through the forest and she wasn't confident the car's suspension could have taken much more of a beating.

After clipping the lead on Molly, Hughey got out of the car to get his bearings.

To Bridgette's relief, he pointed towards a gap in the tree line and said, "Through there. We gotta walk about two minutes."

Bridgette followed Hughey and Molly up a small path that didn't look like it had been used in years. She began to understand why people got lost and perished in the forest as they walked further away from the clearing. After another minute of walking, they emerged out of the forest into a small meadow.

Bridgette stopped for a moment to admire the view as she looked across a large valley to the mountains on the opposite side. The meadow was reasonably flat but fell away down an almost sheer rock face as it merged with the valley below.

"So where are we, Hughey?"

"This is the end of Saddleback Ridge."

Hughey pointed at the valley below and said, "They call that the Cathedral."

Bridgette nodded as she took in the view. "How did it come to get that name?"

Hughey shook his head. "I don't really know. My Dad took me up here to camp one year just before winter when I was a boy. He said when it snowed, the valley became peaceful like being in church."

Bridgette tried to imagine what the valley would look like under snow. She could understand why its narrow base might be referred to as a cathedral with fir trees framing it on three sides.

Hughey pointed at a solitary fir tree over to his left and said, "I'm pretty sure that's where the cabin was."

Bridgette followed Hughey and Molly across the meadow. As they approached the fir tree, Bridgette could see the remnants of a charred structure which had long since burnt to the ground.

Bridgette noticed Hughey stop short of the hut, almost as if he was afraid to go on.

"Are you okay Hughey?"

"My dad and I camped here one night. We slept in the shack because it was too cold to put up our tent... It kinda makes me sad."

Bridgette pulled the Tyson photos out of a plastic envelope and said, "Hughey you can stay here. I'll go check if it's a match for the photo and then I'll come back and see you. Okay?"

Hughey nodded.

Molly tugged on her lead and whined as Bridgette made her way forward. She could clearly see flat rocks placed on the ground to form a stepping stone path up towards what was left of the structure. Bridgette stopped a few feet short of the remains of the structure and looked at the burnt, blackened beams that had somehow survived the fire. Cast about at odd angles, the beams had been overtaken by years of meadow undergrowth leaving little in the way of tell-tale signs that this had once been a hut. At the western side of what she imagined was once the hut, she noticed a large pile of scattered rocks.

She pictured a hand-built chimney and fireplace that years ago would have kept its occupants warm. Bridgette flipped through the photos until she found the one she was looking for. She held it up at an angle and then walked several paces to her left before stopping again.

As she held up the photo to compare the image to what was in front of her, she whispered, "Bingo."

Satisfied that she now had the location for at least one of John Tyson's photos, she looked back towards Hughey and said, "Good job Hughey. This is definitely the place."

Hughey nodded and said, "Okay" but made no move to come forward.

Still holding onto the photos, Bridgette walked back to Hughey and Molly. "We know one of these photos is of the construction site, which is not in this area, but now we're here, a lot of these photos look like they could have been taken in this area."

Hughey nodded. "We can go for a walk if you like?"

Bridgette held up the photographs one by one to compare them to the vista that surrounded them.

She pointed towards the Cathedral Valley. "Is there any way we can get down to the valley from here?"

Hughey shrugged. "I'm not sure. I haven't been up here in a

long time."

Bridgette walked towards the edge of the Meadow. "Let's see how steep this rock face is. Maybe there is a way we can climb down it?"

They stopped just short of the edge and peered over the side. Bridgette estimated the drop was about thirty feet although it wasn't quite as sheer as she first thought. She walked a few feet to her left and then stopped again and pointed out a narrow, overgrown path that zig-zagged its way down to the valley below.

She looked back at Hughey and said, "Do you think you can get down this path Hughey?" Hughey walked over and stood next to Bridgette and looked down the path.

He looked a little reluctant, but said, "I think so?"

"Does Molly need to stay on the lead? If you're not afraid that she will run away, it might be best if you just concentrate on getting yourself down in one piece?"

Hughey replied, I only keep her on the lead because the dogcatcher can take her away from me if he finds her without a lead on."

Bridgette smiled and said, "I don't think you need to worry about a dogcatcher out here Hughey."

After unclipping Molly, the pair made their way down the trail without incident. In spite of his bulk, Bridgette was impressed with how light on his feet Hughey was. Molly, who had gone ahead, greeted them with a soft bark and a wag of her tail when they both reached the bottom. Bridgette held up photos in turn as she looked down the Cathedral Valley. Several of them were almost a perfect match for where they now stood.

"Well Hughey, John Tyson definitely came this way."

She wondered what John Tyson had been up to and why it was important to take photographs of the burned-out ruins of a hut?

And why more photos from this point of the valley? Was he collecting evidence or just using the photographs as a reference point to help him find his way back later?

She knew she wouldn't find any answers here and said, "Let's keep walking Hughey. I have a feeling we're going to find a match for some of these other photos when we get to the bottom of the valley."

With pockets of snow already forming on the ground, Bridgette enjoyed their walk down through the valley. She tried to imagine what it would look like in the middle of winter — fully covered in snow and framed by the enormous fir trees on the left and the right. She understood why they had called it the Cathedral Valley and imagined herself standing in the middle of the valley as soft snow fell on her face in the peaceful stillness. When they reached the bottom of the valley, Bridgette held up the photos again and turned around on a three hundred and sixty-degree arc, checking each photo against the backdrop. She put all but two photos back into the plastic envelope before walking back twenty paces towards the western side of the valley.

Turning to face the eastern side of the valley again, she held each of them up again and nodded — an almost perfect match for the tree line and the small break that looked like it led to a walking trail.

As she walked back towards Hughey, he asked, "Are they the same?"

"Yes, Hughey, this is definitely the way he came. We have two photos that are almost a perfect match."

Pointing towards a small break in the tree line on the eastern side, Bridgette said, "I'm not sure where he was heading, but the photos seem to indicate that's the general direction."

As Bridgette went to move off, she noticed Hughey remained

perfectly still.

"What's wrong Hughey?"

In an almost stammering voice, he asked, "Are we going to be much longer?"

Bridgette looked at her watch — it was close to eleven thirty a.m. She realized if they went any further, they may not make it back for Hughey's one o'clock appointment. She looked back at the forest, keen to continue exploring but knew that would have to wait.

Smiling, she said, "Hughey, thanks for bringing me out here today. We've made some good progress, but we've got to get you back for your appointment."

Bridgette could see the instant relief on Hughey's face as he replied, "Sorry."

"No need to apologize, Hughey — we're helping each other."

As Hughey clipped Molly back on her lead, Bridgette looked back at the forest wondering where John Tyson had been headed and what he was up to.

She whispered, "I'll be back soon," before turning to head back up the valley.

Chapter 17

Apart from the odd snore from Molly who had fallen asleep on the backseat, the first part of the car trip back to Sanbury was quiet. Focusing her energy on getting down off the mountain in one piece, Bridgette left Hughey to his thoughts. She knew his court appearance was weighing on his mind as he spent most of his time staring out the car window.

Bridgette started to relax as they passed Jack Sutton's house. Knowing that the worst of the trip was now behind them, she said, "You're awfully quiet Hughey?"

Hughey nodded and said, "I guess," as he continued to gaze out the window.

"Are you worried about court today?"

"I don't want to go back to jail. The men do bad things, and nobody cares 'cause they think I'm a murderer and stupid."

Hughey turned to face Bridgette and continued, "But I didn't kill her. Olivia was my friend. I would never have done anything to hurt her."

Bridgette replied, "I believe you, Hughey," and for the first time genuinely believed he was innocent.

Bridgette sighed as she tried to think of words of comfort. She found it hard to even fathom the depravity someone as vulnerable as Hughey would suffer in a prison system built around the survival of the strongest.

She knew Hughey had no friends, and she wasn't about to invest him in false hope. Now that he was talking again, she tried to steer the conversation in a more positive direction.

"Hughey, if you don't mind me asking, what exactly is your court appearance about today?"

"They're gonna talk about whether I go back to jail or not."

Bridgette nodded, but Hughey's answer didn't help. She had noticed with Hughey's limited intellect she sometimes had to ask a question in two or three different ways before she got the answer.

"So why did they release you from prison Hughey?"

"They made a mistake when they arrested me. They thought I was eighteen, but I wasn't."

Bridgette pondered the answer for a moment and replied, "So you were tried and sentenced as an adult, not as a child?"

Hughey nodded his head.

"Dan said they made a mistake. Even though I'm a grownup, I wasn't when it happened. He says they can't keep me in jail, but they're trying to."

Bridgette now understood a little more about the court hearing. She had taken some basic law subjects as part of her criminology degree and knew that Hughey's case could turn into a legal minefield if there were no precedents. Now only two minutes from the main center of town, Bridgette wondered if there would be a media presence at the courthouse.

"Hughey, did Dan mention anything about cameras and reporters being at court today."

Hughey nodded again. "He said, there'll be lots of them and I should keep my head down and say nothing. He's got a room around the back that I gotta meet him in."

Bridgette thought about how she might be able to get Hughey

into the courthouse without subjecting him to the media attention.

"Hughey, on the back seat next to Molly, you'll find a blanket. I want you to push your seat as far back as you can and when we get close to the court, I want you to slide down as much as you can and cover yourself with the blanket. When we drive up, it will look like it's only me in the car. I'll park around the back. You should be able to get out without being seen by the media — okay?"

With a slightly relieved look on his face, Hughey said, "Thank you, Bridgette."

"You're welcome."

Hughey's face turned to concern as he reached in the back to get the blanket.

"I forgot about Molly — I can't take her to the courthouse."

"It's okay Hughey. I'm planning on driving out to the construction site that you recognized in one of John's other photos, but I'll drop her home first."

Hughey replied, "Thank you Bridgette," with a relieved look on his face.

"Do you want me to come back and pick you up Hughey?"

Hughey shook his head as he replied, "Dan normally drives me home."

Bridgette replied, "Okay," and focused on the driving again.

As they approached the main street she said, "It's time for you to cover up Hughey, we're almost there."

Bridgette turned left and drove down the main street. Hughey had done a good job of concealing his bulky frame and was all but hidden from the view of pedestrians. She observed two media trucks and a small group of reporters waiting out front of the courthouse for Hughey's arrival and whispered, "Not today guys," as she drove past the group and headed for the rear parking lot.

"We're just heading into the parking lot now Hughey. None of the cameras are following us, so it's looking good."

Bridgette heard a muffled "Okay," from under the blanket and smiled to herself as she realized she was growing fond of the gentle giant. She pulled up in a far corner of the car park behind the main two-story brick building and looked back towards the parking lot entrance. With no sign of any reporters following her, she decided Hughey should get out of the car and into the building as quickly as possible.

Ripping back his blanket she whispered, "We haven't been followed Hughey, so you're good to go."

Hughey tentatively raised his head and looked around. When he realized they were alone he said, "Thank you, Bridgette," and opened the car door.

Reaching a hand into the back of the car, Hughey gave Molly a pat as tears welled in his eyes. Bridgette could see he was trying to put on a brave face and said, "You can tell me all about it tonight Hughey."

Hughey wiped his eyes and replied, "Can you take her to Jack's place if I don't come home?"

Bridgette nodded and said softly, "Of course Hughey."

She watched as the hunched form of Hughey trudged across the car park. Molly whined softly as her master disappeared inside the building.

Bridgette let out a sigh as she put her car into reverse.

She looked at Molly. "There's nothing more we can do here girl, let's drop you home."

As she drove out of the car park, she looked at the reporters and camera crews milling around on the lawn in front of the courthouse. She hoped they wouldn't be reporting on Hughey going back to jail later in the afternoon.

Chapter 18

Bridgette only had a rough idea where the construction site was from Hughey's directions. But as she headed out of town on the northern road towards Rochford, she needn't have worried. With major billboard signage every few hundred yards promoting the construction of the Snowbridge Resort, she had no trouble finding the exit.

After turning left and heading back into the forest down a road that looked scarred from constant heavy truck use, she got the impression Snowbridge was a new development.

Bridgette drove on for several minutes before she emerged through the tree-line at the top of a picturesque valley. Beyond the construction site was a lush green valley that was covered in large pockets of snow and already looked well in the grip of winter. She drove into a large makeshift parking lot that had turned to mud due to heavy vehicle traffic and parked next to an old red Ford pickup — the only other vehicle on the site. She pulled the one photo that John Tyson had taken in this location from the file before sliding it back under the seat.

Bridgette sat in the car for a moment and looked through the building site at the view of the valley below. She knew it would be close to freezing outside and looked around to get her bearings before getting out. She studied each of the three large buildings under construction. All of them were not much more than two story steel frames on concrete slabs. She looked down the valley and saw a long row of large steel poles rising up in a straight line from deep in the valley — each set in a large concrete block that rose out of the ground.

As she got out of the car, she tried to imagine what it might look like in the future with thousands of people skiing down the mountain at the height of winter.

Buttoning her jacket against the cold, Bridgette looked left and right before deciding to head off toward the largest of the structures and four portable pre-fab office buildings that sat to its right on concrete blocks. Careful to avoid the large semi-frozen pools of mud and water that tried to block her way, she circled her way around but saw no signs of life in any of the portables, which were all locked up tight. She continued her walk around towards the front of the building. Even though it was not much more than a frame, she could see it would be a large building — easily the size of six basketball courts. Although it was only just after two o'clock in the afternoon, the site was quiet. She wondered why there were no construction workers on site on a weekday as she came around to the front of the structure. She stopped for a moment and took in the breathtaking views of the valley below again before continuing on around the side of the building.

Bridgette stopped and pulled the photograph from her pocket. She held it up and compared it to the view in front of her for several seconds before whispering, "Close enough."

She put the photograph back in her pocket. Tyson might have been standing another twenty or thirty paces further to the right, but there was no doubt she was in the right place. As she stood contemplating why he would have photographed the valley, she heard a man's voice behind her.

"Can I help you?"

Bridgette turned around to see a man standing next to a steel beam at the edge of the building. He was in his early sixties and was wearing an orange safety jacket with the word 'Security' emblazoned across the front. The man's overalls looked in need of a good wash and his disheveled appearance made her wonder if he really was a security guard. He looked warily at her and she immediately knew she wasn't welcome here.

Without waiting for an answer, the man stepped down off the concrete slab and said, "This is a construction site. If you don't have a reason to be here, you're trespassing."

Bridgette decided not to reach for her police badge and instead replied, "Sorry, I didn't see any sign. I thought it was okay."

The man stopped a few feet short of her and placed his hands on his hips.

"What are you doing here?"

Bridgette pulled the photograph from her pocket again and said, "Someone I know took this photo from up here. I wanted to see the location for myself. It's very pretty."

To her surprise, the man's sullen features dissolved as he said, "Maybe not for much longer."

Eager to keep the conversation going, Bridgette replied, "Why do you say that?"

The man frowned and responded, "This place will be crawling with tourists inside two years. I'm not sure you could call it pretty when that happens."

Bridgette got the feeling the man didn't like what was going on here. She was tempted to ask why he was working here if he didn't agree with the change but resisted the temptation. Instead, she responded, "I guess it will be good for Sanbury?"

The man's shoulders sagged. "That's what they're all saying.

Good for the town, lots of jobs and opportunities."

"But you don't believe that?"

The man shrugged. "I barely make minimum wage for sixty-hour weeks. For someone of my age, I don't see that changing much when Snowbridge opens."

Bridgette nodded. The man didn't seem to be in any hurry to move her on and she got the distinct impression he was lonely.

"I know little about construction, but it seems awfully quiet around here?"

The man nodded. "They shut up for the winter about six weeks ago. It's only me here now to make sure nothing gets stolen."

"But winter's still two weeks away?"

The man shrugged again. "Snowbridge is owned by some Chinese company. Who knows how they work?"

Bridgette thought about the man's response. It seemed odd that a company would shut down operations so far out from winter and wondered again what John Tyson had been doing here?

Deciding she needed to learn as much as she could, she stuck her hand out and said, "I'm Bridgette and I'm actually a detective from Hartbourne."

The man reluctantly gripped her hand. He seemed wary again at the mention that she was a detective and didn't give her his name.

Bridgette asked, "I'm not sure if you've heard of John Tyson or not? He was a Hartbourne detective who was working here as—"

"He's the guy who disappeared a few weeks back."

"Yes. Did you know him?"

The man shook his head. "Not really. You stay here more than a few weeks, and everybody knows your business whether you like it or not. So I knew he was a police officer, but we never actually met."

Bridgette nodded to buy herself some time.

She held up the photograph again. "This photograph was found among some of the files on a case he was working on. I'm fairly sure he took the photo. Do you have any idea what he might have been photographing here apart from the view?"

She passed the photo to the man, who stood there scratching his head as he stared at the image.

The man replied, "Well, that's definitely our valley," and added, "Maybe he just liked the view?" as he handed back the photograph.

Bridgette frowned for a second as she studied the image again. "Does the snow fully melt here during summer?"

"Depends on where you go. On the peaks, you got cover all year round in pockets, but down in the valleys it's mostly gone by late-spring."

Bridgette held up the photograph again. "So this photo would have been taken recently?"

The man studied the picture again and nodded. "The poles weren't here last year, so this is definitely this year's snow. We had our first flurry early — I think about seven weeks ago, which is probably why they shut down construction shortly after. One minute there's dozens of guys here working and the next, it's like a ghost town."

The man paused and pointed to a smaller concrete slab set between two of the buildings, and continued, "That slab for an amenities block is the only thing that they've done since. A team of four men came back for a day and then they were gone again. It'll be just me now until spring I guess."

Bridgette thought for a moment and then asked, "Did they ever have any trouble here? Union disputes, for example?"

"Not that I recall. There was the odd flare up every now and then, but no more than any other place I've worked."

"Do you keep records of everyone that comes in here?"

The man grimaced. "We're supposed to, but the other guys that used to work security sometimes got lazy."

"Do you think we could check? John Tyson disappeared six weeks ago, so it will only be a week or two at the most that we need to check?"

The man looked warily at her again and said, "Aren't I supposed to see a search warrant before I show you something like that?"

"You have every right to say no. I can get a warrant, but I'd rather save everyone the hassle. All I'm really trying to find out is a date when John Tyson might have taken this photograph. It might not mean much, but every bit of information helps."

The man shrugged and said, "Follow me."

As an afterthought, he added, "And the name's Leo."

Bridgette said, "Nice to meet you, Leo, I appreciate your help," as she followed the man back up to the portable offices. He unlocked the door to the largest one which was labeled, 'Site Office' and then turned around to face her.

"You need to wait out here while I check. It would be my job if they found out I was letting a cop poke around inside without a search warrant."

Bridgette nodded and said, "Okay Leo."

She expected the man to return in a minute announcing that there was no record of Tyson's attendance, before asking her to leave. As she contemplated whether it was worthwhile trying to get a search warrant, he appeared at the door with a battered foolscap file of loose-leaf sheets and said, "You're in luck."

The man carried the file outside and placed it on a drum.

As he turned to walk back towards the office, he said, "I think what you're looking for is an entry on the seventh. I'm not sure what it proves other than he wasn't up here sneaking around taking photographs."

The man paused at the door and said, "When I come out again, I expect you'll be gone," before disappearing inside.

Bridgette ran her finger down the handwritten list of entries on the right-hand page. About half way down she recognized John Tyson's handwriting, registering his attendance on the construction site on the seventh day of the previous month. She flipped through to the end of the log and scanned back through the last few pages. The site visits for the last two months were less than three pages of entries and consistent with everything Leo had told her.

She closed the file and called out, "Thank you, Leo," before making her way back to her car.

Bridgette started her car and drove slowly out of the muddy car park. She pulled up just before turning onto the main road to study the construction site notice board. The board listed the companies involved in the project in partnership with the Sanbury Development Corporation. She made a mental note to check on each company later as she wondered which one officially employed Leo.

Bridgette put her car into gear again and pulled out onto the road to head back to town. She looked back at the construction site through her rear-view window as she picked up speed and wondered whether John Tyson's appearance here just two days before he disappeared was just a coincidence.

Chapter 19

Delray sat in his office reflecting on the meeting he'd just had with the Commissioner. He wasn't surprised that Internal Investigations weren't making much progress in the basement shooting investigation, but he was surprised the Commissioner was so willing to admit he needed help. He wasn't exactly sure where he should start as he stared at his crumpled list of names again.

He wondered if it had been wise showing Underwood the list. Even though the Commissioner thought it was an inside job, accusing a senior officer of corruption with no real proof was reckless. The more he thought about, the more he realized he had taken a huge risk adding Cunningham to his list.

He murmured, "What were you thinking Felix," as he put the list back in his top drawer.

He sighed as he thought about Bridgette's father. A respected detective before the incident, Peter Casseldhorf had managed to live in hiding for almost twenty years before he had been gunned down in a professional hit. Delray knew whoever was really behind this was unlikely to have pulled the trigger or personally attempted the murder of his daughter two nights earlier. He recalled the Commissioners words, 'Ninety-nine percent of them are as honest as the day is long, but there's always one who can be turned for the right price.'

He knew the Commissioner was right. It made sense to be focusing on someone active inside the force who knew a lot about Bridgette's movements. Delray pulled a large notebook out of his bottom desk drawer and opened it up to a fresh page. He had twenty-four people working for him in three teams and apart from Bridgette, his latest addition as a rookie detective, and Charlie Bates who had transferred in six months earlier, everyone else had been with him for at least two years. He didn't feel comfortable investigating his own staff, but Underwood was right. Internal Investigations were no closer to finding the culprit now than when it had happened. Something had to change to narrow down the pool of suspects.

Delray sighed again. He couldn't bring himself to write down the full name of each team member. He contented himself with writing down their initials in a column on the left-hand side of the page which somehow seemed to make it less personal. He then drew six columns across the page and chewed on the end of his pen for a moment as he thought about who they were looking for. He knew whoever had been in the basement that night had overridden the security system. He wrote down the word 'security' in the first column. He scratched his chin as he thought about who knew Bridgette was looking into her mother's murder case on her own time. It had been kept quiet and only a handful of people officially knew. He knew the easiest way to find out what a police officer was up to was to check the database log files to see what they were accessing. He knew you needed special system administration privileges for that and wrote down 'system admin' at the top of the second column. He stared at the sheet again before writing 'financial problems' in the third column, knowing an officer who was cash-strapped would be more easily tempted. He chewed on his pen again as he thought back to the incident. Bridgette's attacker had been wearing a mask, but she was fairly confident her return of fire had hit her attacker in the shoulder with a ricochet at least as he fled. He knew from experience that even a superficial gunshot wound wouldn't be easy to hide and wrote 'behavior' and 'absence' in the fourth and fifth columns.

Delray couldn't think of anything else and left the sixth column blank as he thought about his team. He couldn't imagine anyone being involved in something like this, but he knew the Commissioner was expecting nothing less than a thorough assessment of each officer. Delray let out a sigh as he went down the list of names putting a tick in column one against team members whom he knew had higher than normal levels of access to security systems. There were only three that he could think of — Connor, Bates, and Matthews. He would cross check with his team leads later to make sure but was satisfied he had it covered for now. Delray looked at the second column — 'system admin'. Ryan and Bates had both spent time in computer fraud and probably still had higher level privileges than anyone else. He put a tick against both their names in column two and then focused on column three. He knew Sinclair was up to his eyeballs in debt and put a tick against his name. He didn't know enough about any of the other officers in his team and made a mental note to discuss this tactfully with each of his team leaders.

Delray looked at column four and frowned. Behavior was something he was normally on top of. After twenty years of managing people, he was adept at reading people and normally knew when one of his team were having problems.

But he was the first to admit the last two months had been a blur for him. After closing out the Selwood serial killer case and then dealing with the aftermath of losing one of his most senior officers who'd been fatally shot during the arrest, he knew he'd lost touch.

He mumbled, "As if I'm on top of that right now," and moved his focus to column five.

Delray didn't need to guess about absences as he keyed in his password and unlocked his computer. The date that his best detective and close friend had been shot and killed was forever etched in his mind. He opened up the staff leave system and keyed in the date. The screen refreshed and Delray quickly ran his eye down the list of names checking leave dates around that period. There were only two absences, Charlie Bates for three days with a bad case of flu and Cory Johnson whose wife had just had a baby. Delray wasn't worried about Johnson's absence because it had been planned months in advance, but Bates' absence bothered him. He picked up his phone and dialed Bates' supervisor's number.

The phone was answered after the third ring.

"Ty Goldsack."

"Ty, you got a minute? I gotta question for you about staff leave."

Goldsack replied, "On my way Chief," before the phone went dead.

A moment later Goldsack appeared at Delray's door.

Delray said, "Close the door, Ty," and waited for his lanky senior detective to walk in and sit down.

As he settled into his chair, Goldsack said, "I'm usually in for a grilling when you ask me to close the door Chief, but I can't think of anything off the top of my— "

"Relax Ty, you're not in trouble. I just wanted to ask you a question about Charlie Bates."

"Okay."

"You remember the basement incident?"

Goldsack nodded.

"I've just been looking at the leave records. It looks like Charlie took three days leave immediately after that."

Goldsack nodded again, and replied, "I remember sending him home. He looked like death warmed up. He said he had the flu, and I didn't want him sharing it with anyone."

Delray sat impassively behind his desk staring at Goldsack.

Goldsack continued, "What's this about Chief?"

Delray shifted in his chair and then said, "I've been asked by the Commissioner to investigate everyone in my team for possible involvement in the basement shooting incident. I'm fifty-seven years old and I've been on the force for over thirty years Ty. I've seen things that would give most people permanent nightmares, but investigating my own staff is by far the worst thing I've ever had to do."

He turned the notebook around and slid it across the desk towards Goldsack. "I promised the Commissioner I would help even though it went against everything I've ever believed in as a police officer..."

As Goldsack studied the page, Delray continued. "The Commissioner is concerned that whoever stole the microfilm record of the murder case must have known Bridgette was working on it. I know it was all kept quiet, so that means—"

Goldsack nodded. "The spotlights on people working closely with her or who can track her access to our databases."

Delray nodded, "I'm going with someone who works close to her. There was very little information on the computer because the murder was twenty years ago. Only people in our team and a couple in archives knew the physical file was missing.

Goldsack continued, "Charlie Bates is an interesting character.

Smarter than most and better than anyone I've ever seen in front of a keyboard but what possible interest could he have in a murder case that's twenty years old? He'd have barely been out of kindergarten when it happened."

Delray pointed at his list and said, "I wrote down the five key things that I could think of that we might be possibly looking for in a suspect. Charlie is a match for more categories than anyone else on the team, but it's his absence straight after the shooting that bothers me most."

Goldsack thought for a moment. "I remember seeing him sitting at his desk working away on his computer the morning after the shooting. He was sweating up a storm and asked if he could go home."

"If he was that sick, why wouldn't he just ring in?"

Goldsack shrugged. "I'm not sure Chief. There was a lot going on with the Selwood murder case, so maybe he felt obligated?"

Delray fixed Goldsack with a stare and asked, "Could he have been hiding a gunshot wound? Bridgette was fairly sure she hit her attacker in the shoulder with return fire, although perhaps just with a ricochet."

Goldsack sat still as he thought about the question. Delray knew he was deep in thought and let him be.

After almost a minute he responded, "To be honest Chief, on the day after the shooting, it was chaos in here and I didn't give him another thought after I told him to go home."

Goldsack paused for a moment and then continued. "When he returned to work three days later, he looked to be in a lot of pain. I remember him volunteering for all the desk work. He barely left his desk for the next week or so as I recall."

Delray raised his eyebrows. "That hardly seems consistent with flu symptoms?"

Goldsack grimaced. "I can't argue with you on that one Chief."

They sat there in silence for a moment, both lost in their thoughts before Goldsack asked, "So what do we do now Chief?"

Delray let out a long breath as he leaned back in his chair. He thought for a moment and then responded. "For now, just sit tight. I need to take this to the Commissioner. This could all end badly for us if we start accusing someone without enough proof."

Chapter 20

Bridgette parked across the road from the courthouse and sat in her car watching the media. They had spread out across the lawn in front of the building drinking coffee, smoking and talking on mobile phones. It had been well over two hours since she had dropped Hughey off for his hearing and she knew from their body language that Hughey's court case was still in progress. She debated walking over and quietly sitting in a back row to listen to the rest of the hearing but decided that with Payne's threat of jail hanging over her it would be wiser to wait in the car.

She thought about their morning trek to the Cathedral Valley and pulled the photos out of the file again. She sorted through them until she had just the photos of places that she still didn't know the location of. There were five in total. Bridgette fanned them out like playing cards and studied the images. Three of them were close-ups of rock slides and would be hard to place unless you were intimate with their locations. She put them down on the passenger seat and studied the remaining two photographs. They both appeared to be photos of the one gorge but taken from different angles. The gorge didn't appear to be overly deep or wide and the rock faces that formed each side appeared to narrow into a dead end on one side. The gorge was surrounded by large fir trees that looked no different to any others she had seen in the Sanbury area.

Bridgette wondered if the photographs were located somewhere close to either the Cathedral or Snowbridge valleys. It would make sense if Tyson was photographing a series of settings that lead to a specific location, she thought. She knew enough about each valley's geography now to search the surrounding terrain using Google Maps. The gorge had a unique enough shape, and she was confident she could find it if it was in the general region.

Bridgette's concentration was broken by a flurry of activity in front of the courthouse. She looked across to see reporters and camera operators rushing to the courthouse steps.

Bridgette focused her attention on the courthouse's front doors which were now open. She figured if Hughey emerged with his lawyer, he would still be a free man, but if it was just his lawyer, she knew he would be back in custody and most likely heading back to the same jail that had been his living hell.

She had no doubt he was the victim of a grave miscarriage of justice and hoped he could finally catch a break.

Although not overly religious, Bridgette whispered, "God, please let him come out through the front," as she watched as people spilled out through the open doors. She held her breath as the reporters rushed up the steps to get photos and an interview. In the chaos of the moment, Bridgette's heart sank as she could see no sign of Hughey. After two minutes, the flow of people out of the building stopped. She feared the worst until the press surged forward again. She watched as a man dressed in a tailored, dark blue suit walked through the doorway before pausing at the top of the courthouse steps. He was in his late thirties and had wavy dark brown hair and a close-cropped beard. She was fairly sure this was Hughey's lawyer and smiled as she saw her neighbor lumber up and stand quietly behind the man as he made a statement to the press. Hughey tried to bow his head to hide from the photographers, but at six foot five, that was difficult to do. She watched for a minute as the lawyer delivered his statement before he led Hughey around the back of the building and away from the cameras. Moments later she saw a dark gray BMW emerge from the courthouse car park and pull a right onto Sanbury's main street. She could see Hughey in the passenger seat and knew for certain he was still free — at least for now.

Bridgette had seen enough and smiled again.

She whispered, "Maybe there is some justice after all?" as she checked her watch. Bridgette was due to meet Hughey's lawyer at around five thirty p.m. for a quick drink before he headed back to Rochford. She still had over an hour to kill and decided it was time to call Delray.

She picked up her smartphone and dialed his desk number from memory expecting to leave a message and was surprised when she was greeted with Delray's calm, baritone voice.

"I've been meaning to call you all afternoon Bridgette, but the day kinda got away from me."

Bridgette smiled again — she liked the calming effect her boss had on her.

"I'm having one of those days myself Chief."

"Well, this time I've got fourteen minutes to my next meeting, so tell me how the day's panning out. It looks like you survived your little trip into the forest without getting yourself murdered by your neighbor — so that's a good start."

"I've made good progress tracking down the locations of the photos in Tyson's file. Hopefully, I'll know all of them sometime tomorrow."

"Well, that's good progress. If we know where they were taken, hopefully, it will be a little easier to figure out why they were part of the file."

"Yes."

"How are you getting on with Payne?"

"That's what I was ringing about. Has he contacted anyone at Hartbourne today?"

"Not that I'm aware of."

"We had a run in this morning, and he promised he'd be calling my superiors."

"Not this superior. I'm up to date on all my messages and if he rang the Commissioner's office directly, I'd have heard about it by now. So what happened?"

Bridgette gave Delray a quick summary of the encounter and then waited.

There was silence on the phone for a moment before Delray shot back, "So let me get this straight, you give him a list of all the people you want to interview as agreed and he's not happy and wants to know your every movement in Sanbury?"

"Pretty much."

Bridgette could hear Delray mumbling in the background. She heard the word 'jackass' and several other expletives and pictured her boss pulling the phone away from his mouth while he let out his frustration.

In a more composed voice, Delray came back and said, "So then what happened?"

"He told me I wasn't welcome in his station anymore and he'd throw me in jail if I continued with any interviews."

More silence followed. Bridgette could picture Delray scratching his chin as he thought about what to do next.

"So has he had anyone following you today?"

"Not that I know of."

More silence before Delray responded, "I think he's bluffing Bridgette. Payne's a big fish in a little pond. Arresting a police officer from a much larger jurisdiction is a very ballsy move, which he knows could backfire. I'll let the Commissioner know, but for now, continue your work — business as usual."

Bridgette smiled and replied, "If I wind up in jail, you'll be the first person I call."

Delray chuckled. "It's been a long while since I've had to bail anyone out of jail."

There was silence on the phone for a moment before Delray came back and said, "The subject of the shooting in the basement came up in my meeting with the Commissioner this morning. He made it very clear he's unhappy with the lack of progress being made by Internal Investigations and he's asked me to get involved."

"Just while Cunningham's on leave?"

"I didn't get that impression, so next week could get interesting when Cunningham gets back."

"Am I allowed to ask what the Commissioner wants you to do?"

"He thinks someone close to you had to be involved and frankly, the more I think about it, the more I agree with him. I've been tasked with conducting an investigation of my own team."

"I'm sorry Chief, this is—"

"Stop right there Bridgette. Your mother's murder was never resolved, and you had permission to investigate on your own time. What happened down there should never have happened, particularly inside a supposedly secure police facility."

"I'm not sure there's anything I can do to help Chief, but if you need anything else from me, I'm just a phone call away..."

Bridgette could hear Delray let out an audible sigh over the phone. "I started looking into it today and I've found a couple of irregularities I'm working through."

"Okay."

More silence before Delray said, "This is just between you and me Bridgette and is absolutely confidential — you don't repeat a word of it to anyone, not your colleagues or anyone, okay?"

"Of course."

"I'm hoping I'm wrong, but one of our team isn't checking out. He was in the building and working alone when you were attacked and took three days leave immediately after the incident."

Bridgette's eyes widened. The whole incident had been a shocking blur she was still trying to come to terms with. One minute she was reviewing her mother's murder file on a microfilm reader and the next, she was scrambling across a floor covered in broken glass searching for a hiding place while she dodged gunfire. She rubbed what was left of her left ear lobe, which had been grazed by a bullet during the attack, as she thought back to the nightmare.

Delray continued, "Right now, I'm not telling you who is under suspicion, but I might come back to you in the next twenty-four hours with some questions and I just want you to be prepared for that..."

"I'll help however I can Chief."

"I'm sorry to lay this on you Bridgette, but I'd like this resolved before you get back here if possible, so I'm going to press this hard for the next few days..."

Bridgette mumbled a few words of support and said goodbye as her boss disconnected. She put her phone down and rubbed her left earlobe again as she replayed the conversation back in her mind. If it was one of Delray's team, that meant someone who had worked closely with her had tried to kill her in the basement.

She looked out her car window and barely noticed the flurry of activity as the media contingent packed up for a rapid departure. She remembered insisting on working the day after the incident as Delray's team made final preparations to set a trap for Kayne Selwood, a serial killer who had murdered at least seven young women. One team member had gone home sick with the flu — a police officer she had worked closely with and considered a friend.

She frowned and whispered, "Charlie Bates," hoping for the first time in her life that Felix Delray was wrong.

Chapter 21

Bridgette walked into the Summit Sports Bar at the top of Main Street. She was a few minutes early and looked around the sparse crowd of patrons for any sign of Hughey's lawyer. The bar was no different to most sports bars she had been in. With its heavy wood paneling, low-level lighting, and dark carpet, most of the light came from the large flat screen TVs that were spread around the walls playing sports channels at low volumes. The long bar, which took up most of the left-hand side of the room, was tended by two men in white shirts — both of whom looked bored by the low turnout on a Tuesday evening. Bridgette ordered tonic water on ice and continued to scan the crowd until she saw Hughey's lawyer tucked away in a booth in a rear corner. A woman in her late-thirties, with shoulder length dark hair, sat opposite him and they looked like they were engrossed in deep conversation.

Bridgette decided to leave them be for a moment and sat on a bar stool. She sipped at her tonic water and watched the traffic on Main Street through the front glass window and wondered what Hughey was doing now. She was relieved he had not gone back to jail and pictured him in his home preparing an evening meal, content with a simple life far from the threat of other inmates.

She heard a noise behind her and turned to see Hughey's lawyer standing behind her.

The man stuck out a hand. "You must be Bridgette. I'm Dan Strickland, Hughey's lawyer."

Bridgette responded, "Nice to meet you, Dan," as she extended her hand.

Strickland had a firm grip and after letting go, he pointed at the booth where the woman was still sitting and said, "I'm just catching up with an old law school friend. Please come and join us."

Bridgette responded, "Okay," and then followed.

The woman slid out of the booth on Strickland's approach to wait for introductions. She was about Bridgette's height and looked professional in a tailored dark blue woman's pantsuit.

"Bridgette, I'd like you to meet Andi Butler. Andi and I went to law school together."

Butler nodded once in Bridgette's direction and said, "Hello," as Bridgette shook hands with her.

Butler motioned Bridgette to slide into the booth first and said, "I can't stay long, I've got a class to get to."

Bridgette obliged and slid into the booth and sat opposite Strickland.

Strickland said, "Besides practicing law, Andi runs a martial arts class here a couple of times a week."

Bridgette nodded and said to Butler, "That must help you stay in shape."

Butler nodded. "When I came back to Sanbury and found out no one was running martial arts classes here, I started my own. It's turned into a nice little sideline."

Strickland rolled the ice around in his glass and said, "I did a little research on you after our call on Sunday night Bridgette. In addition to being a cop, you're also a state martial arts champion if I'm not mistaken?"

Bridgette half smiled and responded, "A long time ago, but I don't compete anymore."

Butler said, "We have a mixed class on Thursday night at six. Why don't you join us?"

Bridgette was about to say no but realized it might provide her with an opportunity to meet some local people who may have known John Tyson. "Okay, that would be nice."

Butler pulled a card from her pocket and slid it across the table to Bridgette. "We work out of a place called The Fitness Factory — it runs parallel to Main Street. If you have trouble finding it, just call me."

Butler smiled at Strickland and said, "I have to go, Dan — it's never a good look when the instructor is late."

Strickland rose out of his seat and leaned across the table to kiss Butler. They whispered their goodbyes to one another, and Bridgette got the distinct impression they were more than just old friends.

Butler turned to Bridgette and said, "Nice meeting you, Bridgette. I hope we see you Thursday night."

Bridgette waited until Butler had made her way out through a rear door of the bar, before she turned back to Strickland and said, "I hope I wasn't intruding."

Strickland smiled knowingly. "Not at all. Andi and I had a thing for each other back in our student days. We still catch up, but it's mainly when she's in Rochford on business these days."

Bridgette glanced down at Butler's card which had little more than her name, phone number and email address on it and asked, "So what does she do here in Sanbury?"

"She's a corporate lawyer. Most of her career has been spent working for big companies. She grew up in Sanbury and came back about two years ago to help get the Snowbridge Resort development up and running."

Bridgette nodded. "So how did the hearing go?"

Strickland frowned. "Not as good as I hoped. The judge reserved his decision. We're due to reconvene on Friday, so I'll know more then, but frankly, it could go either way."

"I asked Hughey what the hearing was about. He seemed a little vague on the detail, but from what he told me, I gather he was charged as an adult rather than as a minor?"

"You got it. They charged him with murder as an adult when he was only seventeen and still a minor. Being a cop, I'm sure you're aware that being charged as an adult carries a vastly harsher sentencing penalty?"

Bridgette nodded.

Strickland continued, "I guess you've figured out Hughey isn't overly bright?"

"Yes. He does his best, but it's obvious he struggles if you spend any time with him."

Strickland continued. "Hughey has an IQ of sixty-eight and while not quite low enough to be legally classified as intellectually disabled in this state, he is simple."

"Okay."

"To put it bluntly, Hughey has the mental capacity of an eleven-year-old. He had a difficult birth where he was deprived of oxygen. It's not helping with his case because he gets nervous in court and comes across as someone who is unpredictable and potentially violent."

"I've spent some time with him in the last two days and I find it hard to see him squashing a bug, let alone killing another human being."

"Like I said on the phone, Hughey's no murderer. He was framed and had an incompetent lawyer who couldn't even figure out they had his date of birth wrong."

"So somebody got away with murder?"

Strickland nodded. "I'm almost sure Hughey was deliberately chosen as the fall guy because he's big and not very bright."

"I'm not familiar with all the legal technicalities, but most juveniles only serve fifteen years for murder?"

"In this state even less depending on the circumstances. I've been his lawyer for three years and I'm not trying to convince the court that he's innocent, even though I think he is. I'm just trying to get him out of jail anyway I can."

"Which is why you're trying to get the charge corrected?"

"If we can get the charge amended, he'll have served his time and can go free."

"So what's the problem? I thought that would have been straightforward?"

"The problem is Olivia Hodder was a beautiful young seventeen-year-old girl, and this is a small town. Her body was never discovered, and people haven't forgotten. When the judge said he's going to take his decision under advisement, that's doublespeak for he knows he's going to take a lot of flak from the residents of Sanbury and a bunch of politicians if Hughey is paroled. My guess is he's going to spend the next two days going through legal cases trying to find a precedent that would allow the conviction as an adult to stand because he doesn't want to cop any flak."

"So that means you're back in town on Friday?"

Strickland grimaced and said, "Yeah — that's when we get the verdict."

"And if the judge finds against you, then Hughey goes back to jail?"

"For the remainder of his sentence. I got him out on bail while the state figures out how they want to play this. But that will come to an end very soon."

Strickland paused for a moment and then continued in a quieter voice. "Hughey was reasonably settled in jail up until about three years ago. The state cut the prison budget, and he was moved from Hartbourne maximum security to Rochford, which was where I got involved. Hartbourne was like a three-star hotel compared to what he's had to endure at Rochford. He's been raped repeatedly by other inmates and there is almost nothing we can do to stop it. His mental condition has become very fragile... I can't see him surviving another twelve months, let alone twelve years if he's sent back there."

They were both quiet for a moment as they sipped on their drinks.

"Thanks again for looking out for him on Sunday night Bridgette. The big guy has no friends and if you hadn't stepped in, God only knows what would have happened."

"I only did what any reasonable person would do."

Strickland shook his head. "I know you're a cop, but things work differently here. You spend enough time in Sanbury, you get to realize the police own this town and can do pretty much what they want. Most local folks would have just turned a blind eye to what you saw on Sunday night."

Cocking his head to one side, Strickland continued, "So I've been meaning to ask — how is it that a Hartbourne detective winds up in Sanbury and living next door to my client?"

Bridgette gave Strickland a quick rundown of the John Tyson case and her role in the investigation. Strickland was attentive and asked a few questions that showed he was genuinely interested. She concluded by giving Strickland a brief summary of her confrontation with Payne that morning and his threat to put her in jail if she continued investigating.

Strickland shook his head. "Like I said, the police are a law unto themselves around here."

Bridgette took another sip of her tonic water and replied, "So, I may be here on Friday, or I may already be back in Hartbourne. It really depends on whether Payne wants to brawl with Hartbourne's Police Commissioner."

"Well, if you're not here, I'll phone you and let you know the outcome of the hearing."

"Thanks, Dan, I'd appreciate that. I'm really hoping Hughey can catch a break on this. He's suffered more than enough."

Strickland looked at his watch and said, "I've got to hit the road. I've still got a couple of hours prep to do for court tomorrow."

"It was nice meeting you, Dan."

Strickland smiled and said, "You too Bridgette. I hope I see you on Friday," as he slid out of the booth.

Bridgette watched Strickland as he walked out through the same rear door as Butler had. She wasn't sure what to make of Hughey's lawyer. The intimate kiss with Butler and his comments about how they 'still catch up' made her think he had commitment issues. She felt confident he was committed to Hughey, and that was all that mattered.

Bridgette took a final sip of her tonic water and noticed a smartphone had been left on the table as she went to slide out of the booth. It had an expensive black leather case, and she was fairly sure it belonged to Strickland and not Butler. She grabbed the phone and hurried to the rear exit. Pushing through the rear door, she knew she could probably catch Strickland before he left the parking lot if she hurried. As she emerged into a small alleyway, Bridgette stopped in her tracks. The alleyway was narrow and poorly lit, but the light was good enough for her to make out the partially silhouetted figures of three men. Bridgette wasn't sure what she'd stumbled into as she made out the outline of a knife being pressed into the neck of the tallest of the three men who had been pinned against a wall. She willed herself not to panic as she locked eyes with the man who had the knife held against his neck. The man was doing his best to remain calm, but she could see the terror in his eyes and knew Dan Strickland feared for his life as he stared back at her.

Chapter 22

Bridgette knew enough about human anatomy to know that Strickland would bleed out in under two minutes if the knife held against his throat severed his jugular vein. She wasn't sure what she'd walked into, but instinct told her Strickland's best hope of survival was for her to stand her ground and not escalate the situation any further. Both assailants wore ski masks, but that didn't help her understand if they were intent on robbery, murder, or something else. She moved her gaze from the assailant who had the knife up against Strickland's neck to the other man. He had a stocky build and looked edgy as the knife he held in his right hand started to twitch.

Bridgette made no attempt to move forward or backward — the next move had to be made by one of the two men. She watched as they made brief eye contact with each other. With his knife still held at Strickland's throat, the taller man nodded once at his accomplice. Bridgette watched as the shorter man tightened his grip on the knife and took one step forward. The man made no sound and stood with his knife hand extended slightly from his body ready to strike. Separated by four steps, she wondered whether the man was expecting her to panic and run. She stood staring into the man's eyes, her posture neither aggressive nor submissive. The man took another step forward. Bridgette's body tensed — three steps separated them. The man was still one step short of being able to attack her without lunging first. She had no doubt he was trying to get her to panic and run. The man looked confident and as his mouth spread into a grin, it was contorted by the ski mask which was too tight for his face.

She had practiced knife attacks as part of her martial arts training and knew what to do. Apart from a gun, she knew her best defense against handheld weapons was to stay still and balanced and let the attacker come to you. The man feigned a lunge forward and then let out a short laugh when Bridgette's body twitched. For a stocky guy, he was quicker and nimbler than she expected. As they both stood their ground, Bridgette decided she needed to goad the man to get him to make the first move.

Doing her best to control her breathing, she said, "Your ski mask is too tight. It contorts your face."

The man's grin disappeared as he feigned a second strike. Bridgette's body went tense as she flinched again.

Now positive the man wanted her to make the first real move, Bridgette continued, "You've made a mistake. I know who you—"

Bridgette never expected to complete her second sentence. She knew the man was right handed and like most right handed people, he would probably pivot off his right foot and lunge with his left. Probably, but not certainly. She had pretended to be watching the knife blade, but her focus had been entirely on the man's left foot. The man's two feigned lunges had been made using his upper body only. Bridgette knew it wasn't possible to lunge without lifting one foot and stepping in closer. She had gambled on the left foot and had rehearsed her move over in her mind in the split second she had while the stocky guy had been advancing.

Her brain reacted before his left foot had fully lifted off the pavement. Shifting her balance slightly to her left foot she brought her right foot up swiftly in a swinging arc. Her kick needed to be fast and accurate, precise enough in her timing to strike the knife hand and dislodge the knife. Too slow and she would be stabbed, too quick and she would be kicking at air — the kick had to be perfect.

Bridgette wasn't sure if it was adrenaline, a sixth sense, or her bodies' innate desire for survival, but the knife thrust almost appeared to happen in slow motion. She felt her right foot tense and straighten as it lifted off the ground, just as it had done thousands of times during martial arts training and practice. As her foot swung through an arc towards the blade, she realized her reaction time had been a fraction slow. There was no time to adjust. Just like a bullet's trajectory couldn't be altered once fired from a gun, neither could her kick. By the time she registered the kick wasn't going to connect with the knife blade she heard the unmistakable snap of bone breaking as her foot struck the assailant's knife arm just behind the wrist.

Bridgette ignored the knife as it flew through the air and the stocky guy as he crashed to the ground writhing in pain. She focused on the assailant who still had Strickland up against the wall. The alleyway went quiet for a moment with the only sound coming from the stocky guy as he moaned softly as he cradled his broken wrist.

Keen to take advantage of the situation, Bridgette said to the man holding Strickland, "You're one man down. The smart move would be to get out of here while you can."

To her surprise, the man shoved Strickland back towards her and pulled a snub-nosed pistol from his pocket.

Pointing it at her chest he said, "The smart move for you would be to go back inside."

Bridgette held up her hands and backed up to the door. Strickland was a step behind her. Without taking her eye off the weapon, she reached out and opened the door. Strickland took the cue from Bridgette and with his hands in the air, back walked through the open doorway.

The man with the gun walked forward and stood over his partner and motioned Bridgette to move back inside with his gun.

"Last chance or you'll be on the ground as well."

Bridgette nodded once and eased through the open doorway and shut it behind her. She breathed for about the first time in ten seconds and then looked across at Strickland whose features had turned pale.

She handed him his phone and said, "You forgot this."

* * *

Strickland leaned up against the corridor wall and stared at Bridgette as his chest heaved in and out. Neither of them spoke for close to a minute as they silently processed what had just happened. Bridgette watched the color return to Strickland's face and was relieved he hadn't suffered any serious injury.

She expected him to thank her for stepping in and helping, but was surprised when he said, "That was a ballsy move out there."

Bridgette shrugged. "I didn't have much choice."

"Before you broke that guy's wrist, you said something about him making a mistake."

"I needed to get him to make the first move."

Strickland stared at her for a moment and said, "It sounded like you recognized him?"

"I'm almost certain it was Mitch Conden, the cop who assaulted Hughey on Sunday night."

"A Sanbury police officer?"

Bridgette nodded. "The mask was too small for his face and I got a reasonable look at his facial outline."

"Well, that makes this interesting."

"So, what was this all about Dan? I can't imagine a cop being involved in a simple robbery?"

"They threatened me. They said if I come back on Friday to defend Hughey, they'll put me in hospital."

"I can't believe a cop would be dumb enough to get involved in something like this."

Strickland shrugged. "Many people around here liked the status quo. They had a murderer in jail and they just want him back there."

"Are you going to press charges?"

Strickland shook his head. "You can't give a positive ID, so there's no point. Even if Payne's brother turns up with a broken arm, he can say he slipped in the bathroom and it's all a nasty coincidence."

Strickland massaged his throat for a moment and continued, "No harm done. I'll just be more careful in future."

Bridgette nodded. She wasn't so sure Strickland was doing the right thing and asked, "Are you at least going to report this to the police?"

"No. Like you, I've got more than enough problems with the Sanbury Police. I don't want to turn this into some kind of circus and give the judge any reason to think I'm grandstanding to get Hughey's sentence overturned."

Strickland paused for a moment and pulled his car keys from his pocket before looking warily at the rear door. "Do you think they're still out there?"

Bridgette responded, "There's only one way to find out," and slowly opened the rear door again. They both stared out into the alley. There was no sign of either man and everything was quiet.

Chapter 23

Bridgette sat in her car in the carport at the back of the Summit Sports Bar and contemplated ringing Delray. It was well after six p.m. and she was still a little rattled by the encounter with the two masked men. As she sat and reviewed the incident in her mind, she decided she first needed answers to some of her questions. She picked up her mobile phone and dialed a local number from memory. The phone was answered after three rings.

"Jack Sutton."

"Good evening Jack, this is Bridgette Cash. I came to interview you yesterday about John Tyson."

"And are you making any progress Detective?"

"I think so. I discovered a file hidden out the back of John's house late yesterday. It included some photos I believe he took out in the mountains that I would like to show you and get your opinion on."

"Swing by whenever you like. I'd be happy to take a look."

"There's one other thing I'd like to talk to you about if that's okay?"

"And what's that?"

Bridgette gave Sutton a brief rundown on the attack on Strickland in the alleyway. She concluded by saying she thought she recognized one of the assailants as Sanbury police officer, Mitch

Conden.

Sutton was silent and Bridgette wondered whether she had reached out to the wrong local.

She continued, "I'm not sure how the police force really works around here, but I'd like to ask someone local that I trust a few questions."

"You eat chicken, Bridgette?"

"Yes."

"I'm just pulling a casserole out of the oven. Why don't you stop by and join me for dinner? I can't promise I can answer all your questions, but hopefully, I can answer some of them."

"Thanks, Jack, but you really don't have to feed me as well."

"No trouble. Sounds to me like you could do with some company after what you've been through today."

"Can I bring anything?"

"Just yourself."

"I'll be there in fifteen minutes."

* * *

Bridgette knocked twice on the front door and was suddenly hungry as she picked up the faint aroma of apricot chicken casserole wafting out from inside the house.

Sutton opened the door and with a concerned look asked, "Are you okay?"

Bridgette responded, "I'm fine, not a scratch on me."

"You better come in before you freeze to death."

Bridgette thanked Sutton for seeing her on such short notice as she followed him through to a large rustic kitchen. The kitchen had a large wooden island workbench complete with a ceiling hanging rack of pots and pans. It was clean and tidy and looked like it got plenty of use. She could see a large casserole dish cooling on a rack next to the sink and said, "That smells amazing Jack."

Sutton grinned a little as he spooned out the casserole onto two white dinner plates. "It was my mother's family recipe. I don't cook it that often because it feeds me for a week, but with winter almost on us, I felt in the mood."

Sutton nodded to a shallow woven basket that contained several bread rolls as he picked up the two plates and said, "Grab the basket if you don't mind and follow me."

Bridgette followed Sutton into a dining room that featured a sturdy wooden table surrounded by six equally sturdy chairs. There were several landscape paintings on the walls and a wooden sideboard that looked older than she was. The room looked as though it hadn't been remodeled in a long time. She wondered if Sutton kept it that way in memory of his wife.

Sutton said, "I don't get many visitors here, so I thought we'd use the dining room."

Bridgette sat down and placed the Tyson file on a chair beside her. She watched as Sutton carefully placed their meals at two place settings he had laid earlier at one end of the table.

Pretending not to notice his hand tremors she said, "Thanks for seeing me on such short notice Jack. You really didn't need to go to this much trouble."

"No trouble at all Bridgette. By the sounds of things, we've got a lot to talk about."

Bridgette savored the first mouthful of the casserole. "This is really good Jack. My aunt used to cook something similar when I was a little girl. This brings back a lot of nice memories."

"Glad you're enjoying it. I'm no chef, but no one ever goes hungry at my table."

Bridgette decided to leave her work questions until the end of the meal and instead asked, "So what do you do for work Jack?"

Sutton swallowed a mouthful of his meal and put his fork down. "I'm just about retired. My MS is starting to make a lot of things difficult that used to be easy. I had a panel and spray shop in town, but I sold that to my business partner about six months ago. Most of my money is tied up in the Snowbridge development now and I still make a bit of furniture in my metal shop out back on my good days."

"I visited Snowbridge today. It looks like it's going to be a huge development."

"Hopefully not too big. We don't want it to change our town totally, but we have high hopes it will bring a lot of tourists our way. We get the best snowfalls in the state most years, so I can't understand why it's taken this long."

"I met Andi Butler earlier. She seems to be one of the key players?"

"That she is. There's a lot of Chinese money backing this investment, but a lot of locals have bought in as well. She's working with the local chamber of commerce to make sure we don't get railroaded by some overseas company. We like our town the way it is and don't want to see it change too much."

"So how long until Snowbridge will be up and running?"

"About eighteen months. Now that all the investment funding is in, construction is expected to take off in spring. This time next year, all the buildings and the ski lifts should be nearing completion."

"And the locals are happy?"

"Mostly. There's always a few that complain, but most of us realize how important this development is. Unemployment is high around here and this gives a lot of people hope."

They were quiet for a moment as they enjoyed their meal until Sutton broke the silence with a question.

"So I'm intrigued. What's in this file you found at John's place?"

Bridgette opened the file and slid it across the table to Sutton. "I'm still trying to figure out what it's all about. There's a bunch of printouts from geology websites and some photographs of forest areas and clearings. There's also several handwritten pages of notes which seem to be related to the photographs."

Sutton put on a pair of reading glasses and continued eating as he scanned the file's contents.

He murmured, "Definitely John's writing," as he came to the handwritten notes.

Sutton scanned the website printouts and said, "These all look like they relate to rock slides in the area. What on earth was John up to?"

"I'm trying to find a link between the reports and the photos. Maybe he thinks Olivia's body is hidden under a rock slide, but figuring out where all the photos were taken is the first step."

Sutton scanned the photos for a moment and then held up the one of Snowbridge Valley as he looked at Bridgette. "That one's easy — you were there today."

Sutton put the Snowbridge photo down and then skimmed through the others. "I recognize the ones here from Cathedral Valley..."

Sutton paused and stared at the photo of the burnt-out shack. His facial expression hardened for just a moment.

Bridgette said, "Hughey showed me the site today. He said the shack burnt down a long time ago."

Sutton nodded. "That it did. It had special memories for me. My father and I were part of a team that built it. It was used by hikers as a place of shelter and a spot to camp overnight without having to pitch a tent. Such a damn shame it burnt down."

"Was it deliberate or an accident?"

Sutton put the photo down and said, "Nobody knows. It could have been just a careless hiker who left a lamp going. All we know is that in the spring after Olivia disappeared, a team that went out looking for her after the snow melted came across the shack pretty much as you see it in that picture."

"Is it possible it's somehow connected to her disappearance?"

Sutton shrugged. "Olivia's body was never discovered among the ruins or anywhere else for that matter, so who knows?"

Bridgette picked up the photo to study the burnt-out ruins again.

Sutton continued. "You think the two are connected?"

"Maybe. I'll research the local newspaper archives tomorrow to see if there's any other information that might help."

They both went quiet as they continued to eat.

After finishing the last fork-full of her meal, Bridgette smiled and said, "That was great Jack. I don't think I'll eat for a week now."

Sutton laughed. "You're welcome, Bridgette. So what else have you got planned for tomorrow?"

"I'm going back out to Cathedral Valley to continue to see if I can find where the remaining photos were taken."

"The gorge may not be anywhere near Cathedral Valley."

"No, but all the other photos, apart from the one taken in Snowbridge Valley, seem to be in a series. I figure it can't hurt to spend an hour or two exploring. If I can find the gorge, it might answer some questions."

"You got an emergency beacon?"

"No."

"You going alone?"

"That's the plan."

Sutton pushed back from the table, and mumbled, "Follow me."

Bridgette followed Sutton through his house to a room at the rear. It was the size of a small bedroom and had been fitted out as an office. The wooden desk contained several neat piles of papers and documents and one battered and aging laptop computer. Bridgette wasn't sure what Sutton was looking for and waited patiently at the doorway as he began rummaging around in an overhead cupboard.

A moment later he mumbled, "Hah," and withdrew a small yellow device made of hardened plastic.

After wiping the dust off it, he handed the device to Bridgette and said, "Take this. It might just save your life."

The device fitted snugly in Bridgette's hand and looked like a small walkie-talkie. Even though she never had a need to use one, she knew it was an emergency locator beacon.

Sutton pointed to a large red button on the side of the device and said, "You slide that on if you get into trouble and it will send out a distress signal. It's waterproof and uses satellites to help find your location."

"Thanks, Jack."

"Hopefully you won't need it, but you shouldn't go walking in the mountains, particularly at this time of year, without one."

"I would have thought the middle of winter is the worst time?"

"Not really. The mountain range that we live in is unpredictable. The first real dump of winter snow can be mild, or it can be feet deep. It can come on sudden if the weather conditions line up and that's when hikers get caught out. You should keep an eye on the weather conditions. They can turn nasty very quickly and they're forecasting a possible great storm for the end of the week."

"A great storm?"

"That's what the locals call it. It's where we get feet of snow dumped in one hit. Everything pretty much shuts down. Even the roadways in and out of Sanbury can be cut off for a period."

"Does it happen very often?"

Sutton thought for a moment and said, "I've seen three or four in my lifetime. The worst one was when I was a kid. We were stuck at home here for close to three days while they cleared the road."

"I'll keep that in mind."

Sutton said, "Let's go back to the living room. I'll make you a cup of tea — peppermint, right?

Bridgette followed Sutton back into his lounge room. She sat in one of the large armchairs and looked around the room while Sutton prepared the tea. With its large old-fashioned furniture and a bookcase full of ancient hardbacks, the room reminded Bridgette of her aunt's house. She relaxed a little as she studied photos on the wall opposite. There were several pictures of Sutton as a young man with a pretty young woman by his side — his wife she assumed. There were also photos of the same couple with two small children — all happy photos of a family from a bygone era.

Sutton returned moments later with two steaming hot mugs of tea. He tried carefully placing one of the mugs on a coffee table next to Bridgette but spilled some of the tea because of the tremor in his hands. He didn't seem embarrassed as he mumbled an apology.

Bridgette pretended not to notice the spill as she thanked Sutton for the tea.

After settling into a chair opposite and taking two sips of his tea, Sutton said, "So tell me about what happened in town tonight? It sounds like you're one lucky lady not to be in the hospital or worse."

Bridgette sighed. "It all happened so fast, Jack. One minute I'm having a quiet meeting in a bar with Hughey's lawyer and the next minute someone's trying to stab me in an alleyway."

"You said on the phone you thought one of the men was Mitch Conden? The police officer?"

Bridgette nodded. "I think so. The man's mask was tight, and I got a fairly good look at his facial outline."

Sutton frowned. "The local police aren't the most professional outfit I've ever seen operate, but this is out of character, even for them."

"I agree."

"And you're sure you broke his arm?"

Bridgette nodded again. "I heard it crack."

Sutton winced. "Well, we'll know one way or another in the next day or so. It's almost impossible to hide a broken arm, so he's going to have a lot of explaining to do."

"Maybe not. He can say he slipped in his bathroom and was nowhere near the alley. I can't see Payne challenging his version of events."

"So, what are you going to do about it?"

"I'm not sure Jack. At first, I was fairly convinced they were just trying to threaten Hughey's lawyer to stop him going ahead with the case on Friday..."

"But now you're not so sure?"

"As I was driving over here I asked myself, why would they be threatening Hughey's lawyer now? Friday's hearing isn't about defending Hughey, it's a formality to hear the judges' verdict on whether Hughey goes back to prison or not. So why would they wait until now to pull a stunt like this?"

Sutton frowned. "So, if the lawyer's not the reason for the attack then what is?"

"Hughey's lawyer left before me. I think they expected us to walk out to the car park together. They bailed up Dan, but never made any attempt to hurt him. It was only me they tried to stab."

"Why on earth would they want to attack you, Bridgette?"

Bridgette held Sutton's stare and responded, "That's a very good question, Jack."

Chapter 24

Roman Quinn sipped coffee as he stood watching the sun come up through his home office window. Unable to sleep, he'd been up for almost an hour waiting for the call. He picked up his phone when it finally buzzed and made no attempt to hide his frustration as he answered, "This is getting out of control."

"Can you talk?"

"I'm alone. Cindy went to her mother's yesterday. She won't be back for a week."

In a slightly amused voice, the caller responded, "So you'll never see her again."

"That doesn't concern you. Why is that cop still walking around?"

"We underestimated her."

"Clearly."

"Nobody expected her to be able to fight off two grown men."

"So what are you going to do about it? We can't afford to have her running around."

"I will take care of it myself."

"Is that wise? The last thing we need is for you to—"

"I'm reasonably confident she'll be continuing her search in the mountains at some point today. I won't need to get that close."

"That's how it should've been handled in the first place."

"What about Conden?"

There was a pause while Quinn thought about the question. "He called me when he got home from the hospital last night. He wants more money."

"After what happened last night?"

"He knows this is coming to an end. It's his way of squeezing us for as much as he can."

"How much?"

"He hinted at another twenty thousand."

"Will that keep him quiet?"

"Maybe, but I'm not prepared to take the risk."

"So what does that mean?"

"It means you take care of the cop and I take care of Conden."

"We're drawing a lot of attention to ourselves?"

"The local cops don't know their head from their ass. We'll be long gone before they make any connection."

"I'll call you tonight."

Quinn stared out the window for a moment as he took another sip of his coffee.

In his own time, he responded, "No. I'll call you after I'm done with Conden."

* * *

Bridgette pulled up in the forest clearing and waited for Delray's call. Her morning had been full, and she was thankful for the few moments of peace. As she rested her head on the car seat backrest, she closed her eyes and listened to the sound of bird calls breaking the silence. She found her thoughts returning to the incident the previous evening. While still a long way from having all the answers, she was confident she at least had some of them. Her rest was short lived as her phone rang.

She pressed answer without looking at caller ID and said, "Hi Chief."

"Sorry, it's taken me so long to get back to you Bridgette. I've been in back-to-back meetings all morning."

"No problem, I've been busy myself."

"So how goes the investigation?"

Bridgette knew she would need to discuss the incident in the alley at some point but decided to give Delray her progress report first.

"I interviewed Olivia Hodder's mother this morning. She's never given up hope of finding her daughter alive someday."

"I can't imagine that was easy."

"No. She's still grieving. I don't think she will ever get closure until they find her daughter's body. I feel so sorry for her."

"So what did she have to say?"

"She started by telling me everything she could remember from the night Olivia disappeared. Olivia had been attending an end of term dance at her school and disappeared around 9 p.m. She then told me everything she could remember about the search for Olivia in the weeks that followed and how tough it had been on her family."

"I've got a daughter myself. I can't even begin to imagine how hard it must have been for all of them."

"She was devastated when the police finally called off the search but has never stopped looking. When John Tyson came to town, she pleaded with him to take another look at the case."

"That's understandable."

"Tyson told her he was already looking into Olivia's disappearance because of a request made by Hughey's mother, Della

Warren. While she wasn't overly happy about who Tyson was working for, she was desperate to hear of any progress and kept in close contact with him."

"Okay."

"According to Jenny Hodder, he seemed to think the police did a reasonable job because he wasn't able to find anything new."

"Interesting."

"Jenny said he didn't give up but turned his attention to the search zones and he began interviewing people who had been directly involved in the search. He even went as far as to research rock slides in the area during the winter Olivia disappeared, thinking her body might be out there somewhere buried under tons of rock and dirt."

"That would account for the research information you found in his file."

"I don't think so."

"You don't think so?"

"About a month before he disappeared, he visited Jenny and told her he was sorry, but he'd done all he could. She was upset but understood."

"So he stopped searching a month before he disappeared?"

"Not exactly. That's when he started the long treks into the mountains."

"I'm sorry Bridgette, but you've lost me."

"Tyson's treks into the mountains were well documented. Everyone assumed he was still searching for Olivia Hodder's body. I went over his hidden file again after talking to Jenny Hodder. There's no mention of Olivia, not even in the handwritten notes."

"So what was he up to? John Tyson doesn't strike me as the kind of guy that needed to go for long walks to discover himself."

"I'm not sure Chief. He may have stumbled upon something

else entirely different while investigating Olivia's disappearance."

"It wouldn't be the first time that's happened."

"If I can find the location of the last two photos in the file, it might shed some light on what he was up to."

"So that's what you're planning next?"

"I'm currently parked in a small clearing just before the Cathedral Valley. I didn't have time to finish exploring here yesterday, so I'm going to spend a couple of hours on it this afternoon."

"You're alone today?"

"Yes, but I do have an emergency beacon and a compass."

"Please be careful Bridgette. I don't want you taking unnecessary risks."

"There's something else you need to know Chief."

"And what's that?

Bridgette took a deep breath and then gave Delray a brief rundown of the attack in the alleyway the night before. When she had finished, there was silence on the other end of the phone.

Finally, Delray came back and said, "What the hell's wrong with that town?"

"I'm trying to keep a low profile, but that doesn't seem to be working for me."

"So was Strickland the target?"

"That's what I thought at first. It made sense because he's defending Hughey and he's received a couple of phone threats in the past. But the trial is all but over and while they bailed him up, they only attempted to stab me."

"And that's when you broke the guy's arm?"

"Yes."

"And you're fairly sure it was the sergeant you had a run in with on Sunday night?"

"I can't be certain Chief, but the mask was tight, and I got a good look at his facial outline."

"It doesn't sound like a couple of thugs out robbing people."

"No."

More silence followed. Bridgette waited while Delray had his thinking time.

Finally, Delray came back and said, "Are you carrying your service pistol?"

"It's locked in the safety box back at the house. We're not licensed to carry outside our jurisdiction Chief, and I didn't want to give Payne any more ammunition against me; if you'll excuse the pun."

Delray said flatly, "Well I applaud you playing it by the book Bridgette, but that changes right now. As soon as I get off the phone, I'll send you an email giving you permission to carry and then I'll square it away with the Commissioner. We cannot have you out there without some form of defense."

Delray was quiet for a moment and then asked, "So what's your take on all this Bridgette? Why are they targeting you?"

"I've tried to keep an open mind on this, but I'm now positive John Tyson was murdered. I'm not sure what he's stumbled onto, but someone around here is desperate to keep it covered up."

"This was supposed to be an easy assignment Bridgette — a chance to get you out of the city for a while and away from the situation here... but it looks like you've gone from the frying pan into the fire."

Bridgette tried to downplay the situation. "No harm done so far Chief and I'll feel a lot safer if I can carry my gun."

"I'm going to convene an urgent meeting with the Commissioner on this. Until then, no more interviews. When you've finished up what you're doing go home and wait for my call. I'll try and get some reinforcements down there by the end of the week."

"Okay Chief."

There was a short pause before Delray came back and said, "Promise me you'll be careful Bridgette. I know you're very capable, but nobody's bulletproof."

"I promise Chief."

Delray ended the call and Bridgette was once again alone in the forest. She picked up the two photos of the gorge off the front passenger seat and studied them for a moment. She figured this was probably the last part of the investigation into John Tyson's disappearance she would be conducting on her own. After carefully placing them into her jacket pocket, she got out of her car and locked the door. She stood and listened to the sounds of the forest as she buttoned her jacket and strapped on her backpack. The forest remained eerily quiet as she took one last look around the clearing.

After checking the battery level on the emergency beacon, she whispered, "You're as ready as you'll ever be," and set off down the pathway towards the Cathedral Valley.

Chapter 25

It took Bridgette fifteen minutes to walk across the meadow and down to the base of the Cathedral Valley. Despite the cold, she was thirsty and stopped for a drink of water before entering the forest again. After retrieving a water canteen out of her backpack, she frowned as she looked up into the sky. The dark gray nimbostratus cloud cover had thickened and seemed noticeably closer to the ground than when she'd left her car. She could no longer see any glow from the sun and noticed the conditions had become more threatening. Bridgette felt an ice-cold wind stirring and noticed some tiny snow particles beginning to randomly swirl through the air in front of her.

She checked her watch again. It was just after one p.m. Bridgette took a sip of water and then studied the sky again as she debated what to do. She had planned on spending two hours exploring before heading back to avoid walking out in darkness. She studied the pathway in front of her that lead into the forest as she screwed the cap back on the canteen. This was as far as she had come with Hughey yesterday. The path was barely wide enough for one person and she imagined it was only used by seasoned hikers.

Taking one last look at the sky, Bridgette set off again, deciding to walk for fifteen minutes to see what she could discover. With no sun overhead, the forest was dark, which made it feel like she was walking at night. She stuck to the trail to avoid getting lost and kept up a steady pace.

After five minutes she noticed the forest becoming slightly lighter again. Relieved to see a break in the tree line ahead, she quickened her pace and moments later emerged from the forest into a large clearing. She stopped and looked back along the dark trail she had just come from and frowned. Normally, she enjoyed her own company and being on her own didn't bother her. She wasn't sure whether it was the dark aura of the trail or something else that made her edgy.

Shaking it off as best she could, Bridgette took a few more steps into the clearing before stopping to survey the view in front of her. The clearing was about the size of a football field and surrounded by tall forest on three sides. The bottom of the clearing intrigued her. The soil was covered in rocks and ended abruptly in what looked like a sharp drop. She pulled the photos of the gorge from her pocket and held them up to compare them to the landscape in front of her. While the angle was wrong, the geography in the photos was similar and gave her hope. Bridgette placed the photos back in her pocket and began walking down the gentle slope. Her cheeks were almost frozen as she got to the halfway point and she wondered how much the temperature had dropped since she had left her car.

She stopped for a moment, mesmerized by the snow flurries. They were getting heavier, and she noticed the ground in front of her turning a powder white before her eyes. She knew she should hurry, but she had always loved the feel of snow falling on her face. She closed her eyes and leaned her head back. Suddenly, she was eight again and building a snowman with her aunt. As she slowly turned in a three hundred sixty-degree loop, memories of the day came flooding back. The experience had been bittersweet.

Still reeling from the death of her mother, she remembered laughing for the first time in months as tiny snowflakes had fallen on her face for the first time. She opened her eyes again and smiled at the memory.

Bridgette knew she needed to keep moving and started walking again. As she approached the bottom of the clearing her spirits were buoyed. She didn't need the photo to know she had found the place where John Tyson had taken the photographs. Stopping just short of the rocky outcrop, Bridgette peered over the edge. The gorge wasn't overly deep and narrowed to a dead end just like in the photos. She smiled as she realized her search efforts had been rewarded. Bridgette tried to take another step forward to get a better look, but the shale rock beneath her left foot moved. She studied the edge of the gorge and was certain the unstable surface she stood on had given way in a rock slide at some point in the past. Stepping back, Bridgette surveyed the perimeter as best she could looking for a way down. The slope down into the gorge varied from about seventy degrees where she currently stood to an almost vertical drop everywhere else. While not deep, she knew she would need a rope to get in and out.

She whispered, "Another day," and thought about asking Hughey to come back with her the following day.

The snowfall was now heavier and as it settled on her coat, Bridgette knew she needed to head back. She turned to walk back up the hill, but only took two steps before she heard a sound like a distant whip crack breaking the silence. Bridgette froze. She'd spent enough time at the police gun range to be familiar with the sound of a rifle shot and began rapidly scanning the top of the clearing to get a bearing on the direction it had come from. Bridgette wondered if it was just someone out hunting, but as she caught sight of a figure stepping out of the forest to shoulder a rifle, she knew she was the target. She had a fraction of a second to decide. She was at least forty yards from forest cover — close to seven seconds for someone in peak physical shape running across loose rock in winter clothing. In that time, she realized the shooter could squeeze off another three or four rounds and her odds of survival were poor at best.

Bridgette spun back towards the gorge as the man lowered his head over the rifle scope and jumped as a second shot rang out. Landing hard on the shale rock face of the embankment, she tried desperately to grab at the shale rock to stop her momentum, but she quickly picked up speed as she slid down the steep slope. Totally out of control, Bridgette put her hands and arms up around her head to protect herself as she tumbled and bounced off rocks. Completely disorientated, she continued to fall and let out an audible groan as she slammed into a large boulder at the bottom of the embankment.

Winded and unable to move, Bridgette lay on her back and stared up into the dark gray sky as her body began to shake. She knew she needed to keep moving even though the pain in her left shoulder was excruciating. She tried to sit up, but her body refused.

Chapter 26

Bridgette fought off waves of nausea as her vision drifted in and out of focus. She knew she needed to get to cover and finally willed herself into a sitting position. Ignoring the searing pain in her left shoulder, she used the boulder for support as she struggled up into a standing position and then frantically looked around for a place to hide. The gorge was covered in rock and a mix of spindly plants that were nowhere near big enough to use for cover. She saw two fallen trees, but they were both small and offered no protection either. She looked down the gorge to where it narrowed into a dead end and focused on a boulder. Lying just in front of the dead end, it was about five feet high and about the same width across. With no other options, Bridgette hobbled forward and pushed the pain out of her mind as she worked her way up into a sprint. With the pain from her shoulder now raging like a fire throughout her upper body, Bridgette pushed it out of her mind as she focused all her energy on getting to the rock before the shooter reappeared. She braced for the sound of more gunfire and did her best to suppress the image of a bullet ripping through her spine and cutting her down as she ran.

Just steps away from reaching her destination, Bridgette dove to the ground as she heard a third shot and saw a bullet ricochet off the boulder in front of her. She knew from the direction of the sound that the shooter was standing somewhere near the point where she had jumped. She scrambled around to the left-hand side of the boulder as she heard the crack of a fourth shot.

Bridgette heard the sound of footsteps running across the loose shale surface at the top of the embankment. Looking up and to her right, she just caught sight of the shooter as he disappeared into the cover of the forest. She knew he was moving around to a point where he would be at the edge of the gorge directly above her. She looked up and knew the boulder would offer her no protection. Leaving the cover of the rock, Bridgette quickly moved across to where the two rock faces merged and looked up again. She hoped the slight overhang would protect her, but her heart sank as she realized the shooter would still have a clean shot.

She cursed under her breath and began desperately scanning left and right for another possible place to hide. As she heard the sound of the footsteps on the shale rock above her, she felt a cool breeze on her legs. She looked down at a small bush that was growing out of the base of the wedge. It was only knee high and she could see a gap in the rock behind it. Bridgette quickly reached down and pushed the plant over on its side and stared at a gap where the two rock faces didn't quite meet. The gap was little more than knee high and just wide enough for her to crawl into. As several small rocks began landing on the ground around her, she knew the shooter was almost at the edge. Without thinking, Bridgette dropped to the ground and began crawling into the crevice. She prayed it would be big enough to hide her as she crawled forward. She stopped and let out a deep breath when she estimated she'd crawled about eight feet forward and was safe from gunfire for the moment. With almost no light penetrating the gap, Bridgette stuck her hands out into the blackness but couldn't feel any walls. Realizing she had room to turn around, Bridgette maneuvered around on her stomach until she was facing the entrance again. She cautiously crawled forward, doing her best not to make any sound. When she reached the entrance, she realized she had crushed the plant as she had crawled in through the opening and wondered if the shooter had noticed as she watched and waited.

Silence followed for almost five minutes. She barely dared to breathe for fear of giving away her position and slowly moved her position until she could see most of the way around the top rim of the gorge.

Bridgette let out a gasp as the shooter reappeared at the top of the shale slope where she had jumped. Her body went tense as the shooter shouldered the rifle and began to slowly scan the entire base of the gorge with the scope. Not daring to move a muscle, she watched as the man made long and slow deliberate sweeps with the rifle as he searched for his quarry. The scene seemed surreal as the shooter started to turn white in the falling snow. The man seemed to notice the snowfall getting heavier and turned his head skyward for a moment as the wind picked up. Bridgette hoped he would give up the hunt, but bit down on her lip as she watched the man settle over the top of his rifle scope again. The man continued his sweeping scan and only stopped when the rifle was pointing directly at the hole in the rock she now occupied.

Bridgette could feel her heart begin to race and her mouth go dry as the man held the gun still. She was positive there wasn't enough light for the shooter to make her out with the naked eye, but she began to wonder if the scope has some form of night vision as she braced again for the shot that would end her life. The wind speed continued to increase, and the man looked up again.

To Bridgette's relief, the man lowered his rifle as he continued to study the skyline. Bridgette still didn't dare to breathe as she watched the man take one step back from the edge of the gorge. As the snow continued to fall, she wondered if she had survived as she saw the man turn and walk away. She watched for almost two minutes but saw no sign of the man. She wondered if he had simply shifted position and was waiting for her to come out of hiding. She knew she needed to be patient and as the snow continued to fall, she realized she was safe for the moment and out of the cold.

Bridgette briefly turned her head and looked back into the darkness. She could still feel the breeze and wondered how big the cavity was. It didn't feel cavernous, but in the dark, it was impossible to tell. She didn't risk turning on her torch yet for fear of alerting the shooter to her position if he was still watching.

Relieved to still be alive, Bridgette ignored the pain in her shoulder as she rolled onto her side to release the straps on her backpack. She dragged the bag around in front of her to take advantage of the small amount of daylight at the entrance to her hiding place. Bridgette's whole body went tense as she noticed a huge tear on one side of the bag. Frowning, she resisted the urge to panic and calmly unzipped the bag and began searching its contents. As she pulled out her water canteen and flashlight, she realized the backpack must have caught on a rock and torn as she tumbled down the embankment.

Unable to find any sign of her emergency beacon or phone, she refused to be discouraged by the setback and whispered, "You're still alive," as she thought about what she would do next.

She knew it was too risky to go out looking for either device as she watched the snow continue to fall. The man could be anywhere, lying patiently in wait for her to surface. She knew she would at least have to wait until nightfall and even then, there was no guarantee she would find either device if the snow kept up. As she began to contemplate spending the night in the cold, she realized how trapped she was. With no emergency beacon or phone to call for help and no way to escape the gorge, she knew a shooter lying in wait for her was only the beginning of her problems. Realizing she had little option but to wait, Bridgette wondered how far the cavity in the rock extended as she turned her head and looked back into the blackness. She wondered if she could find an alternate way out. Holding onto the torch, she decided to risk turning it on to see what was behind her.

Bridgette switched the light on. The torch glowed dimly, and she wondered if it had been damaged when she had tumbled down the embankment. She held it up and pointed the feeble beam into the darkness. The cavity was more like a small cave about twenty feet deep and no more than four feet high. She shone the dim beam around on the back wall looking for any gaps or cracks that would offer her a way out. When she couldn't find any, she turned the flashlight to her left and played it along the length of that wall as well.

Undeterred when it also appeared solid, Bridgette flicked the beam around to the opposite wall. The cave stretched about fifteen feet to her right and was barely illuminated by the glow from her flashlight which seemed to be growing weaker by the minute. She slowly played the light down the right-hand side of the cave and stopped when she got half way.

Bridgette held the torchlight steady and did her best to compose herself as she stared into the gloom. There was just enough light for her to make out what looked to be the remains of a woman's shoe. Trying not to be unnerved by what she was looking at, Bridgette slowly played the light further down the wall and gasped when the light illuminated the remains of a human skeleton, still partially covered with clothing and slumped against the wall. Almost mesmerized by what confronted her, Bridgette's shock was short lived as she heard the sound of small rocks spilling down onto the ground just outside the cave entrance. Switching the light off, Bridgette lay still and listened to the unmistakable sound of footsteps as the shooter walked to the edge of the gorge above her.

Chapter 27

Delray sat in one of the four leather visitor's chairs outside the Commissioner's office and tried to look relaxed. He watched the hands of a large electric clock on the wall opposite as they silently closed in on six o'clock and wondered if his meeting would be rescheduled? He used the time to think about what he would say to Underwood as he reflected on the conversation he'd had earlier in the day with Bridgette. The alleyway attack on his rookie detective worried him. Now convinced that John Tyson had been murdered, it was imperative that Bridgette got immediate support or return to Hartbourne while they thought about their next move. He knew the Commissioner well enough to know that he would act quickly and decisively.

He wasn't so sure how the Commissioner would react to his initial investigation into the basement shootout. Delray ran his fingers through his dark curly hair and let out a long breath before pulling the grid page of notes he'd made on his team members out of his coat pocket. As he smoothed the notes out on his trouser leg, he kept returning to the three crosses he placed against the line for Charlie Bates. He wondered if it was enough to bother the Commissioner with. He'd casually engaged Bates in conversation earlier in the day. Bates moved okay now and seemed happy as he went about his daily routine. Delray knew enough about human behavior from almost thirty years on the force to know outward appearances meant nothing.

Delray heard footsteps and folded up his page of notes as he saw the Commissioner striding up the corridor. Delray watched as Underwood stopped briefly at his executive assistant's desk to pick up a couple of messages. Underwood gave Delray a brief nod and motioned him to follow as he headed for his office.

Holding the door open, Underwood said, "Come on in Felix. I'm running late so we're going to have to make this quick."

Delray walked in ahead of Underwood and went to take a seat in one of the three designer timber and leather chairs that sat opposite Underwood's huge desk.

Underwood said, "Over here Felix," and motioned Delray to join him at an eight-seat conference table on the left side of his expansive office. Delray had never sat at the table and knew it was normally reserved for meetings Underwood wanted to hold in private.

As he sat down, Underwood explained, "I've got a crime prevention dinner to attend this evening with the Police Minister and I need to be out of here in under ten minutes." Pointing at his large wooden office desk, Underwood continued, "If I sit over there Felix, I know I'll get stuck, so let's talk here."

Delray nodded and said, "Fine by me Commissioner."

"My executive assistant tells me you have another matter other than the basement shooting to discuss as well?"

"That's right sir. I have some grave concerns about leaving Detective Cash on her own in Sanbury."

"And why is that?"

Delray gave Underwood a brief rundown of the attack Bridgette had suffered the night before.

Underwood sat and listened patiently. When Delray finished,

he responded, "So, she's okay then?"

"For now, although I've told her not to go anywhere without her service pistol even though she's not licensed to carry there."

Underwood replied, "That won't be necessary Felix. As of right now, this investigation is suspended."

Underwood clasped his hands together and thought for a moment before he continued. "Contact Detective Cash and tell her to prepare a statement for me of what happened. Reinforce that I'm pleased with the work she's done, but for now, we need to pull back to fully consider our next steps. I'll need to have a phone conference with her first thing tomorrow morning and then I'll make contact with Chief Payne."

Underwood paused for a moment and then said in a more conversational tone, "This could get ugly Felix. As you know, we have no formal jurisdiction in Sanbury so this could be one for the politicians to sort out — particularly if Payne refuses to cooperate any further. We have to be careful we're not sidelined."

Delray nodded and didn't try to hide his disappointment. "I understand sir. I'll call Detective Cash as soon as we're done here."

Underwood looked at his watch. "We've got five minutes Felix, so let's go through what you've learned about the basement shooting."

Delray pulled the page of notes from his pocket and flattened it out on the table. "Sir, I did up a grid earlier — each team member and then a column for each of the five key things I think we're looking for."

Delray slid the page across to Underwood and spent a minute explaining each column and the markings he'd made against each police officer.

Pointing at the entry for Charlie Bates, Delray continued. "Sir this is the one that stands out. I might be jumping at shadows, but in addition to his above average security privileges and computer access, Detective Bates took three days leave after the shooting incident and had noticeably diminished physical capacity for several weeks following his return to work."

Delray went on to give a brief summary of Goldsack's observations.

Underwood listened intently and then asked, "So what's your take on this Felix? Should he be considered a suspect?"

Delray paused for a moment to think about the question. It pained him to think one of his team could be involved in something so contemptible. "Sir, I haven't had a lot of time to think about it. I like Bates, but to be honest, I don't know him well enough to really give an opinion."

Underwood nodded and said, "Well there's one way to find out for sure."

"And what's that?"

"We're within our rights to call him in for a drug test at any time and there's no reason why that can't be extended to a medical, particularly as he's formally requested desk duties."

Underwood paused a moment and held Delray's gaze. "If the doctor discovers he's got a recent shoulder wound, then he's got a lot of explaining to do."

* * *

Quinn pressed the answer button on his mobile and said, "I didn't expect to hear from you until tomorrow?"

The caller said, "Where are you?"

Quinn looked at his closed office door and replied, "I'm at the office, but it's late. Everyone's gone home."

"We have a problem."

Quinn shook his head and said, "Tell me she's not still alive?"

"I didn't get a clean shot. She escaped down into a gorge behind Cathedral Valley."

"Did you go after her?"

"She's trapped. You can't get out of the gorge without a rope. I walked around the top for over an hour trying to find her, but the snow made it impossible."

"You're positive she can't get out?"

"Not on her own."

Quinn took a deep breath to keep his anger in check. "This is a complication we don't need."

"I plan on going back tomorrow. I will—"

Quinn interrupted. "No. You'll create too much suspicion."

"We can't leave her there. Someone may go looking for her."

Quinn thought for a moment. "We'll get Clement. After the debacle in the alley the other night, he owes me."

"Clement doesn't get off until mid-day tomorrow."

Quinn said, "Make the call. As soon as he finishes his shift, tell him to head up there and finish it. He's not to come back until he's positive she's dead."

"What do you want me to do with the rifle? Clement won't want it."

Quinn thought for a moment and then responded, "Wipe it clean and then hide it in the house that Cash is staying in. If by some miracle she manages to get out, we'll tip off the police that she's in possession of an illegal weapon. That should keep her out of the way for long enough."

"Okay, I'll get onto it."

Quinn responded, "Call me when you're done at Cash's place. There's something else we need to discuss," and then disconnected.

Quinn sat in his chair for a moment and stared into space. Cash was a loose end he couldn't afford to have walking around. If she learned the truth, there was still time for the whole deal to come crashing down. He looked at his watch as he picked up his phone again. He needed to leave the office within the hour and still had three phone calls to make.

Chapter 28

It was well after nine p.m. when Roman Quinn pulled up out front of the small timber clad house. The house was about five minutes out of town at the top of a dirt road and backed onto the local saw mill. The road wasn't lit and with no other houses close by, the dwelling was barely visible against a backdrop of darkness.

Quinn studied the house for a moment and then picked up a small mobile phone he rarely used and dialed Mitch Conden's home number.

Conden picked up after three rings. "Hello."

"I'm out front."

The phone line went dead. Quinn switched the engine off and waited a few moments until a dim porch light came on. The feeble light barely illuminated the front porch of a house that was run down and badly in need of maintenance. Quinn mused how the house was a sad reflection of Conden's life as he walked up the cracked and overgrown footpath. After knocking on the front door, he resisted an urge to stick a finger over the peephole as he waited for the door to open.

Conden opened his front door and stood warily in the doorway, dressed in a pair of wrinkled jeans and a dirty shirt that was too tight for him.

Quinn ignored Conden's invitation to step inside and shook

his head in disdain as he looked down at the cast on Conden's right wrist.

Conden replied aggressively, "She got a jump on me. If you'd allowed me to put a bullet in her like I wanted, this wouldn't have happened."

Quinn tightened his mouth to feign anger as he responded, "I told you, we don't need another dead cop right now."

"And you think putting her in the hospital wasn't going to attract attention?"

"You were supposed to make it look like a mugging. Just to slow her down for a few days, but clearly, you failed."

"I want my money. I know you're getting ready to leave town and—"

"I don't owe you anything."

Slightly emboldened, Conden took half a step forward and said, "I've been keeping a close watch on you and that partner of yours. I know you're getting ready to do a runner. Trying to have that nosy cop taken out only proves it all the more."

Quinn shook his head. "You get paid on results. That's how it works."

"The price has gone up too. I want fifty thousand."

Quinn stifled a laugh. "Are you out of your mind?"

"I'll make this easy for you. I know you're leaving, but I'm prepared to keep my mouth shut."

Quinn paused for a moment as he studied Conden's body language. He could smell alcohol on his breath and assumed he was probably high as well.

He realized getting into an argument was pointless and replied, "I'll pay you five thousand to keep quiet, but that's all. I've got the money in the car. I pay you now and then we're done."

Conden's face broke into a conceited grin. "We go way back

Roman. I've been covering up your dirty little secrets since high school. What I know is worth a lot more than five thousand."

Quinn stared back and gave no reaction.

Conden continued. "So, let's start with Olivia Hodder. Do you remember that night Roman? You wanted her so bad and when she turned you down—"

"Olivia Hodder was just a school girl who's been dead for seventeen years."

"Seventeen years is nothing. I've seen people charged with murders they committed over thirty years ago."

Quinn decided he needed to take control of the conversation. In a more conversational voice, he replied, "So let's talk about it then, Mitch. You were there and held her down. I'm not a cop, but by my reckoning, that would make you an accessory?"

Conden responded confidently, "Murder is a complicated thing, Roman. Remember, I didn't pull the trigger — you did."

Quinn put on a concerned look as he responded, "You're bluffing. You're not about to make any confession that would implicate you as well."

"You remember your watch, Roman? The one she ripped off your wrist when you tried to pin her down?"

Quinn said nothing. He needed to learn as much as he could before he responded and waited for Conden to continue.

"We never found it did we? Even when we went back and tore the hut apart afterward."

Quinn could see Conden was enjoying himself. The condescending smile was nauseating, but he kept his expression neutral as he waited patiently for the overweight cop to continue.

"When we put a match to it, it got me thinking. If it wasn't there, then where was it? I always wondered if she'd held on to it when she escaped. It's a pity for you, you weren't a better shot."

Quinn said nothing.

"When I came back home after the police academy, I started looking for her. I had a big advantage over the search teams because I knew where to look..."

Conden paused for dramatic effect and then in a softer voice said, "It took me nearly three years on my own time, but eventually I found her."

"So, what does that prove?'

"The body was badly decomposed, and it looked like it had been ravaged by animals. Bones were scattered everywhere, but I took my time. I guess wild animals aren't much interested in watches, even expensive ones that are personally engraved."

Quinn pretended to be exasperated as he replied, "So what do you want?"

"The watch and a few of her bones are in a safe deposit box at my bank. I've kind of kept them as an insurance policy. It's all yours for fifty thousand."

"You know I don't carry that much cash on me."

Conden chewed his lip for a moment and said, "I'll take the five as a deposit now. You can give me the rest at the bank when I give you the box."

Quinn nodded. "And then we're done?"

Conden nodded. "It's a fair deal. I get a final payment for loyal service and you get the only evidence that will ever link you to a murder."

Quinn had all he needed and nodded. "Give me a minute. The cash is locked in the back of my car."

Conden grinned as he stepped back. "You're letting all my heat out. I'll wait inside."

A moment later Quinn was left standing under the dull porch light staring at Conden's closed front door. He suppressed a smile as he turned and walked back to the car. Conden thought he was smart, but he'd given up far more information than he should have. Quinn opened the passenger door and retrieved a rifle off the front seat. He'd deliberately left the interior light for his car switched off and wasn't worried about Conden being able to see anything he did in the darkness. Casually, he walked back to the front door with the rifle down by his side.

After stepping up onto the front porch, Quinn knocked on the front door twice and then took two steps back. Calmly, he raised the rifle to his shoulder and pointed it directly at the door's peephole. He counted off three seconds and pulled the trigger.

The stillness of the night was shattered by the sound of the rifle shot as it echoed across the valley below. Quinn waited for several seconds and then stepped forward and kicked the front door open.

After stepping in through the doorway, he looked down impassively at the lifeless form of Mitch Conden. Lying on his back in a rapidly expanding pool of his own blood, Conden was almost unrecognizable. Quinn studied the face for a moment admiring the work of his high-power rifle, which had almost totally obliterated the upper left-hand side of his face.

He nodded approvingly and remarked, "A definite improvement Mitch," as he looked up the short hallway he now stood in.

He debated searching the house for any other incriminating evidence but decided it wasn't worth the risk of staying any longer than necessary.

Using a handkerchief from his pocket, Quinn turned off the porch light and then pulled the door closed behind him. He walked back to his car at an unhurried pace and mentally reviewed what he needed to do next. Tomorrow would now include a trip to Conden's bank. He knew the manager well and figured the five thousand cash in his top pocket would be more than enough to get him five minutes of alone time with Conden's deposit box.

Chapter 29

Bridgette awoke to the sensation of something wet pressed against the side of her face and recoiled as she tried to brush it away. Fighting off the urge to panic as she stared up into the darkness, she heard the unmistakable sound of a dog barking. Confused, she shook her head to clear the fog and realized she wasn't dreaming as the presence barked a second time and continued to lick her. She relaxed a little as she realized the dog, or whatever it was, probably meant her no harm.

In the background she heard a voice she recognized calling out, "Molly, Molly," and knew she was sharing the darkness with her neighbor's dog. Now fully awake, she realized she was still in the tiny cave in the gorge as the image of the skeleton lying just a few feet away came back to haunt her.

She heard Hughey call out Molly's name again, only this time louder. She tried to raise up her head to call back but was overcome by dizziness and lay back down again.

Dehydrated and with a splitting headache, she called out to Hughey, but her voice was barely louder than a raspy whisper.

Bridgette cleared her throat and called out again, only this time her voice was slightly louder.

She was relieved when her neighbor shouted back, "Where are you, Bridgette?"

"In the cave behind the rock."

Bridgette had no idea how long she had been asleep. She heard Hughey's voice frantically call her name again, only this time much louder.

Comforted by the presence of Molly who began to lick her hand, she responded, "There's a small opening in the rock behind the boulder. Can you see it?"

Bridgette heard scuffling outside the entrance to the cave and then Hughey's voice call out, "Bridgette are you in there?"

She tried to raise her head to look back to the entrance but still felt nauseous. Reaching her left hand back over her head, she said, "I'm near the entrance Hughey."

Tears welled in her eyes as she felt the warm contact of another human as Hughey gently squeezed her hand.

"We found you, Bridgette."

She whispered, "Thank you, Hughey."

"I don't think I can squeeze into the cave to get you out Bridgette — I'm too big."

Bridgette reached her right hand over her head as well and said, "Just drag me out, Hughey."

"I don't want to hurt you."

"I'll be okay Hughey. Just take it slow."

Bridgette felt the reassuring grip of Hughey's hands around hers and then felt herself being pulled slowly forward. She was surprised to see blue sky above her as she was pulled from the cave. Hughey continued to gently drag her until she was well away from the entrance. She looked up into her neighbor's concerned face as her eyes adjusted to the daylight.

Hughey's concerned, "Are you all right Bridgette?" question was drowned out as Molly barked again and continued to lick her hand.

Still slightly dazed, she responded, "How did you know I was missing?"

"I was worried when you didn't come home last night, so I rang Jack. We both knew you were up here, so he came and picked me up. It was after midnight when we found your car, so we slept in the truck until it was light enough to start looking for you."

Hughey gently lifted Bridgette up into a sitting position. She leaned her head back against the boulder and said, "Thanks, Hughey, I think you saved my life."

Hughey handed her a water canteen. After taking a long sip, Bridgette asked, "How did you know where to look for me?"

"You said you were going to explore the trail through the forest. We weren't sure where you went after you got to the clearing, but Molly picked up the trail and led us here."

Molly let out a small bark at the mention of her name and seemed content to be sitting beside Bridgette.

Bridgette stroked the dog and said, "She's very clever."

Hughey continued, "I got worried when she went over the edge and down the gorge, but she seemed to know where she was—"

Hughey stopped mid-sentence as he heard his name called. They both looked up to see Jack Sutton standing close to the edge of the gorge directly above them.

With a concerned look, Sutton called down, "Are you okay Bridgette?"

Bridgette nodded, "A little cold and dehydrated Jack, but no broken bones."

Sutton shook his head. "I can't believe we found you alive. You're incredibly lucky."

Bridgette smiled as she patted Molly again. "Neither can I."

Sutton shifted his position slightly to get closer to the edge. "Can you walk Bridgette?"

Bridgette tried not to shiver as she responded, "I'm a little weak, but I'll give it a try."

Sutton pointed across to the embankment she had tumbled down yesterday. "We got a rope going down the embankment over there — that's how Hughey got down. I'll fashion a sling for you to help us lift you out."

"Thanks, Jack, I'm sorry to have put you out."

"No problem, we're just glad we found you alive."

Sutton frowned as he asked, "So what happened Bridgette? You don't strike me as the type who falls into a gorge they can't get out of."

Bridgette took a couple of minutes to explain what had happened."

Sutton's mouth dropped as he listened. "Did you get a look at him?"

"Not really. He was wearing some kind of snow goggles and had a scarf covering most of his face."

Sutton paused for a moment and then said to Hughey, "Bridgette looks to be suffering some hypothermia, Hughey. We need to get Bridgette out of here now. If she can't walk can you carry her?"

Hughey nodded and said, "I can carry her easy."

Bridgette held out her hands and motioned to Hughey to help her up as she said, "Let's see if I can walk first."

She took a moment to get her balance and then looked up at Sutton again. "Jack, there's something else you need to know."

"And what's that?"

"There are human remains in the cave."

Sutton looked stunned. "Well, this day is full of surprises."

Bridgette let go of Hughey's hand and leaned up against the boulder for support.

She still felt weak, but the nausea was clearing. "It's not much more than a skeleton now. Whoever it was died a long time ago. I didn't get close, but there was a woman's dress shoe near the body... I'm thinking it may even be Olivia Hodder."

Sutton nodded and said, "I'll ring Payne as soon as we get you out of here, but I don't think it will be high on his priority list today."

Bridgette frowned. "Why?"

Sutton responded, "I rang Sanbury Police after we located your car last night, but nobody wanted to talk to me. When I rang again this morning, I found out why."

Bridgette looked confused and replied, "So what's happening Jack."

Sutton grimaced. "Mitch Conden was found dead in his house from a gunshot wound. No weapon was found near the body so they're treating it as a murder."

Chapter 30

Bridgette opened her eyes and blinked rapidly as she tried to bring her vision back into focus. Her mouth was dry, and her shoulder still hurt, but she felt warm and comfortable. Turning her head to her right she saw the faces of Hughey and Jack Sutton drifting in and out of focus.

In a weak voice, she managed, "Where am I?"

"Sanbury Base Hospital Bridgette," replied Sutton.

Bridgette closed her eyes again. "How did I get here?"

Hughey responded, "You collapsed Bridgette."

Sutton asked, "Do you remember what happened Bridgette?"

Bridgette shook her head. "Not really."

Sutton said, "We got you out of the gorge, okay, but you insisted on walking back even though we both told you it was a bad idea."

Bridgette managed a weak smile. "That sounds like me."

Sutton continued, "You collapsed about halfway up the Cathedral Valley. Hughey had to carry you the rest of the way. After we got you back to my truck, we brought you straight here."

Bridgette nodded and opened her eyes again. "How long have I been here?"

Sutton looked at his watch. "About three hours. It's almost one o'clock."

Bridgette said, "I don't know how to say thank you to you guys.

If you hadn't been looking out for me..."

Sutton responded, "We're just glad you're alive Bridgette. The doctor came and looked at your chart a few minutes ago. He said you've got a mild case of hypothermia, probably some concussion and some torn muscles in your shoulder. But the good news is, with a few days rest you should be fine. He wanted us to leave you in peace, but we're not so keen on leaving you until we know more about who shot at you and why."

Bridgette winced in pain as she sat up in bed. She reached out to pour a glass of water from a jug on the bedside table, but Hughey insisted on pouring it for her.

Bridgette thanked Hughey as he handed her the glass. After taking a few sips, she felt the fire in her throat subside and asked, "Did the doctor say how soon I could leave?"

Sutton said, "I asked the same question. The doctor said you won't be going anywhere until he clears you and the police have been to interview you. I called the station not long after we arrived and they promised to get a detective here today, but they didn't say when. I figure with the murder of Mitch Condon, you're low on the priority list."

Bridgette nodded and then asked, "So what happened to him?

Sutton replied, "The word around town is he was shot with a high-power rifle. They found the body inside his house. He's pretty badly messed up..."

Bridgette nodded. She knew Conden's death had to be connected with what happened to her but wasn't sure how all the pieces fit together.

Sutton continued, "So are you up to telling us what happened Bridgette?"

Bridgette replied, "There's not a lot to tell really," and then explained how she had walked through the forest to the clearing and then down to the edge of the gorge. She concluded by adding, "When I got to the bottom of the clearing and looked down at the gorge, I realized I was at the location where John had taken the last of his photos. It started to snow hard, so I decided to head back. That's when I heard the gunshot."

Sutton asked, "Did you see the shooter?"

"I saw him stepping out of the forest to take a second shot at me. I knew I was exposed and there was no chance I could get to cover before he fired again, so I jumped off the embankment to escape. When I hit the bottom there was nowhere to hide except behind the boulder at the bottom of the gorge. When he started shooting again, I had to move further behind the boulder to avoid getting shot. That's when I found the cave."

Sutton responded, "You got lucky."

Bridgette nodded. "Yes. Very lucky."

Sutton shifted in his seat and then said, "I'm not sure I should be telling you this just yet, but you're lucky it didn't snow much last night."

"What do you mean?"

"It looks like we've got another great storm coming. If it had hit last night that whole area could have been covered in snow. If that had happened, Molly wouldn't have picked up your scent."

Bridgette grimaced. "And you would have had no idea I was in the cave."

Sutton nodded.

"I need to buy Molly a big bone as soon as I get out of here."

Sutton grinned as he responded, "I'm sure she'd like that. So tell us what happened next."

"I could see the top of most of the gorge from inside the cave. I watched him walk around both sides of the gorge for almost an hour trying to find me—"

Sutton interrupted, "You told us straight after we got you out that you didn't recognize him?"

Bridgette nodded. "He was wearing ski goggles and had a scarf up over most of his face. All I can tell you is he had a slim build and wasn't overly tall, but that's not much to go on."

They were all quiet for a moment. Bridgette shivered as she thought about how close she'd come to dying.

In a more reflective voice, she said, "My backpack tore when I rolled down the embankment. I lost the emergency beacon and my phone. I debated going back out to try and find them but decided it wasn't worth the risk... just in case he was still out there waiting."

Sutton pointed to the top drawer of the storage unit beside her bed. "Hughey found your phone about half way down the embankment wedged between two rocks. The screen's broken, but it still works. You've got a few missed calls I think."

Bridgette replied, "Sorry about your emergency beacon Jack."

Sutton waved her off. "No big deal Bridgette. You're alive — that's all that matters."

Bridgette looked towards the door and frowned a little.

Sutton said, "Problem?"

Bridgette grimaced. "Not really, I'm just hungry."

Hughey jumped up and said, "I'll go see the nurse. Would you like ice cream? That's what they gave me when I was in the hospital."

Bridgette smiled as she responded, "Something simple would be fine Hughey. Maybe a bread roll?"

Sutton waited until Hughey left the room and then said, "You okay to keep talking or do you need a break?"

"I'm okay Jack."

"I don't know if you remember, but just after we pulled you

out, you told us you found a body in there?"

Bridgette nodded. "I briefly turned my torch on just after I entered the cave to see if there was another way out. That's when I discovered the body. I didn't want to give my position away, so I switched it off again and waited until well after dark before I turned it back on again."

"That must have been creepy, lying in the dark knowing you were sharing the space with a body."

"Kind of."

Sutton raised his eyebrows. "I think I'd find that pretty hard, regardless of the circumstances."

"I only had time to study the body for a few seconds before I had to switch my flashlight off. But it was long enough to give me a lot to think about while I lay in the darkness."

Sutton frowned. "Sorry Bridgette, I'm not following."

"The body wasn't much more than bones, so it was fairly obvious it had been there for a long time."

Bridgette paused for a moment as she relived the moment. "There was something very strange about the body..."

Sutton leaned forward and waited for Bridgette to continue.

"On one side of the body, the bones were scattered everywhere, which is what you would expect if a wild animal had been feeding on the remains."

"And the other side?"

Bridgette frowned for a moment. "They were gathered together — almost in a pile."

Sutton frowned as well. "So what do you make of that?"

"I'm not sure. As I lay there in the dark trying not to freeze to death, I thought about it from different angles. No animal that I know of would pile up bones like that."

"So, you're suggesting a person did this?"

Bridgette nodded. “I’m positive somebody’s been in the cave, Jack. Somebody knew about the body.”

Chapter 31

Bridgette picked up her phone and dialed Delray's mobile number again. To her relief, he answered after the third ring.

"Sorry Bridgette, it's been a crazy day here. I'm glad I finally get to talk to you. Did you get the message I left earlier?"

"Yes Chief, but I wanted—"

Delray didn't seem to hear Bridgette's response and kept talking. "I'm really sorry Bridgette, but the Commissioner has suspended the investigation. Until we get a better handle on what the hell is happening there and why you were attacked—"

Bridgette interrupted. "Chief, I'm in the hospital."

"You're what?"

Bridgette sighed. "It's kind of a long story, but I was shot at yesterday afternoon while I was out exploring the area around the Cathedral Valley."

Bridgette could hear the growing alarm in Delray's voice as he asked, "Are you all right?"

"Some mild hypothermia and maybe some concussion, but I'm going to be okay."

"No bullet wounds?"

"No, but I came close."

"Hang on a minute."

Bridgette could here Delray get up and close a door — she

presumed to his office.

After he settled again, he said, "Okay, tell me what happened — top to bottom."

For the second time that day, Bridgette recounted her story. Delray listened mostly in silence, but, like Jack Sutton, he questioned her on whether she recognized the shooter. When she had finished describing her ordeal, she gave Delray a brief rundown of how she had discovered a body in the cave.

Bridgette waited in silence while Delray had his thinking time. She was glad Sutton had taken Hughey across to the police station for his daily parole check in. She had a feeling the next part of the conversation would be better held in private.

"I can't believe this has all deteriorated this badly Bridgette. When are you going to be released?"

"I'm not sure. I'm still under observation and Sanbury Police want to interview me."

"Will you be well enough to drive when you're released? I don't want you staying in that town a minute longer than is absolutely necessary."

"I think I'll be okay to drive. But I might be asked by Sanbury Police to hang around until after the body in the cave is recovered — just in case they have more questions. Also, there's something else you need to know..."

"And what's that?"

"You remember Mitch Conden, the officer who arrested my neighbor Hughey on Sunday night?"

"The cop who likes to get heavy handed?"

"Yes."

"What about him?"

"He was murdered last night."

Delray tried to muffle an expletive and then replied, "What

happened?"

"I don't have a lot of details, but according to some of the locals, he was shot with a high-power rifle. They found him dead inside his house."

"Is suicide a possibility?"

"That's not what I'm hearing."

"Sanbury isn't a big town Bridgette. This must all be connected."

"I agree with you, Chief. There's a lot of pieces of the puzzle on the table right now... we just have to figure out how they fit together."

"Bridgette right now we have to make sure you're not the next victim in all this. We need to get you out of there as soon as possible. I'm going to organize for someone to drive up there and pick you up."

Bridgette felt uncomfortable. She didn't want someone from Hartbourne Metro coming to rescue her but played down her response. "I'm safe while I'm in hospital Chief."

"I don't want you there on your own Bridgette."

"I'm not really on my own Chief," Bridgette explained how Jack Sutton was insisting she come and stay with him until she left town.

"You trust him?"

"He and Hughey rescued me from the gorge early this morning. If it wasn't for them, I'd still be there."

Delray thought about it for a moment. "I'll have to brief the Commissioner on what's happened, so he'll get the final say. But promise me you'll leave town as soon as Sanbury Police have what they need from you?

"I promise Chief."

"Good and I want to know where you are at all times, okay?"

Bridgette felt relieved that Delray wasn't going to send someone to escort her home. Providing him with an update on her movements was a small price to pay.

"I'll text you whenever I move locations if that suits you Chief?"

"That'll work. Now is there anything I can do for you? Do you need me to call Payne or anything?"

"Can I ask a favor?"

"Fire away."

"I don't have my laptop here. Would you mind getting someone to do a couple of searches for me?"

"What kind of searches are we talking about?"

"Background checks on a couple of companies here that I have concerns about."

"Can this wait until you get back?"

"I'm sure it can, but I'm hoping this information may help us get to the bottom of what's happening here a little quicker. Also, it may be useful background information for the Commissioner if he has to negotiate with Payne."

"Let me get a pen."

Bridgette waited a moment until Delray came back and said, "Okay, fire away."

She pictured the noticeboard that she had seen in the entrance to the Snowbridge resort parking lot and then spelled out the two company names she was interested in.

Delray read the names back to make sure he had the details correct and then said, "I'll get someone onto this right away."

"Can Charlie do it? He'll be much quicker than anyone else."

There was more silence on the phone.

When Delray didn't reply straight away, Bridgette frowned and said, "Have I missed something Chief?"

"I can't go into details right now Bridgette, but Charlie can't help you at present. Keep this confidential for now — we'll talk more about it when you get back."

Bridgette knew not to push Delray and replied, "Okay."

Delray replied, "Bridgette, I need to set up some time to see the Commissioner. Please be careful and as soon as anything changes there, you call me, okay?"

"I will Chief, I promise."

Bridgette heard her boss disconnect and sat for a moment replaying the conversation over in her mind. Charlie Bates was by far the best computer analyst they had, and he'd been getting good results for the team since joining the Homicide unit six months ago. She reflected on an earlier conversation with Delray about the shooting and realized Bates was probably his prime suspect. Her thoughts were interrupted as she looked up to see the large figure of Corey Payne standing in the doorway of her room staring at her.

She held his stare as he walked into the room and stopped about three feet from her bed.

Payne stood still and stared at her for a moment. The hostile glare wasn't as prominent as it normally was, and she wondered how much he'd been affected by the death of his cousin.

She decided to break the silence and said, "My condolences to you on the loss of your cousin."

Ignoring her sentiment, Payne said, "We've started a full investigation into Mitch's murder first thing this morning. After your run-in with him on Sunday night, you're one of our prime suspects..."

Bridgette decided not to respond. She wasn't sure whether Payne was trying to bait her to get a reaction or if he was working a different angle.

Payne continued. “We visited your house this morning and conducted a search — all legal I might add.”

“I’m not sure it’s filtered all the way up to your level yet, but I spent the night out in the mountains. I got stuck in a gorge after being shot at and had to be rescued.”

“So I’ve heard.”

Bridgette decided not to respond.

Payne stepped in closer and pulled a photograph out of his pocket. As he handed it to her, he said, “Perhaps you’d like to explain this. We found this under your mattress when we conducted our search.”

Bridgette stared at a photo of her bedroom. It looked exactly the same as she’d left it yesterday morning, except now there was a high-powered hunting rifle lying on her bed.

Chapter 32

Delray looked up when he heard a knock on his door and did his best to hide his surprise as he saw Commissioner Underwood standing in the doorway.

Delray said, "Sir, this is unexpected. Did I miss an appointment?"

Underwood responded, "No Felix, this is a spur of the moment thing," as he walked into Delray's office.

Delray knew the Commissioner rarely left the fourth floor and when he did, he usually had a convoy of advisers in tow. He decided to let the Commissioner take the lead with the conversation.

After sitting down, Underwood said, "I've been giving this business in the basement a lot of thought Felix. Your list of suspects, and particularly Bates, is bothering me. I didn't get much sleep last night... and for me, that's unusual."

Delray nodded and said, "Sir, it's been weighing heavily on my mind too."

Underwood said, "Is Bates at work today?"

"Yes, Sir. He should be at his desk right now as a matter of fact."

"Call him in. I'd like the three of us to have an informal discussion. Maybe we can clear this up without the need to get Internal Investigations or anyone else involved."

Delray picked up his phone and punched in Bates' extension. After waiting for several seconds, he said, "Charlie, it's the Chief. You got a minute; I'd like to speak to you in my office?"

They waited in silence until there was a knock on the door.

Delray looked up to see a slightly concerned looking Charlie Bates standing at the door staring at the Commissioner.

Delray said, "Come in and close the door, Charlie. The Commissioner and I won't keep you long, but there is something we'd like to clear up."

Bates mumbled, "Okay," as he walked in.

When he was seated, Underwood nodded at Delray to start the discussion.

Delray clasped his hands together and leaned forward on his desk. He studied Bates for a moment before he spoke. If Bates was nervous, he was hiding it well.

"Charlie, as you know, we're trying to get to the bottom of the shootout incident in the basement."

Bates nodded but said nothing.

Delray continued, "I've been working with the Commissioner on this and there are a couple of things we'd like to discuss with you."

Bates frowned and said, "Do I need a lawyer?"

Delray looked at Underwood to take the lead.

Underwood responded, "I'm told you took three days leave immediately following the shooting, Detective?"

Bates shot back, "Sir, I had the flu. I didn't know that was a crime?"

Underwood remained calm and said, "I'll ask you to remember who you're speaking to Detective. No one's accusing you of anything yet. But as you can appreciate, one of our officers was fired upon and I intend to get to the bottom of it."

Bates nodded.

Underwood continued. "I've read the report filed by Detective Cash. She believes a round she fired struck her assailant in the shoulder, either directly or by way of a ricochet."

Bates shot back, "I wouldn't know Sir, I wasn't there."

Underwood glanced at Delray and then continued. "The easiest way for you to clear this up is to remove your shirt and show us you have no injuries to your shoulders."

Bates replied, "I'm not saying anything else without a lawyer."

Underwood said, "If you've got nothing to hide, why do you need a lawyer?"

Bates looked away and thought for a moment. "I have an injury to my left shoulder. I ride a push bike for fitness and came off a couple of weeks back. There's a lot of bruising..."

Underwood nodded and said, "Show us."

Bates replied, "Not without a lawyer."

Underwood replied, "As a police officer, Hartbourne Metro is entitled to examine or drug test you any time it likes. So, either you take your shirt off, or I'll have you charged for disobeying an order."

Delray watched as Underwood held Bates' stare.

When Bates didn't reply, Underwood added, "What's it going to be Detective? You're making this far harder than it needs to be."

Bates replied, "I've already told you I'm injured. Taking my shirt off will prove nothing. Like I said, I want my lawyer."

Underwood said, "Don't force me to have you arrested Detective. That's a blemish you don't want on your record..."

Bates shook his head and did little to hide his fury as he stood up. Delray and Underwood watched as Bates removed his tie and slowly unbuttoned his shirt. He gingerly removed his shirt to reveal a huge black bruise across the top of his left shoulder.

As Delray and Underwood stared at the injury, Bates said, "Like I said, I fell off my bike."

Underwood got up from his chair and motioned Bates to follow him across to the window where the light was better.

Bates stopped a few feet from the window and did little to hide his anger.

Underwood motioned Bates to move even closer to the window and said, "I used to ride competitively in my youth. Mainly road races... I had a couple of top ten finishes, but never won anything."

Delray watched as Underwood examined Bates' shoulder. The bruising was right across the top of his left shoulder, but it didn't look recent.

Underwood examined Bates' shoulder for close to a minute and then stepped back. "I've had my fair share of tumbles off bikes, Detective and I've never seen an injury like that from a bike accident."

Without waiting for any further instruction, Bates said sullenly, "This was a mistake. I want a lawyer."

Underwood nodded and said, "You're going to need one Detective. I've also seen a few bullet wounds in my time, including a couple from ricochets. You've got a major trauma site at the top of your shoulder consistent with being hit by shrapnel or some other object."

Underwood pulled a smartphone out of his pocket and pressed speed dial. After waiting a couple of seconds, he said, "Come in," before disconnecting and turning back to face Bates again. "Detective Bates, I've just called Aaron Sterling from Internal Investigations. He will take you upstairs for a formal interview in relation to your possible involvement in the shooting incident in the basement. When you get upstairs you are to call your lawyer or the police union immediately. I have a doctor on standby to examine you once you have legal representation..."

Underwood paused for a moment and held Bates with a long stare before he continued. "Based on my preliminary examination, I'm not buying your bike story for a second."

He paused as Aaron Sterling knocked once before opening the door to enter Delray's office.

Underwood fixed Bates with a laser stare again and said, "I can't tell you how disappointed I am," before he headed for the door.

Delray watched as Underwood paused long enough in the doorway to say, "We need to talk about Sanbury Felix, but I need to make some calls first. I'll see you upstairs in half an hour."

Delray mumbled, "Okay Sir," as he stood behind his desk watching as Bates was placed in handcuffs and read his rights.

Chapter 33

Derek Sirocca was fifty-two years old and spent most of his working life in a three-piece suit. Today was different. A rare day in his calendar with no court appearances or client appointments, he had swapped the suit for a pair of tan chinos and a white linen shirt.

His boutique list of clients had made him a millionaire several times over. Organized crime figures, dirty politicians, and even a few A-list media celebrities all had his number on speed dial — he was the ultimate Mr. Fix-it. They hired him more for the additional services he offered, rather than his expertise as a lawyer. When it came to finding a way to keep someone out of jail or the media spotlight, there was no one better than Sirocca.

He worked alone without an office, secretary or associates other than two men with criminal records whom he referred to as his private investigators. His boutique list of clients liked it that way. Few people ever knew their inside story and they could always count on Sirocca's discretion.

He worked sixty-hour weeks — not because he had to, but because he enjoyed the rush of being able to outmaneuver the legal system to his client's advantage. He kept his circle of friends small and didn't have time for relationships unless they were short, involved rough sex and the exchange of money.

Today, he sat in his home office reviewing a file for one of his

A-list clients, a TV star who'd been caught with a prostitute and a small quantity of cocaine in a police raid at a celebrity pool party. The client had come to him begging for help. Sirocca knew his client's career would be over if he was prosecuted and negotiated a fee of one hundred thousand dollars to make the charges disappear. In under two days, he had managed to get the prostitute to agree to take the rap for the cocaine possession and deny any involvement with his client for twenty-five-thousand in cash. He had also greased the wheels of two prominent local journalists who had agreed to write news stories casting doubt on the legality of the police raid and who had been arrested. He stood to clear sixty-five thousand for less than two days' work — God, how he loved being a lawyer.

Sirocca closed the file and felt in the mood for celebrating. He got up from his iKon leather office chair and gazed out the window at the Hartbourne city skyline. He'd had the fourth bedroom of his lavish penthouse converted into an office soon after he had purchased the property. It was the only one of the four bedrooms that afforded him a view of the city and he'd chosen it as a constant reminder that the greed and corruption of the city's inhabitants enabled him to live such a privileged existence. He was in the mood for a little fun and debated whether it would be a blonde or a brunette this time. He moved across to look into a narrow ornate mirror he'd had fixed to the wall. The mirror was supposed to resemble art, but Sirocca used it to study his appearance several times a day. He was diminutive in size and offended when people called him short. He turned sideways to study his profile. Still the same trim weight he'd been in his early twenties, he knew he looked good for someone over fifty. He curled back a fleck of graying hair behind his left ear. Some of his clients said his hair was too long, despite his immaculate grooming. He didn't care — they hired him, anyway.

His train of thought was interrupted by one of his mobile phones as it rang on his desk. He frowned. The phone was for his VIP clients only — five of them in total — and was never far from his reach, twenty-four hours a day. If it had been his normal phone, he would have allowed the call to go through to voicemail, but for these clients, that wasn't an option.

He read the caller ID on the screen as he picked up the phone and said, "It's been a while."

The male voice responded, "I have an urgent job for you."

Sirocca suppressed the urge to say, "They're always urgent," and instead responded, "What do you need?"

The voice said, "One of my informants inside Hartbourne Metro has been discovered."

"What happened?"

"I've only got sketchy details, but it appears his superiors have charged him with stealing microfilm and shooting at a police officer."

Sirocca worked with this client frequently and was familiar with his client's business. He was aware his client collected intelligence from inside police headquarters and asked, "I take it he was stealing the microfilm for you?"

"Yes."

"Does he know your identity?"

"No, and we need to keep it that way."

Sirocca knew full well what was coming but asked anyway. "How can I help?"

"The officer's name is Charles Bates. He is in his early thirties and very intelligent, particularly with computer systems. He's had no good reason in the past to learn my identity, but that all changes now he is looking at a prison sentence."

"Do you want me to represent him?"

The voice responded, "Yes, for your usual fee. He is due to be arraigned downtown within the hour. He has already been instructed that you will represent him and that he is to keep his mouth shut. I need you to reinforce that message with him and after you've interviewed him, give me your professional opinion of what we should do next."

The caller hung up. There was no need for any further instruction — he'd given Sirocca enough information for now.

Sirocca walked through to his expansive living area with its floor to ceiling double glazed windows and stared out at the panoramic view of the ocean. The view was lost on him as he went over the conversation in his mind and began planning what he needed to do next. If he thought Bates was open to a plea deal in exchange for information and a lighter sentence, they would need to make sure the case never got to court. He had helped his client stay out of the police spotlight for many years and with careful planning, this would prove no different.

Sirocca punched in a number in his smartphone and pressed connect.

The call was answered after three rings. "I'm alone — you can talk."

Sirocca replied, "I have a job for you," and then explained the meager details he knew about the arrest of Charlie Bates.

The man who called himself John listened without interrupting and replied, "What do you need?"

"I need you to work up a background profile on Bates. I'll get what I can from him when I get downtown, but people in his situation never give you the full story and its vital I have it."

"I'll start on it right now and send something through later today."

"Good. Also, I need you to get a schedule of where Bates is likely to be held while he awaits trial."

"You don't think he'll make bail?"

"That depends on how my interview goes with him. If it looks like he's a risk, I'll make sure he doesn't. He will be far easier to take care of where he is than if he's out roaming the streets."

"Okay."

Sirocca added, "We'll start with your usual retainer and go from there depending on how complicated this gets."

"I'll be in touch."

Sirocca disconnected. He sighed as he stared at the ocean view — he would need to put on a suit after all.

Chapter 34

Bridgette stared at the photograph for a moment and then asked, "Where did you find it?"

Payne took a step closer to her bed and said, "In the ceiling cavity of your house, wrapped in plastic."

Bridgette realized she shouldn't say anything else without a lawyer being present and simply nodded.

She could see from Payne's body language he felt in control as he said, "We're running ballistics on it now against the bullet that killed Mitch. You're going to be in a lot of trouble if we come back with a match."

Bridgette did her best to control her anger and responded, "Like I said before, I was shot at and stuck in a gorge. There's no way I could have killed Mitch Conden."

Payne shook his head. "I'm not buying it. For all we know, you shot Mitch and drove out there afterward and left enough of a trail to make sure you were found again."

Bridgette said, "It makes you wonder doesn't it?"

Payne frowned. "Wonder what."

"If I'm smart enough to set up such an elaborate alibi, why would I leave the murder weapon in a location where it could be so easily found?"

Payne grabbed the photograph back and said, "You're not as smart as you think you are. You might be some hotshot detective from the city with a fancy university degree, but you're out of your depth out here. I know you broke into Tyson's house and you're lucky you're not up on a break and enter charge."

Bridgette called Payne's bluff. "That's a serious accusation you're making Chief Payne. Do you have any proof?"

With a menacing grin, Payne shot back, "You're very ballsy for someone who's a primary suspect in a murder."

Bridgette knew she wouldn't win an argument with Payne and decided to diffuse the situation. "Chief, I will cooperate in whatever investigation you run on this. I've got nothing to hide."

"That's what they all say Detective."

Doing her best to control her exasperation, Bridgette responded, "What motive would I possibly have for killing a Sanbury police officer?"

"I wouldn't know."

"Wouldn't know what Corey?"

They both turned around to see Jack Sutton and Hughey standing in the doorway to Bridgette's hospital room.

Payne shot back, "This is official police business, Jack, so back off!"

Sutton replied, "I spoke to the Doctor on the way in. He hasn't authorized you to be in here, let alone to be conducting an interview."

Payne said flatly, "I'll decide where and when I conduct my interviews."

Sutton stood his ground and said, "You know Corey, a lot of people in this town say you don't know your head from your ass. Mostly, I've defended you, but when you pull stunts like this, I'm inclined to agree with them. Hughey and I rescued Bridgette from a gorge this morning — she was half frozen to death and lucky to be alive. I've already provided a statement to one of your detectives and I'm sure Bridgette will be happy to do the same when she's given the all-clear from her Doctor."

Payne held Sutton's stare for a moment and said, "You need to be careful Jack. This doesn't concern you."

To diffuse the situation, Bridgette said to Payne, "Chief, I have nothing to hide and I'm more than willing to cooperate."

Sutton added, "But only after the Doctor has given his approval."

Payne looked back at Bridgette and said, "I'll be back shortly. You better organize yourself a lawyer, because you're going to need one."

Without another word, Payne stormed out of the room leaving Sutton and Hughey in his wake.

Bridgette waited until Sutton and Hughey both sat down and said, "Someone planted a gun in my house."

Sutton nodded. "So I've heard. I told the detective who took my statement that there was no way you could have been involved. Once he realized we'd camped next to your car all night he believed me. Payne will eventually get the message — right now he isn't thinking straight."

Bridgette said, "Do they have any suspects other than me?"

Sutton shook his head and said, "Not that they were willing to share. So what do you make of the rifle?"

Bridgette had had enough of lying around in bed. As she swung her legs out over the edge of the bed, she answered, "Someone wants me out of the way and is getting desperate."

Hughey frowned and said, "What are you doing Bridgette?"

"I'm getting up Hughey. I've had enough of lying in bed and I'd like to ring my boss back and get some advice before I let Payne interview me."

Sutton walked across to the window. As he stood looking out at the falling snow, he said, "I think the Doc was wanting to keep you here overnight Bridgette."

Bridgette said, "I don't want to sleep here tonight Jack. I don't feel safe. There's no security — anyone can just walk in."

Sutton nodded and said, "I think that's wise Bridgette," as he continued to stare out the window.

"If your offer's still good Jack, I think I'd like to stay at your house?"

Sutton turned and responded, "I think that's wise Bridgette," before he returned his gaze to the snow.

Bridgette frowned. Sutton seemed distracted which prompted her to ask, "Is there a problem Jack?"

Sutton pointed out the window at the snow which continued to fall. "It's almost a whiteout out there. Hughey and I got a storm update on the radio as we drove back here. We're likely to get a super storm tonight."

Bridgette frowned, "As in we could be snowed in?"

Sutton nodded and looked at Hughey. "You better come and stay too Hughey. Without a car, you're too isolated where you are."

Turning back to Bridgette, Sutton said, "We'll wait downstairs. I'm sure the Doctor will want to check you over again before he gives you the all-clear. Once you're released, we'll go and pick up your stuff from your house."

"What about my interview with Payne?"

Sutton said, "We'll call into the station on the way back to my house. But with this storm coming, my guess is he's not going to have a lot of time to interview you. If that snow keeps up like it is, no one will be going anywhere within a couple of hours."

Chapter 35

Bridgette pushed through the glass front doors of the Sanbury police station and shook the snow from her hair and jacket. Pimply cop with the red hair was manning the front counter and eyed her with suspicion as she approached.

"You're not allowed in here anymore Detective. Chief Payne has suspended your investigation."

"I'm here to make a statement for Chief Payne in relation to a search that was conducted at the house I'm staying in."

Pimply cop said, "Hang on a minute," and picked up the desk phone. Bridgette stepped back from the counter and waited while he had a whispered conversation — she assumed with Payne.

After hanging up, Pimply cop said, "Chief Payne has asked you to wait."

Bridgette sat in a chair. After ten minutes of waiting patiently, Bridgette wondered whether they would leave her there for hours like they did with Hughey. She approached the counter and said to Pimply cop, "I've got two friends waiting outside in a car for me. They're going to freeze to death if I leave them out there much longer."

He replied smugly, "Not my problem Detective, I don't control the weather."

Doing her best to remain calm, Bridgette responded, "Is your boss going to be long? If so I'm happy to—"

Bridgette noticed the large figure of Cory Payne striding through the open work area of the office toward her and didn't bother finishing her question.

He looked to be in a dark mood and made no attempt to hide his irritation as he came up to the counter and demanded, "What are you doing here?"

Bridgette answered, "You said you wanted to interview me. I've been discharged from the hospital so I thought I'd make myself available as soon as I possibly could."

Payne's face broke into a mocking grin as he pointed out the large window behind her. "Maybe you haven't noticed Detective, but we've got a major snowstorm coming in. Right now, assisting emergency services is my priority."

Bridgette nodded and said, "Fine by me."

She turned to Pimply cop and said, "Like it or not officer, you're a witness that I have attended the Sanbury Police Station with the full intent of being interviewed by Chief Payne in relation to a search and seizure of an unlicensed firearm. If at some point—"

Payne bellowed, "You leave my officers out of this. This is between you and me."

Bridgette responded, "Really? And here I was thinking this was an official police investigation."

Payne moved forward two steps until his bulky frame pressed up against the service counter. He put his hands on his hips and grinned slightly as he said, "You're a cocky little bitch, aren't you?"

"Thank you for the character assessment, Chief, but I was simply following your instructions."

Payne pointed a finger at Bridgette and snarled, "You've been obstructing local police work ever since you got here and have no respect for my authority. I'm over it and intend to make a formal complaint about your behavior to your Commissioner."

"As you wish. Am I free to go now?"

Payne nodded and said, "For now, but you're not to leave town. Right now, I have higher priorities, but as soon as this storm passes, I'll be calling you in for an interview."

Bridgette nodded and said, "You have my mobile number, but if for some reason you can't get through on that, I'll be staying at Jack Sutton's house until I leave town."

Bridgette turned to leave, but Payne called her back.

"Detective Cash."

Bridgette turned back to face Payne. In a more controlled voice, he said, "Police officer or not, I'm quite within my rights to arrest you and place you in a holding cell until we get to the bottom of that illegal firearm we found in your house. But right now, I don't need one of my officers babysitting you."

Bridgette nodded and then asked, "Do you seriously think I'd be involved in a murder and dumb enough to leave a weapon in my house?"

Payne replied, "Criminals do the strangest things Detective, you of all people should know that."

Bridgette was mindful that Hughey and Jack were sitting in his truck in freezing conditions and didn't see the point in laboring the conversation any further.

"If there's nothing else Chief, I'll let you get back to your job."

Payne responded, "You're on notice Detective and consider this your final warning. If I get any inkling you're still conducting an investigation, or anything else comes up that remotely connects you to Mitch Conden's murder, I will put you behind bars. Are we clear?"

"Perfectly clear."

Payne studied her for a moment and then said, "Right now,

you're in the cross-hairs Cash. If I get a ballistics match on that rifle for Mitch's murder, you're going to need a lot more than a very good lawyer."

Bridgette debated whether she would respond or not. She knew Payne was goading her and she was still feeling weak and drained from her overnight ordeal in the freezing cave. She didn't fancy spending her remaining time in Sanbury in a holding cell and knew she had to be careful in how she responded.

"I've been dealing with bullies most of my adult life and you're no different to most that I've encountered. You can threaten me as much as you want, but your evidence is flimsy at best. There's no doubt in my mind that John Tyson was murdered, and I suspect Mitch Conden's murder is probably connected. I'm not who you're looking for Payne."

Bridgette held Payne's stare and waited for him to make the next move. She doubted he wanted the grief and embarrassment of arresting a fellow police officer from another jurisdiction when they had voluntarily come in for an interview. But Payne was unpredictable, and she knew anything was possible.

He pointed a finger at her again and said, "You'll be hearing from me, Detective," and then turned on his heel and stormed back toward his office.

Chapter 36

Felix Delray had mixed emotions as he walked towards the holding cell. While he was angry and disappointed with what Charlie Bates had done, above all, he was confused. Bates had been a good detective and he wondered where it had all gone wrong as he knocked on the door.

A young uniformed officer Delray had never met opened the door.

"Can I help you, Sir?"

"Chief Inspector Delray for a private word with Detective Bates before he is transported downtown for his arraignment."

"Sir, I'm under instructions not to allow the prisoner out of my sight."

Delray was in no mood for an argument and said, "This is a private conversation between a detective and his boss. Unless you want me to take it up with the Commissioner, you can wait outside."

The officer's eyes widened at the mention of the word 'Commissioner'.

He stood aside to allow Delray to enter and said, "Let me know when you're done Chief."

Delray waited until the young officer had closed the door behind him before he turned to look at Bates.

Bates sat in one of two chairs at a meeting desk in the middle of an austere room of the ground floor of the Hartbourne Metro South building. He looked disheveled, and the jovial smile had been replaced by a sullen stare. He almost looked like he was in a trance and refused to make eye contact with Delray as he sat down opposite.

Delray studied Bates for a moment, barely able to believe one of his team had turned on him. He let out a sigh and said, "Most days in your career blur into one another... but there are three days in the past month I will never forget. The first was when Bridgette was shot at in the basement, the second was when Lance Hoffman was killed... and the third is today."

Delray studied Bates' reaction. The young detective still refused to make eye contact. "Look at me, Charlie."

Bates responded without looking at Delray, "I have nothing to say without my lawyer."

Delray nodded. "That's probably wise — you're in a lot of trouble."

They room fell quiet while Delray tried to figure out what to say next.

Finally, he said, "What I can't figure out is why you did it? You're a smart guy — it didn't cross your mind that one day you'd get caught?"

Delray let the question hang. Bates didn't respond and still refused to look at him. "And why would you want to kill Bridgette? How could you turn on one of us like that?"

Bates turned and faced Delray. Through gritted teeth, he responded, "I'm not sure if you're aware of this Chief, but I rank in the top five percent of police officers in Hartbourne Metro for accuracy with a pistol. If I was in that basement and wanted her dead, she would be..."

Delray was taken aback by the answer. Bates wasn't admitting to anything, but his message was clear enough. He wondered what had caused Bates to go off the rails like he had. It was usually quick money, but he wasn't about to pursue that now. Instead, he nodded and said, "Let me give you one piece of advice. Internal Investigations have already told me Derek Sirocca is representing you and I know you can't afford him, not on your salary."

Bates looked away again.

Delray continued, "To my knowledge, Sirocca only has a handful of clients — all of whom are filthy rich and belong in jail..."

When Bates didn't respond, Delray placed his elbows on the table and clasped his hands together. Leaning forward he continued, "You're involved with a bad crowd, Charlie. They might say they'll look after you, but you're a liability now. Frankly, there's no upside for them keeping you around..."

Delray let the message hang for a moment, but Bates wouldn't look at him. Delray continued, "One final question Charlie, and I don't expect a straight answer. Were you involved in any way with the murder of Bridgette's father?"

Bates responded, "This meeting is over Chief. I'm not saying anything without my lawyer."

Undeterred, Delray pressed him. "You realize you're working for whoever was behind the murder of her father, don't you? And when we catch him, you could be implicated as well?"

Bates closed his eyes and in a voice barely above a whisper replied, "I have nothing more to say."

Delray nodded as if to say he understood. As he stood up, he said, "You need to decide quickly how this is going to play out Charlie. If you decide to come clean and tell us what you know, I can offer you protection in jail and a lighter sentence. If you don't, then you're on your own and I shudder what to think might become of you..."

Bates looked up at Delray and shook his head. "You forget I've been a cop for six years. I know what jail is like. Nobody can protect me—"

"Charlie, you're a small fish in a big pond. The people who Sirocca represents play for keeps. I'm not trying to scare you, but I'm the only one that can offer you any real protection. You co-operate and I'll get you a new identity and a lighter sentence in a minimum-security facility with white collar criminals."

Bates shook his head. "I'm not prepared to take that risk. For the right money, anyone can be found and taken care of."

Delray didn't have the energy to argue. He dropped his business card on the table and said, "My offer's good for twenty-four hours but no longer. Think about it. You've made one stupid mistake — it doesn't have to be two..."

Delray rapped on the door and then turned back to Bates and asked, "Is there anyone you want me to call?"

Bates shook his head.

As Delray turned to leave, Bates said, "There is one thing you can do for me..."

"Okay."

"When you see Bridgette... tell her I'm sorry she got hurt."

Delray nodded. He wasn't sure what to make of Bates' last remark as he pointed at the business card that Bates was now holding. "Call me Charlie, I'm the only one who can help you."

Delray walked out and didn't look back. He didn't expect Bates to call him but at least he'd made the offer. He didn't like Bates' chances of making bail. Sirocca was good, but most judges took a dim view of attempted murder, particularly cop on cop. He pressed the button at the elevator to go back to his office. He made it a rule never to drink at home on weeknights, but that rule would be broken tonight. The elevator door opened, and he stepped in. After pressing the button for the second floor, he thought about Lance Hoffman. It had been over a month since his death. In that time Delray had had his fair share of bad days as he adjusted to life without his most trusted senior detective. Delray missed his friend, but no more so than now. He whispered, "What I wouldn't give to able to talk to you now Lance," as the elevator doors closed.

He made a mental note to send an email update to the Commissioner when he got back to his desk and then he would head home. Delray wondered what he would say to Bridgette. She respected Bates and enjoyed working with him. He decided he would leave it until they were face to face before he said anything further.

Chapter 37

Bridgette's gaze was drawn away from the flames that danced across the logs in the open fire as she saw movement in her peripheral vision. She looked up to see Jack Sutton standing in the doorway to his living room.

"Dinner will be ready in about two minutes Bridgette."

"Thanks, Jack. It smells amazing. What are we having?"

"Chicken and vegetable soup — homemade of course."

"I can't wait."

Sutton grinned a little as he looked back towards the kitchen. "I've also baked us some bread. Provided Hughey doesn't eat it all, it will make a nice side to the soup."

Bridgette laughed and said, "Keeping him away from it for another two minutes could be quite a challenge."

Sutton nodded. "I sent him outside to get another load of firewood. Hopefully, that will keep him occupied long enough until I get everything ready."

"Good plan. Is there anything I can do to help?"

Sutton shook his head. "All taken care of Bridgette. After what you've been through, you need to rest. I'm still surprised the Doctor actually let you out of the hospital."

Bridgette shrugged. "I didn't give him much choice and when I told him I was coming here; he relaxed a little."

Sutton nodded. "So how are you feeling after your latest run-in with Payne?"

Bridgette shrugged, "It could have been worse. At least I'm not in jail."

"When do you have to front up again?"

"I'm not sure. Payne will call me in for an interview about the rifle they found in the house once the ballistics have been run, but they also want to interview me about the body in the cave."

"Do they think it's Olivia?"

"It's looking that way. They had an advance team out there on site today. They've determined it's the skeleton of a female and that she's been there a long time. But then the storm closed in and they had to abandon the recovery. I'm not sure when they'll get back to complete it."

"It could be days if this storm keeps up."

Bridgette nodded. "I got the impression that the storm has put everything on hold — even Mitch Conden's murder investigation."

Sutton walked over to a large exterior window and drew back the curtain. As he stared out into the darkness he said, "When you've lived through one, you'll understand."

"Any idea when this will break Jack?"

Sutton shook his head. "The weather reports say it could go on for another twenty-four hours or more. If that's the case, everything will shut down and people will be forced to stay at home to ride it out. The police turn into the emergency services just to keep everybody safe."

Sutton dropped the curtain and turned back to Bridgette. He pointed at the two photographs she had been absently holding like playing cards and said, "Are they the photos John took of the gorge?"

Bridgette nodded. "I was just sitting here thinking about

them."

"I'd like to know how he figured out the body was down there."

Bridgette frowned a little. "I'm not sure he did."

"What do you mean?"

Bridgette picked up a third photograph from the coffee table and handed it to Sutton. "This photograph has always bothered me."

Sutton studied the picture for a moment and said, "This is the one he took at Snowbridge — two days before he died, right?"

Bridgette nodded. "It doesn't fit with the other photographs. It's a totally separate location and yet somehow they have to be connected."

"Maybe the photograph just got mixed up with the others?"

"I don't think so. It was hidden away with everything else in his file. I think he was very careful with what he chose to include."

"So... it's just luck that you found the body?"

"I don't think John Tyson had any idea she was down there. I think his motive for photographing the gorge was totally unrelated."

Sutton said, "I'd like to continue this conversation, Bridgette," as he handed back the photo, "but I need to tend to my soup before it burns."

Bridgette watched Sutton leave the room and then returned her gaze to the fire. She found it hard to believe that fourteen hours ago she had been trapped in a gorge and well on her way to freezing to death. Now, safe and warm in a house with people she trusted, she realized how close she'd come to being another victim of the Sacred Mountains. As she studied the photos again, she was now certain there was a lot more at play behind Tyson's murder than someone simply trying to prevent a body being discovered. Her thoughts were interrupted as Hughey walked into the living room carrying a large load of cut wood.

As she watched him make a neat stack next to the fireplace, she said, "That should keep us going well into tomorrow Hughey."

Hughey nodded as he brushed snow off his jumper. "I hope so. It's freezing out there and I don't like going out in the dark."

"I'm sure Jack appreciates your help."

Hughey slumped into a chair beside her and said, "My mom always taught me to be kind to other people, so I try my best."

After a moment of sitting quietly and watching the fire, Bridgette said, "I never really got to thank you properly for rescuing me, Hughey. If it hadn't been for your concern last night, I'm just not sure what would have happened today."

Hughey looked embarrassed and leaned down to pat Molly who was sprawled out asleep in front of the fire. "It was Molly who found you Bridgette, not me."

Bridgette said firmly, "Molly helped for sure, but if it hadn't been for you and Jack, I doubt I would have survived another night. So... thank you."

Hughey frowned and then looked away.

"Are you okay Hughey?"

Without looking back at her, Hughey mumbled, "Yeah."

Bridgette sensed that there was something wrong and said, "Hughey, what's the matter?"

Hughey shrugged. "Nobody says thank you in prison..."

Bridgette tried to put herself in Hughey's shoes. She realized the thought of going back to prison would have been weighing heavily on his mind.

"Are you worried about your court appearance tomorrow Hughey?"

"Dan rang me today. He said it's been postponed to next week."

Bridgette said encouragingly, "Dan is a good lawyer. If anyone can get your sentence overturned, he can."

Hughey nodded as he stared into the fire. Bridgette noticed her normally talkative neighbor was very quiet tonight.

Bridgette thought for a moment and then said, "If you go back to prison, how long will it be for?"

"Dan says another five or six years."

Bridgette knew that may as well be an eternity for someone like Hughey. She knew what it was like not to have hope and said, "Will anyone come and visit you now that your Mom is sick?"

Hughey bit his bottom lip and shook his head as he stared into the fire.

Bridgette wasn't sure whether she could see tears forming in his eyes or not. She felt for Hughey and said softy, "I really hope you don't go back to jail Hughey. But if you do, would you like me to come and visit you?"

Hughey turned to Bridgette and nodded. "No one's ever visited me except my Mom and the lawyers. It's not a very nice place."

Bridgette managed half a smile as she responded, "You know Hughey, I'm a police officer. I'm used to prisons. Remember how I saw you in prison on Sunday night?"

Hughey nodded again and said, "Thank you Bridgette, but I don't want to be any trouble."

"It's no trouble, Hughey. Friends stick together."

Sutton appeared at the door and said, "Sorry to interrupt folks, but dinner is ready."

The mention of food seemed to draw Hughey out of his funk. He got to his feet and said, "I'm ready."

Bridgette went to stand up, but her phone rang. She looked down at the screen and recognized the number and said, "Do you mind if I take this Jack? It's a callback from Hartbourne Metro that I've been waiting on."

Sutton said, "Take your time Bridgette. I'll try and make sure Hughey doesn't eat everything."

Bridgette thanked Sutton and pressed answer. "Hello, this is Bridgette."

"Bridgette it's Paul Foley here. Chief Delray asked me to check out a couple of company names for you."

Bridgette had heard of Paul Foley but never met him. She knew he worked within the criminal fraud team and had had a lot of success with organized crime. She was happy Delray had been able to get his help and said, "Thanks for calling me back Paul. I didn't think I'd hear from you tonight seeing as it's so late."

"You're lucky. My wife and kids are out of town for a couple of days, so I'm happy to work some overtime."

"So did you find anything?"

"I've spent most of the afternoon on this, and I'm still trying to get my head around it, but the short answer is, yes."

Bridgette tried to contain her excitement as she responded, "Okay."

Foley continued. "From what I can work out so far, Snowbridge is a consortium of companies that are building a new ski resort — that much is fairly clear. From there on it gets messy. The construction company you asked me to check on are Bowman and Moss Construction. I got off the phone from their CEO about ten minutes ago. They managed the last phase of the construction, which mainly involved pouring slabs, but don't have a contract for any further work. They've been in business for about seven years and seem legitimate."

"Okay."

"The project was initially financed by a consortium that included the Chinese company Kwan Wei Investments. I couldn't find out a lot about them, other than they pulled out of the project about eighteen months ago."

"Do you know why?"

"Not yet, but I'll keep digging. From there it gets interesting. About twelve months ago a new company by the name of Snowbridge Securities joined the consortium."

"Another Chinese company?"

"No. Snowbridge is local."

"Okay."

"But that's just the beginning Bridgette. Snowbridge Securities has money on cash deposit with a local bank in Sanbury. I rang the manager late today and got confirmation. He said this is the company that has been financing all the construction at the resort."

"Did he say how much money?"

"No, but I got the feeling it's a lot of money because he said I'll need a warrant before he's prepared to say anymore. Also, there's a new company by the name of Amorand Investments that has just been set up in Rochford as part of the consortium. According to the national companies register, they become a legal trading entity tomorrow."

Bridgette frowned. "Tomorrow?"

"I pushed the manager about this, but he wouldn't tell me anything other than Amorand will be co-funding the remainder of the construction."

There was silence on the phone for a moment while Bridgette thought through what Foley had just told her. Finally, she said, "I'm not a big fan of coincidences Paul. This might be nothing, but it could be everything..."

"I agree with you, Bridgette. I wish there was more that I could tell you, but that's as much as I know right now..."

"Thanks, Paul. This has been really helpful."

There was more silence before Foley came back and said, "Bridgette, it's almost eight and I'm starving. I'm going to head home now, but after I've eaten, I'm happy to go back online and keep searching if you like? I'd like to find out who runs Amorand and what their deal is."

"That would be great Paul and if you find anything, can you please call me?"

"You got it, Bridgette."

Bridgette thanked Foley for his time and disconnected. She stared into the flames of the fire as she replayed the conversation over in her mind. She felt like they were slowly connecting the dots, but she knew she was still a long way from having the full picture. She opened John Tyson's file again and pulled out the handwritten notes and wondered if she had missed something. Like John Foley, she too was starving and the smell of the chicken soup wafting into the living room reminded her she should join her friends. She put the file back on the coffee table knowing she would come back to it shortly. Paul Foley hadn't told her much, but it was enough for her to start a whole new line of investigation.

Chapter 38

Roman Quinn stood at the window of his downtown office and stared out into the darkness. Normally, the street lights provided him with a good night view of the main town center, but not tonight. The heavy snowstorm had reduced the visibility to almost zero. Too on edge to focus on any work and consumed by what the storm was doing to his plans, he was relieved when his desk phone finally rang.

Moving back to his desk, Quinn picked up and said, "You should have called me an hour ago."

The caller responded, "Cool your jets, I've been busy and this storm isn't helping."

"Right now, the storm is the least of our problems."

"Why is that?"

Quinn sat down and said, "I had a call from Seymour at the bank. Some cop from Hartbourne rang him this afternoon asking about Amorand."

The caller asked, "What were they trying to find out?"

"The cop asked a bunch of questions about its incorporation. Seymour tried to find out why he was after the information, but he got the run-around."

"It has to be Cash's investigation."

Quinn rolled his eyes. "Obviously and I hear she's been released from the hospital?"

The caller said, "Yes."

"Did the police find the rifle at her house?"

"Yes, I planted it in the ceiling and then phoned in a tipoff."

"Then why isn't she in jail?"

The caller replied, "Payne is playing it safe. He's not prepared to start a war with Hartbourne Metro without more evidence directly linking Cash to Conden's murder."

Quinn turned around and looked out through the window at the storm again. "If Hartbourne Metro have figured out what's in play, they could ruin everything." He paused as he studied the falling snow for a moment and then said, "Every road out of Sanbury has been cut off. And that's not likely to change for the next forty-eight hours. We can use this storm to our advantage."

"How?"

"I'm going to call Hollingway. There's more than one way to get out of town."

"Isn't that risky in this weather?"

Quinn spat out, "We have no choice. The transfer goes through tonight and storm or no storm, people will soon figure out what's happened. The plan was to be gone from Sanbury by tomorrow and that doesn't change. If Cash or someone gets on to us, tomorrow could turn into the worst day of our lives."

"So what's the plan?"

Quinn thought for a moment and said, "I'll organize the pickup for nine o'clock tomorrow morning."

"Will I meet you at the office?"

Quinn formed the word 'yes' with his mouth but paused. He thought for a moment and then said, "No. Pick me up from my house at eight-thirty. It's on the way."

"And what happens if the roads are shut?"

Quinn declared, "Given the obscene amount of money you're

about to make, I'm sure you'll find a way," and then hung up.

He picked up a small bottle of single malt whiskey off his desk and drained what was left of the bottle. He'd already had two glasses and knew he would be over the limit if he was breathalyzed on the way home. He thought it was unlikely that any cop would be out patrolling in this weather as he pulled on his coat.

Pausing at the office door, Quinn took one last look around his office. He knew whatever happened tomorrow, he would not be back. He had never been the sentimental type — everything was a means to an end, and this was no different. He switched off the light and headed for the elevator. There were several phone calls he still needed to make, but they could wait until he got home and out of the storm. As he stepped into the elevator and pressed the button for the basement, he was surprised at how liberating it felt to be leaving Sanbury. He would miss the power and the wheeling and dealing of course, but not his wife or his family.

Quinn thought about his conversation with the caller as the elevator door opened and he walked through the basement parking lot to his car. He had always resented sharing so much with someone who had done so little. Now that the deal was done, they weren't required anymore. He contemplated paying them a visit tonight like he had done with Condon. But as he drove out of the car park and into the blizzard, he knew that wasn't about to happen. He would wait until tomorrow. His house was isolated enough, and they would meet like planned.

As he inched his BMW down Sanbury's main street, he nodded approval to his plan. It was brutal but effective and he wouldn't need to worry about covering his tracks this time. By the time they found the body, he would be out of the country.

Chapter 39

Bridgette looked up from her notes as Jack Sutton walked into the dining room carrying two steaming mugs of tea. He shakily set one of them down alongside her and said, "Peppermint tea for you Bridgette. It's a cold night and this will help keep you warm."

Bridgette smiled. "Thanks, Jack, you really are spoiling me," as she motioned Sutton to join her.

"I hope I'm not interrupting?"

"Not at all. I'm going over John's notes again just in case I missed something. Where's Hughey?"

Sutton glanced back towards his kitchen. "He insisted on washing up and I wasn't about to argue."

"He does like to keep busy."

"I know he's nervous about the court case and anything we can do to take his mind off it is helpful. That's part of the reason why I wanted him to come and stay as well..."

They were quiet for a moment as they enjoyed their tea. Sutton finally broke the silence and said, "So we didn't get to finish our conversation before dinner. You said you didn't think John was looking for Olivia Hodder anymore?"

"I'm sure he still wanted to find her. But the contents of this hidden file and the fact that I was shot at yesterday make me think there's more going on than just covering up an old murder."

"After that stunt of planting a rifle in your house this morning, I can't help but think Corey Payne is somehow mixed up in all this."

Bridgette sipped her tea for a moment and then said, "The gun was definitely a plant, but that doesn't mean he's responsible."

Sutton frowned. "He got there awfully quick and he's had it in for you since the day you arrived."

Bridgette nodded. "I'm not defending him, but they were responding to a tipoff. Apparently, I'd been seen leaving town early this morning driving at a ridiculous speed."

"How convenient."

"The truth is, someone might be playing Payne. I'm new in town and a logical choice if you're trying to create a distraction."

"So, if not Payne, who then?"

Bridgette picked up the two photos that John Tyson had taken of the gorge. She passed them across to Sutton and asked, "What do you see?"

Sutton studied the images for a moment. "I see two photos of the gorge taken from different angles."

Bridge shook her head. "No, what do you really see? What has he really taken pictures of?"

Sutton put on his reading glasses and studied the photos in more detail. Finally, he said, "They both seem to be focused on the left-hand side of the gorge where the rock face gave way."

Bridgend nodded.

Sutton frowned. "So, he was taking photos of a landslide rather than the gorge itself?"

"That's what I'm thinking."

Sutton looked at the photographs again and said, "The whole Sacred Mountain range is full of shale rock deposits. Landslides like this one are common. We're lucky the township is built in an area of the mountain range where the bedrock is stable."

Sutton took off his reading glasses and said, "So if this isn't about Olivia, then what is it about?"

"The phone call I took just before dinner was from a detective by the name of Paul Foley from Hartbourne Metro. He's been running down some information for me on some of the companies associated with the Snowbridge development."

"You think this has something to do with Snowbridge?"

"I'm not seeing anything else that's new or different in Sanbury, so I figure it's a place to start." Bridgette gave Sutton a quick rundown on the information Foley had provided her. She added, "The timing of the setup of this new company makes me wonder if it isn't somehow connected. I'm re-reading his notes in the hope I can find that connection."

Sutton leaned forward and propped his elbows on the table as he took another sip of tea. "There's a lot of folks involved in Snowbridge Bridgette, but you must have your suspicions?"

"We don't have a lot of evidence yet Jack. I'm trying to keep an open mind until we know more."

"I know this may sound like a dumb question Bridgette, but is there anything that I can do to help? John was a good friend and I want to see whoever did this punished."

Bridgette thought for a moment and asked, "Are you aware the Chinese company is no longer an investor?"

Sutton frowned and said, "The Chinese company is the only reason this project is going ahead Bridgette. It's costing hundreds of millions and there's no way we could have financed it locally."

"According to Paul Foley, Kwan Wei Investments pulled out eighteen months ago."

Sutton shook his head. "That can't be right. We had two representatives of the company here less than six months ago doing a site inspection. They were paraded around town like VIPs. There was coverage in the local papers and everything."

"Did they say who they were working for exactly?"

"They didn't speak much English. We were told they were senior vice presidents from the Kwan Wei company and were here to do a routine inspection and report back to their chairman in China."

Bridgette nodded.

Exasperated, Sutton continued, "So if they weren't representing the company, then who the hell were they?"

"That's a good question, Jack."

"I'm not liking this..."

"Of the locals, who has the most to win or lose on Snowbridge?"

Sutton leaned back in his chair and pondered the question. Finally, he said, "I can think of a few people. Most of them are part of the local chamber of commerce. You've got Conway and Richardson — they own the local timber mill and have invested close to half a million. Jenny Sheldon who owns one of the smaller shopping malls has also invested a similar figure. But there are a lot of other locals like me who have invested smaller sums as part of the local cooperative."

"What about Roman Quinn?"

"As head of your local chamber of commerce, I'm sure he's a significant stakeholder."

"But you don't know how much?"

"Roman Quinn has always played his cards close to his chest, so I have no idea."

Bridgette nodded.

Sutton continued. "Why did you single out Quinn?"

"I interviewed him on Monday. He wasn't interested in helping me find John Tyson but told me in no uncertain terms to stay away from the press."

"That sounds like Quinn."

"He was super aggressive and obviously used to getting his own way. It made me wonder how much power he has."

"Sanbury is a small town and the Quinns have controlled it for almost forty years."

"It's hard to understand one family having that much control for so long."

Sutton drained the last of his tea and then stood up. "There's something I want to show you. Grab your coat, we need to go out to the barn."

Bridgette wondered why Jack Sutton would insist on going outside in the middle of a snow storm but said nothing. After putting on her coat, she followed Sutton out into the cold. The snowfall was still heavy, and the wind had picked up — neither of them spoke until they were safely inside Sutton's middle barn with the door closed.

After switching the barn lighting on and brushing the snow off his jacket, Sutton pointed to the eastern side of the barn and said, "This way."

They walked through a maze of car parts and machinery to the far end of the barn and stopped beside a rusted old tow truck.

Sutton said, "This was the truck I first bought when I started my business over thirty years ago. It was old when I got it, but it was all my wife and I could afford. The night of the last great storm, we were in bed asleep, when we heard someone knocking on our front door. I went to investigate and there standing on the doorstep was Roman Quinn. He couldn't have been much more than nineteen or twenty back then and he looked half frozen to death. We got him inside and I asked him what on earth he was doing, and he told me his car had slid off the road and into an embankment about two miles further up."

"Two miles is a long way to walk in this kind of weather."

"You're telling me, but there are no houses any further up Saddleback Road, so he had no choice. Anyway, I told him he could stay the night, but he insisted we go back and get his car. I said he was crazy, but he told me he'd been out with Mitch Conden and had left him with the car."

Bridgette frowned. "Mitch Conden, as in the police officer who was just murdered?"

Sutton nodded. "This was before Conden went to police training. Quinn confessed they'd been up at the hut drinking and Conden had drunk so much he could barely walk."

"So what happened?"

"I got my truck out and we went back to his car. It had slipped off the icy road and got stuck in a snow bank just like he said. I pulled the car out with my truck and we drove back here. Quinn and Conden stayed the night and then I drove them into town the following day."

Sutton paused a moment as if he was reliving the day and then continued. "By then all hell had broken loose because of the storm. There were cars stuck in snow and lots of accidents. I did what I could for the next two days on roads that were mostly impassable by car. At the end of the second night, the truck developed a knock in the engine on the way home. I managed to get it back here, but I knew it was bad. I parked it where it now sits and got a mechanic out to take a look at it. It had a crack in the engine block that was going to cost me more than the truck was worth to repair..."

Bridgette knew there must be a reason behind the story and

prompted Sutton to continue. "So it's sat here ever since?"

Sutton nodded. "Two days after the storm cleared, I get another knock on my front door. I opened it up and there's Arthur Quinn standing on my doorstep as large as life. He'd heard about my truck and wrote me a cheque for a new one as his way of saying thank you for rescuing his son. He was a tough businessman, but he treated people fair. If it hadn't been for his generosity, my business would have gone under."

"That was very generous."

"You know, his son never thanked me. Not when I drove him back to his car, not when I gave him a bed for the night, and not even when I drove him back into town the following day."

"After meeting him, that doesn't surprise me."

"The darkest day for Sanbury was when Olivia Hodder disappeared. The second darkest was when Arthur Quinn dropped dead in the main street of a heart attack. Roman Quinn inherited his father's empire and things have never been the same since."

"In what way?"

"Arthur Quinn was always fair and reasonable. His son is the exact opposite. The town hoped as he got older he would change, but that never happened. Roman Quinn has no conscience and delights in stepping on people as he uses his power to get his own way. As far as Snowbridge is concerned, we've got everything locked up with a very tight legal contract because nobody trusts him..."

Sutton lightly tapped the bonnet of the rusting vehicle and said, "My wife was always at me to have this old girl hauled off to the scrap yard. But I couldn't part with it."

"Too many fond memories?"

"Partly, but mainly it was a reminder for me of how to do business. Nobody minded Arthur having so much control when he was alive. He drove a hard bargain as a businessman, but he was fair and gave back to the community. As I built my business, that's how I wanted people to see me."

Bridgette responded, "It's a pity his son didn't follow his father's example."

She waited for Sutton to respond, but he didn't seem to be listening. As he stared off into space, Bridgette said, "Jack, are you okay?"

In a distracted voice, Sutton responded, "I just thought of something, I should have realized a long time ago."

"Sorry Jack, but I'm not following you."

Sutton turned to Bridgette and said, "What was Quinn doing up on Saddleback that late in the middle of a storm?"

"You said he'd been drinking?"

"During a raging storm? I never gave it a thought. Even when Olivia was officially pronounced missing, but now..."

Bridgette felt her stomach begin to churn as she realized where Sutton was going. She responded, "You think Quinn and Conden were involved in Olivia's disappearance?"

Sutton nodded and said through gritted teeth, "Saddleback Road is the only way to get to Cathedral Valley and onto the gorge without a half-day hike. If it is Olivia's body that we found in the gorge, then those two assholes..."

Sutton couldn't finish his sentence. Bridgette watched as he looked away to hide his anger.

Bridgette gave him a moment and then said, "Don't beat yourself up, Jack. You only made the connection because of where we found the body. Until you knew that, you had every reason to assume they were just two guys who'd been out drinking and got caught in a storm."

Sutton shook his head.

"From what I can gather Jack, it was several months before anyone even suspected her disappearance wasn't connected to the storm."

"That doesn't make it any easier for me Bridgette."

Bridgette couldn't think of anything positive to say to Sutton without sounding patronizing.

Sutton sat down on an old oil drum. Pointing at his truck, he said, "Roman Quinn was the last person to ever sit in the passenger seat. You think there are fingerprints we could salvage?"

"Possibly. In the right environment, fingerprints can last forty years or more, but..."

"But what?"

Bridgette responded gently, "Even if it was Quinn and Conden, we're going to need a lot more than fingerprints in your truck. Without a witness or evidence linking either of them to a crime scene, all we have is enough to prove they were on Saddleback Road that night and needed a tow."

"You know, that's probably why the hut was burnt down within months of her disappearance."

Bridgette could tell by his clenched jaw and facial expression that he was angry with himself for not making the connection sooner. "I'll call my boss in the morning Jack and talk to him. He's been a cop for over thirty years, and he'll have a better idea about what we should do next."

Sutton said, "Thanks, Bridgette, I'd appreciate that."

Sutton stood up and stared at his truck with his hands on his hips. In a quieter voice, he added, "It's times like this, I wish I still drank..."

"How about we go back to the house and I make you another cup of tea instead."

Sutton nodded and they headed back to the front of the barn lost in their own thoughts.

Sutton paused before he flicked off the light switch and said, "I'm positive that's Olivia's body we found today. Do you think in time we can find John too?"

Bridgette pondered the question for a moment. Sutton had been honest with her and now it was time to return the favor.

"I thought about that a lot while I was laid up in the hospital today... I haven't connected all the dots yet, but I'm fairly confident I know where he's buried."

Chapter 40

Bridgette woke up with a cold draft blowing across her back and realized half of her blankets had fallen on the floor. She had tossed and turned for most of the night and after dragging her bedding back in place, she checked the time on her smart phone. She cursed when the display informed her she had missed a call from Paul Foley.

Bridgette tapped in her password and dialed her voicemail to retrieve the message. It had been almost midnight when Foley had called back. Normally, her phone would have woken her, but the exhaustion from spending the previous night freezing in the cave had taken its toll. Hoping that Foley had discovered some solid information, Bridgette held her breath as she listened to his message.

"Hi Bridgette, it's Paul here. Sorry I'm calling so late, but I think I've found something. Call me as soon as you can, we've got lots to talk about."

Foley left his phone number and ended the message.

Bridgette whispered, "Let's hope you're awake Paul," as she dialed his number.

A groggy voice answered after five rings. "This is Foley."

"Hi Paul, it's Bridgette. Sorry I missed your call last night — I hope this isn't too early."

Foley seemed more awake when he realized who it was and

responded, "No need to apologize, Bridgette — it's good you've called."

"You said you'd found something?"

"I think so. I went through everything that I could find on Snowbridge when I got home. It looks like this new company, Amorand, will operate as the trading company for Snowbridge from today onwards."

"So what does that mean exactly?"

"It means Amorand will be used as the company to pay out all the money to the contractors and suppliers involved in the next phase of the development."

"Is this kind of change normal?"

"Not really. It usually only happens when a company is sold or undergoes a major restructure. Neither is the case here and the old company seemed to be working fine. From what I can gather, there's only one difference with the way Amorand is set up."

"And what's that?"

"The old company had six directors, whereas Amorand appears to only have two."

Bridgette frowned. "I'm not very familiar with company structures, but two directors would seem to mean fewer checks and balances for paying money out?"

"You got it. From today onwards, two people will control all the money for Snowbridge."

"How much are we talking about Paul?"

"Without access to a proper balance sheet, I'd be only making a guess."

"Do you have a ballpark figure at least?"

There was silence on the phone for a moment before Foley responded, "You can't hold me to this Bridgette, but based on the company's last financial year transactions, I estimate it's somewhere close to nine million."

Bridgette let out a breath. "Nine million?"

"I could be getting in a wad over nothing Bridgette, but if this is not on the level, that money could all be siphoned out as early as today..."

Bridgette thought for a moment. She was now fully awake and increasingly uncomfortable with what Foley was telling her. "Is there anything we can do to put a stop to this or at least put it on hold?"

"It would have to come through the Snowbridge cooperative. It's possible the executives were duped into signing something without realizing what they'd actually done. If that's the case, they would need to get a lawyer representing them to get a trading embargo put in place until an investigation is completed."

"Do you know who are the signatories for Amorand by any chance?"

"Roman Quinn is one, which shouldn't be surprising given he is the president of the Sanbury Chamber of Commerce."

"And the other?"

Bridgette closed her eyes as Foley told her the name. It was finally making sense for her. She thought for a moment and then responded, "Paul this has been very helpful. I can't see this being a simple coincidence, so I'm going to move on it straightaway. I'll have to call you back for a further update later if that's all right?"

"No problem Bridgette. I'll put together a summary in an email and send it through later this morning. I'll be in at work from about eight o'clock onwards, so if you need anything else just call me, okay?"

Bridgette thanked Foley again for his time and disconnected. She got out of bed and quickly began to dress wondering if they were too late already.

As she emerged from her bedroom, she wondered if she should wake Sutton or head back into town on her own. She was surprised to see her host sitting at his kitchen table listening to a news report on the radio.

Sutton looked up when he saw Bridgette walk into the kitchen and said, "I didn't expect you to be up so early Bridgette?"

Bridgette responded, "We have a problem, Jack," and gave Sutton a summary of the conversation she'd just had with Foley.

Sutton responded, "Maybe we have a little time on our side to figure out what we need to do here. I've just listened to a morning update on the radio. We've had almost three feet of snow overnight and most of the roads are impassable. No one is getting in or out of Sanbury for at least twenty-four hours."

"I wouldn't be so sure of that Jack. There's potentially nine million at play here."

"So what do we do?"

"Roman Quinn is one of two people holding the cards. I'd like to get out to his place and see if he's still in town. We can figure out what to do next once we know."

"There's no way we can get out there in a car Bridgette, not in this snow. He lives out of town like I do but on the opposite side. It's a ten-minute drive in good conditions, but in this snow, it's virtually impossible."

"Virtually?"

"There's no way a car could make that drive."

"Are there any other vehicles that could get through?"

Sutton frowned for a moment as he thought. "Short of a proper snow vehicle, our options are very limited."

Bridgette let out a long breath and didn't try to hide her frustration.

Sutton added, "There may be one way we can get across to Quinn's place, but I'm not making any promises."

"What do you have in mind Jack?"

"I have a snow plow that I can fit to my tow truck when the snow conditions get really heavy. It will take me half an hour to get it bolted on and I can't guarantee you it will get us all the way to Quinn's house—"

"It's worth a try Jack."

Sutton nodded as he stood up.

"We'll need to get Hughey up. I have to winch it into place before I can bolt it on and with my MS, I'll need all the help I can get."

Bridgette responded, "We'll meet you out in the barn in five minutes Jack," and then turned and walked down the hallway towards Hughey's room.

Chapter 41

It took close to forty minutes to get the snow plow fitted to Sutton's truck. Bridgette and Sutton were glad of Hughey's help. His physical strength made all the difference getting the plow fitted quickly in the freezing conditions. After giving Molly a bathroom break and locking her in the laundry with a bowl of food, they had grabbed leftover bread rolls from the kitchen before starting their trip.

The cabin of the truck was proving tight for the three of them, but nobody complained. The coziness was helping keep them warm on a trip that was painfully slow as they plowed through the heavy snow. Bridgette had never seen snow this thick and asked, "Is this as bad as the last great storm Jack?"

"I think the last one was worse, but this one may not be over yet."

Choosing his route to avoid the Sanbury town center, Sutton patiently navigated the large truck through the back streets towards the opposite side of town. After turning left on Cotton Road, he said, "This road will lead us almost to Quinn's front door. He lives on acreage further up with views back over the mountain range and town center."

Bridgette estimated the truck was moving forward at not much more than a walking pace. In a loud voice to be heard over the truck's engine, she asked, "How long will it take from here Jack?"

"About five minutes, give or take. I can't go any faster or I risk blowing the motor."

They were all quiet for a moment lost in their thoughts. Even though the snow had stopped falling, the sky was gray and overcast. Bridgette knew little about the weather conditions but suspected they hadn't seen the last of the storm. The trees that lined the roadway were all heavy laden with snow and there was not a sign of life anywhere as they drove on. She was glad she was wearing her heavy coat and gloves and wondered how anything survived in the sub-freezing temperatures. Hughey seemed to have brightened after a good night's sleep and was keen to talk.

"Is Mister Quinn a bad man Bridgette?"

"We're not sure Hughey, that's why we're going to check on him."

Hughey said, "Maybe I should have brought my gun?"

Sutton responded, "You don't need a gun, Hughey. There's not going to be any shooting."

"Why not?"

Bridgette took the lead and said, "We're just going to see if he's home, that's all. It's called surveillance."

Sutton added, "I hope you're not expecting me to approach quietly Bridgette because with this truck and in these conditions, that's going to be impossible."

"It doesn't matter whether he sees us or not Jack. All we're trying to do is find out if he's still here in Sanbury."

Hughey asked, "Are you going to arrest him, Bridgette?"

"No Hughey. That's a job for Sanbury Police if it comes to that."

Hughey nodded but seemed confused. "So you're just going to watch his house? How will you know if he's in there?"

"We'll figure that out when we get there Hughey."

They were quiet for a moment as they all willed the truck up a steep rise in the road. The snow plow was doing its job clearing the snow off the road, but it was slow going and required all of Sutton's concentration. Finally, they reached the peak and as the truck started its descent into the next valley, Bridgette could see a distinct change in the landscape. There were almost no houses here and the rural setting looked like it belonged in a Christmas postcard.

Sutton pointed through the windscreen at a house on the opposite rise and said, "That's Quinn's house."

Bridgette looked across the small valley at a large stone and timber house about half a mile in front of them. Set back from the road, she imagined manicured gardens would be on show in spring and summer. But under the heavy fall of snow, the garden was just a white slab set against a backdrop of trees that surrounded the house. As the truck got closer, Bridgette was able to make out a separate stone and timber building at the front of the property. It was smaller than the main house and set closer to the road — Quinn's garage, she thought.

Sutton suddenly pulled the truck to a halt and pointed at a small clearing next to the road. Parked in the middle was a small, red Mazda sports car covered in a fine layer of snow.

Sutton said, "There's not a lot of snow on that car so it hasn't been here long. Hughey, would you mind checking it out? We need to see if anyone's inside who needs help."

Hughey mumbled, "Okay," as he opened the truck door.

Bridgette and Sutton watched as Hughey got out of the truck and went to investigate. As they watched him brush snow off the windscreen to look inside, Sutton said, "It's odd that a car would be out in this, let alone parked here."

Bridgette responded, "Maybe they broke down?"

Sutton said, "It's possible," as Hughey climbed back into the truck.

As he closed the door, Hughey said, "There was nobody inside Jack."

Sutton asked, "Did it look like it had been in an accident Hughey?"

Hughey shook his head. "It's got snow chains on the tires, but I couldn't see anything else."

Sutton put his truck in gear and said, "We'll keep going then. Thanks for checking Hughey."

They parked in front of Quinn's house and sat with the engine running to keep the heater working in the cabin.

Bridgette noticed the curtains were drawn in both the upstairs and downstairs windows. To the passer-by, it looked like the occupants were either still in bed asleep or away on holidays.

After a few moments of watching, Sutton said, "What are we looking for Bridgette?"

Bridgette frowned and responded, "I'm not sure Jack. I was hoping to see some sign of life. Maybe smoke coming from a chimney or someone moving around inside."

Hughey chimed in, "It doesn't look like anyone's home Bridgette. You want me to go and check?"

Bridgette answered, "I think I'll go check the garage first. There's a window there that I can look in."

Sutton said, "Quinn drives a BMW 5 series. If the car's there, he may be home, but if it's not, then who knows where he is."

Bridgette motioned Hughey to open the door to let her out of the truck. As she stepped out, she said, "Stay here with Jack, Hughey, I won't be a minute."

After doing her best to rug up against the cold, Bridgette made her way across to Quinn's garage. She kept one eye on the front windows of the main house for any sign of movement. The garage was bigger than she had first imagined, and she wondered if it was used for anything else as well?

Bridgette stopped for a moment at the front of the structure. The building had one large faux timber metal roller door spanning almost the entire width of the building. She noticed the snow was almost knee deep up against the door and knew no one had driven in or out recently. Bridgette made her way around the side of the building nearest to the house to a large side window. The interior drapes weren't completely closed and afforded her a limited view inside. Bridgette waded through knee deep snow and peered in through the window. Her eyes took a moment to adjust to the low lighting, but it didn't take her long to make out the silhouettes of three vehicles inside the garage: a four-wheel drive, a two-door white sports car and closest to her, a dark blue BMW sedan.

While she knew the BMW was no proof that Quinn was home, it made her anxious to find out for certain. She turned and looked back towards the house, wondering what she should do next. She frowned as she focused on the front door and moved forward a few steps to get a better view. As she studied it, she realized its angle was wrong and that it wasn't fully closed. Signaling to the truck for Sutton and Hughey to join her, she waded through the thick snow and up onto the large covered front landing.

When Sutton and Hughey made it to the landing, Sutton asked, "What's up?"

After pulling her Glock service pistol from an interior pocket of her coat, Bridgette pointed towards the door. "The front door is open."

They all stared at the door as it moved slightly in the breeze.

Bridgette continued, "I knocked while I waited for you, but got no answer, so let's go in and see what we can find."

Sutton nodded and with Hughey, followed Bridgette inside to a large foyer area that boasted a marble floor and a large crystal chandelier. There were no lights on, and everything remained quiet.

Bridgette called out, "Hello, is anybody home?"

They waited for a moment but heard nothing. Hughey pointed to an expansive wooden staircase that led upstairs and said, "Would you like me to check upstairs Bridgette?"

Bridgette shook her head. She had an uneasy feeling in her gut about what was happening here. No one in their right mind would leave a door open in such freezing conditions. She played down her response and said, "I think it would be better if we stick together until we know what we're dealing with Hughey."

She motioned them to follow her down a wide corridor to begin their search of the house. The first door on the right led into a large formal living and dining room. The furniture was a combination of expensive leather and mahogany. The room had a formal feel to it and the walls were lined with large original oil paintings. Bridgette did a quick sweep but could see nothing out of place. She didn't think the room was used very much and said, "Nothing here, so let's keep moving."

They moved back out into the hallway again. Bridgette held her gun down by her side as they walked across the hallway to the first door on the left. She opened the door and took one step inside before she froze as she took in the sight that confronted them. She knew she was in Sutton's home office. The room was spacious and fitted out with expensive office furniture that had similar tones to the formal living room. Bridgette stared across at the large mahogany desk that sat in front of an enormous bay window. She heard Hughey and Sutton both gasp behind her. They all stared at the figure of Roman Quinn, slumped in an office chair behind his desk. He stared back at them through lifeless eyes that would never see again — his mouth slightly ajar and his eyes wide open.

She heard Hughey whisper from behind, “Is he dead?”

Bridgette didn’t need to check. The neat bullet hole just above Quinn’s left eye was evidence enough he had departed this world to whatever awaited him beyond.

Chapter 42

Bridgette moved around behind Quinn's desk to get a closer look at his body. Quinn sat in a slumped position, with his left arm hanging over the side of his office chair and his hand almost touching the floor. She saw no sign of a gun and moved in closer to study the bullet wound. The neat entry point above his left eye belied the gaping exit wound the bullet had left in the back of Quinn's skull. Sitting in a pool of his own blood and other body matter she didn't want to think about, Bridgette studied Quinn's eyes for a moment. They were still open, but an opaque film had begun to form over his lenses signaling death had begun its decomposition process. She'd heard some detectives say they could sometimes see surprise on a murder victim's face, but with Quinn, it was impossible to tell. All she could tell so far was he had met a violent end and there didn't appear to be any sign of a struggle.

Sutton stayed on the other side of the desk and asked, "Is it a suicide?"

Bridgette shook her head. "There's no sign of a gun here. It looks like he was shot at close range. My guess is whoever killed him was standing roughly where you are now."

Careful not to step in the pool of blood that had formed in the carpet, Bridgette reached across and placed two fingers on Quinn's neck.

Standing beside Sutton, Hughey asked, "Are you checking his pulse, Bridgette?"

"No Hughey. I'm trying to figure out how long he's been dead."

Looking up at both men, she said, "He's still warm, so this didn't happen long ago."

Sutton said, "This might explain the red Mazda parked close by."

Bridgette nodded as she examined files on Quinn's desk.

Hughey asked, "What are you looking for Bridgette?"

"I'm not sure Hughey. Sitting at your office desk this early in the morning seems a strange place to be murdered."

"Do you think this was his partner?" asked Sutton.

"There are about nine million reasons to think that's a fair assumption, Jack."

Sutton looked a little nervous as he glanced back towards the door. "Do you think the killer could still be in the house somewhere?"

"Probably not. I think they got whatever they came for and left straight away."

Bridgette could see Sutton looked far from convinced and handed him her Glock. "Keep an eye on the door while I search here Jack. The safety is on, so you'll need to slide it off if you think you have to use it."

Sutton mumbled, "Thanks," as he took the weapon and held it awkwardly at his side.

Bridgette withdrew a handkerchief from her pocket and used it to remove the lid from a small, white cardboard box in the middle of Quinn's desk.

Hughey asked, "Why are you using a handkerchief, Bridgette?"

Bridgette absently responded, "So I don't leave fingerprints on the crime scene, Hughey," as she stared into the box.

Bridgette frowned and said, "What do you make of this?" as she slid the box across the desk to give her companions a better look.

Sutton took a step forward and peered into the box. "A dirty old watch and three bones. Are they human?"

Bridgette replied, "I'm not sure, but it seems to be a strange thing to keep on your desk."

Hughey asked, "What are you going to do with the box, Bridgette?"

Bridgette replied, "We'll leave it here for the police to investigate Hughey," as she replaced the lid.

Using her handkerchief again, Bridgette picked up a pencil from the desk and with the rubber tip, began pressing numbers on Quinn's desk phone.

Hughey said, "What are you doing now Bridgette?"

"Quinn's desk phone has a computer display. I'm checking through the last calls he made. It looks like he made two very early this morning."

Bridgette pressed a button to activate the hands-free speaker. "I'm going to redial the first of those numbers."

As Sutton watched, he asked, "What I don't understand is why would his partner shoot him now? Don't they need to go to a bank together to get the money?"

Bridgette answered, "Maybe not. A lot of banking can be done online now, even for very large transactions. All she may have needed is his pin code or his digital security token to authorize a withdrawal."

Sutton frowned and said, "She?", just as the phone call was answered.

Through the phone's speaker, they all heard a voice say, "Good morning, Hollingway Charter, this is Ben."

Bridgette bent down slightly to get closer to the desk phone's microphone. "Good morning Ben, my name is Detective Bridgette Cash and I'm from Hartbourne Metropolitan Police. I'm at the residence of a Mr. Roman Quinn in Sanbury." Bridgette gave Quinn's residential address and then said, "It appears Mr. Quinn rang your company earlier this morning. Do you know what that was in relation to?"

"He has a charter pick up booked for this morning, but because of the storm he rang to confirm we were still coming."

"When you say charter pick up, do you mean a helicopter?"

"Yes. Is Mr. Quinn okay?"

Bridgette looked across at Quinn's body and answered, "I'm sorry Ben, but Mr. Quinn has been murdered."

She ignored the gasp on the other end of the line and pressed on. "Ben, we will give you more information later on, but right now I need your help. Was there anyone else booked on the charter flight with Mr. Quinn?"

"Yes, one other passenger, but Mr. Quinn didn't say who it was."

"That's okay Ben, I think we have that information. Can you tell me where the pickup point was?"

Ben responded, "Hang on a minute, I'll need to check on the computer."

The phone went quiet for a moment before Ben came back and said, "The helicopter is due to land in about twenty-five minutes. Pick up point is Harmer Ridge for a flight directly to Bolton."

Bridgette looked up at Sutton who nodded and said, "I know where Harmer Ridge is."

Bridgette said, "You've been very helpful Ben, thank you."

"I don't know what to say. This is such a—"

"Sorry to cut you off Ben, but I need to keep moving. Someone will call you back later today to take your statement."

Bridgette said goodbye and then pressed another button on the phone with the pencil to disconnect. As she moved out from behind the desk, she said to Sutton, "How far is East Ridge from here, Jack?"

"It depends."

Bridgette frowned. "Meaning?"

As Sutton handed back her gun, he responded, "Harmer Ridge is normally a ten-minute drive from here, further up the road we came in on."

"But in these conditions?"

Sutton shook his head. "I'm not sure Bridgette — it's quite steep. Probably thirty minutes, but maybe longer depending on how thick the snow is."

"We need to get going now Jack, she's got a head start on us."

Sutton frowned and held a hand up. "She? Do you know who this is?"

Bridgette nodded. "I was fairly sure last night. Roman Quinn was at the top of my list of eight suspects. I wondered about the new company name, Amorand. I know he's got an ego, so it got me thinking. It's almost an anagram of his first name, but without the D. I wondered if it was a combination of his and his partner's names. It didn't take me long to figure out who it might be when I played around with letters from his first name and one of the other suspects."

Sutton shot back, "Okay, who is it?"

Bridgette held Sutton's stare and said, "Andrea Butler."

Sutton raised his eyebrows. "The Snowbridge lawyer? Are you sure?"

"Roman Quinn made two phone calls this morning. The first one was to the Bolton charter company, the second was to a mobile phone number I recognized."

Sutton responded, "Andi Butler?"

Bridgette nodded. "She gave me her business card the other night when I caught up with Dan Strickland. The phone number on her card is the same number Quinn called after he finished speaking to the charter company. My guess is he was calling her to say the helicopter was still coming."

Sutton scowled. "Only she decided to make the trip without her partner."

Bridgette motioned Hughey and Sutton to the door. "We need to get moving."

Hughey looked back at Quinn and said, "What do we do about Mr. Quinn, Bridgette."

"We'll deal with him later Hughey. Right now we have to stop Andi Butler from stealing nine million dollars."

Chapter 43

The three hurried out of the house to head back to the truck. As they strode up Quinn's driveway, Sutton stopped mid-step and held up his hand. "How is she planning on getting to Harmer Ridge? There's no way that Mazda will make the trip in these conditions."

Bridgette asked, "How long would it take to walk from here?"

"Hours, even if you cut through the forest. But it's risky. You could easily fall and break a leg."

Bridgette bit on her bottom lip as she tried to think what she would do if she was Butler. "Quinn hasn't been dead that long. Maybe she's organizing for the helicopter to pick up from a closer location?"

Sutton shook his head. "I'm not aware of any location closer than Harmer Ridge that is flat enough for a helicopter to land on, particularly in these conditions."

Bridgette thought for a moment. "Butler doesn't strike me as the kind of person who wouldn't have a plan..."

Turning to look back towards the garage she continued, "Quinn has a four-wheel-drive, which she didn't take—"

Sutton frowned. "We're overlooking something."

Bridgette nodded. "We need to re-check the garage."

Bridgette rushed over to the side access door and tried opening it, but it was locked. While Sutton and Hughey looked around for something to break the door down with, Bridgette peered in through the window again. She looked beyond the four-wheel drive and Quinn's other vehicles at a workshop that had been built into the rear left corner of the building. She wondered if it had its own external access door and headed around the back of the building to check. She only got as far as the rear corner of the building before she had her answer. She'd never been on a snowmobile but had done enough skiing to recognize the unmistakable tracks they left in the snow.

Sutton came and stood alongside her and said flatly, "Well, there's your answer."

As she traced the track marks through the trees across a shallow valley, Bridgette asked, "How long would it take to get from here to the ridge on a snowmobile?"

Sutton squinted and pointed to an area on the opposite side of the valley. "She's going up through the forest which is the shortest route. My guess is about twenty minutes."

Bridgette had seen enough. "We need to keep moving."

* * *

Bridgette found the next ten minutes the most frustrating of her life. After three failed attempts at calling the charter company, she left a message requesting someone call her back immediately. Without taking his eyes off the road, Sutton said, "Maybe we should call Sanbury Police?"

Bridgette sighed. "The first thing Payne will do is tell us to stop interfering in official police business. By the time they get anyone up here, Butler will be long gone."

Sutton mumbled, "You're right," and returned his focus to the driving.

After two more minutes, he looked at his watch and shook his head in frustration. "Sorry, Bridgette, but we're not going to make it. The helicopter is due to land in less than five minutes and at this pace, I'm still a good ten minutes away."

Bridgette looked up at the road ahead. She noticed it seemed to veer hard right and head further into the forest. "Does this road lead directly to the ridge, Jack?"

"No, it circles back around to keep the incline from being too steep. We're actually only about four hundred yards from the top in a straight line."

Bridgette shouted over the engine, "Stop the truck."

"Here?"

Bridgette responded as she motioned Hughey to let her out, "I'm going to run up through the tree line—"

"The snow is very heavy Bridgette—"

"We have no choice, Jack."

Hughey let Bridgette out of the truck and said, "I'm coming with you."

Bridgette frowned. "This could get dangerous Hughey. She's got a gun remember. You'd be better off staying with Jack and the truck."

Hughey shook his head and declared, "Jack doesn't need me in the truck."

Bridgette didn't have time to argue. "Alright, but you need to keep up and do exactly as I say, okay?"

As Hughey nodded in agreement, Bridgette turned to Sutton and said, "We'll wait for you at the top Jack."

After slamming the truck door shut, Bridgette said over her shoulder, "Follow me, Hughey," and bolted across the road.

Chapter 44

Bridgette kept a watchful eye out for the helicopter as they sprinted up through the forest. She was surprised at Hughey's stamina as he managed to keep pace with her through the heavy snow.

When the top of the ridgeline was in sight, Bridgette motioned Hughey to slow to a walk. After getting her breath back, she whispered, "We're not going to show ourselves just yet Hughey. Let's stay back in the trees and watch."

They crept to the edge of the clearing and hid behind a large fir tree to wait. Bridgette could understand why Harmer Ridge had been chosen as the pickup point. The area was almost perfectly flat and clear of trees. She estimated the clearing was about eighty yards across and, with little or no prevailing wind, she figured it was an ideal place to land a helicopter. Bridgette pulled her Glock from an interior pocket of her coat and moved as far forward as she dared.

She couldn't see any sign of Butler as she scanned the area and whispered, "I can't see her yet Hughey, but that doesn't mean she isn't here. Can you keep a lookout behind us, just in case?"

Hughey whispered, "Yes," in a voice that was louder than Bridgette would have liked. The two stood motionless, almost back to back and waited. At first, she couldn't hear anything except the low-pitched whine of Sutton's truck in the distance as it continued its climb to the summit. After almost two minutes, she detected a second sound, a low rhythmic thud, faint at first, but growing louder with each passing second.

Without taking her eyes of the clearing, she whispered, "The helicopter's almost here Hughey. You see anything below?"

Hughey whispered, "I don't see anything Bridgette. It's all quiet."

They waited another thirty seconds for the helicopter to appear. The blue and white aircraft did an overhead pass about fifty feet above the tree line. She watched as it circled the ridge before hovering for a moment and then starting its descent. It was larger than Bridgette had expected with twin doors on each side. Bridgette took a deep breath and re-gripped her gun as the helicopter settled on the snow. She began to re-scan the perimeter of the clearing and only had to wait thirty seconds for Butler to appear. From the opposite side of the clearing, the snowmobile burst from the tree line and accelerated towards the helicopter. Bridgette sprinted into the clearing to get a clear line of site on the snowmobile as it raced across the open ground. Before she had raised her Glock into the firing position, Butler raised a pistol and fired three shots at her in quick succession as she continued to speed across the open ground. Bridgette heard a groan behind her and realized Hughey had followed her and been hit.

Yelling, "Get down Hughey," Bridgette dove to the ground and squeezed off two rounds in Butler's direction. She was relieved to see the helicopter lift off the snow without its passenger and ducked down again as Butler fired another shot in her general direction.

Bridgette debated returning fire as the departing aircraft banked away to its left but decided it wasn't worth the risk knowing Hughey might be hit again if Butler fired back. She watched as Butler gunned the engine and the snowmobile accelerated away toward the eastern side of the clearing.

Lowering her gun, Bridgette turned and looked anxiously back at her companion who was lying on the ground clutching his left shoulder.

As he tried to sit up, Bridgette said, "Hughey, you should be lying still."

Hughey winced and responded, "Sorry I got shot Bridgette," as he willed himself into a sitting position.

"We need to get you to a hospital, Hughey."

Hughey protested, "But she's getting away Bridgette.'

Bridgette responded, "She won't get far on a snowmobile," and motioned Hughey to move his hand away from his shoulder. "I need to see how bad this is Hughey."

Hughey said, "It's not bad," as he dropped his hand, but the look of agony on his face told her a different story.

Bridgette moved closer to examine the wound. The bullet had left a large tear across the left shoulder of Hughey's jacket. The sleeve of his garment was covered in blood, but it was impossible to tell how bad the damage was.

Bridgette could see beads of sweat on Hughey's forehead and said, "I can't see much because of your jacket Hughey. How bad is the pain?"

"It stings a little..."

"Do you feel like you're going to pass out?"

Hughey shook his head. Bridgette studied him for a moment looking for the tell-tale signs he was going into shock. Knowing time could be critical she said, "I know this will hurt Hughey, but I need to unzip your jacket to get a better look at the wound. Okay?"

Hughey nodded and said, "I can't move my arm."

Bridgette lowered the zipper and gently moved the garment off his shoulder to expose the injury. Hughey winced but didn't complain. Bridgette moved around to his left side to get a better look. She couldn't see much more than a ragged tear in his blood-soaked flannel shirt and gently pulled the garment away from his skin. As gently as she could, she ripped at the tear in his shirt until she could see the full extent of the wound. Bridgette let out a long breath as she examined Hughey's injury. The bullet had smashed through his collar bone and had left a huge gash in the top of his shoulder. She could see bone fragment protruding through the exposed wound and knew he would require surgery. The wound was still bleeding, but she didn't think he'd been hit in an artery.

Bridgette said, "The bullet has hit your collarbone and you've lost some blood Hughey, but I think a doctor will be able to patch you up."

Hughey replied, "You need to go after her Bridgette, or she'll get away."

"She won't get far Hughey."

"Even if she gets to the highway?"

"What highway?"

Wincing in pain, Hughey pointed to another ridgeline to the east with his good arm. "She's headed for Easts Ridge. If you walk over the top, you can see down to the highway that goes to Bolton. Can she escape if she gets that far?"

Bridgette looked across the heavily forested valley to the next ridgeline. She estimated its peak was close to half a mile from their current position across rugged terrain. She doubted Butler would get that far on a snowmobile but knew she could probably hike the rest of the way on foot. Bridgette looked back toward the road that led up to the ridge. She could now see Sutton's truck plowing through snow as it inched its way along the road towards the clearing. She estimated it would be several more minutes before he arrived.

Hughey said, "You gotta go after her Bridgette. I'll be okay — Jack will be here soon."

Bridgette weighed up what to do. She didn't think Hughey's condition was life threatening and knew if Butler made it to the highway, she would disappear forever.

Bridgette studied Hughey for a moment and then squeezed his good shoulder. "Tell Jack to call Sanbury Police and take you to the hospital, okay?"

Hughey nodded and said, "What about you Bridgette? You shouldn't be going after her on your own."

Bridgette gave a reassuring smile and said, "I'll be okay Hughey," as she got to her feet."

After pocketing her Glock, she took a deep breath and headed across the clearing at a jog. She had no real plan but decided following the tracks left by Butler's snowmobile was a good place to start.

Chapter 45

The distinctive markings left by the snowmobile made it easy enough for Bridgette to follow Butler's trail. After twenty minutes of hiking through thick snow, Bridgette was fighting cold and fatigue. The temperature was close to freezing, but she refused to slow down knowing every second counted.

Willing herself to keep moving, she frowned as she realized the forest had become quiet. The distinctive rumble of the snowmobile moving through the lower section of the forest had disappeared. She wondered if Butler had abandoned the vehicle and was now on foot?

Knowing her chances of catching her might have improved, she kept moving as more snow began to fall. The heavy conditions made her progress slow, and she hoped Butler was having similar problems. She continued following the trail until she heard the sound of running water. She couldn't see more than fifty feet in front of her because of the forest cover but sensed she was getting close to the bottom of the valley.

After rounding a bend in the trail, Bridgette halted and pulled her Glock from her coat pocket. Ahead and obscured by trees, she stared at the unmistakable rear flap and reflector of the snowmobile. Bridgette knew Butler would shoot her if she had the chance and moved off the path. She stood still for over a minute listening for any sign she might be walking into a trap.

Conscious that Butler could also be getting further away, Bridgette crept towards the snowmobile using the trees for cover. When she was within ten feet of the vehicle, she noticed a single set of footprints leading away from the snowmobile and realized Butler was still on the move. She quickened her pace again and was thankful that the heavy snow cover made Butler's footsteps easy to follow. After another five minutes, the forest lightened, and she realized she was coming to a clearing. She stopped again to listen to the sound of the river and get her bearings. The forest ended about twenty feet in front of her and gave way to a large snow-covered rock ledge which she presumed led down to the river at the bottom of the valley. Bridgette knew as soon as she stepped from the cover of the forest she would be exposed again. She crept forward keeping a wary lookout for any sign of Butler until she got to the edge. Bridgette looked down at the jumbled footprints in the snow in front of her. She pictured Butler looking to her left and then to her right before deciding to head right and follow the river upstream.

Bridgette turned and followed the footprints. She noticed they veered towards the edge of the embankment before moving away again. She realized Butler was looking for potential crossing places as she stopped to peer over the edge. The river was about forty feet below and down an almost vertical drop. She estimated the river was about fifteen feet wide but impossible to get to or cross at this location. Bridgette gazed at the mountainside across the river that led up to Easts Ridge. The forest cover was thick, and she knew hiking to the top wouldn't be easy. Buoyed by the knowledge that Butler still had a long way to go, Bridgette quickened her pace.

She hiked on for another five minutes ignoring the conditions as her fingers began to stiffen. She kept her Glock at the ready and continued to scan the trail ahead for any sign of an ambush. After coming over a gentle rise in the embankment, Bridgette noticed the footprints had turned into an odd mix of shallow indents in the snow. She was puzzled by this until she slipped on snow that had turned to ice. As she regained her balance, she realized Butler must have lost her footing and tumbled down the slope before stopping at the bottom.

Bridgette noticed the sound of the river had turned into a roar and peered over the edge again. The river had narrowed and now contained jagged rocks making her think the water would soon turn into rapids further upstream. Sensing she was closing in on Butler, Bridgette pressed on, following the river as it rose further into the mountains. After coming around another bend, Bridgette was surprised by the view that confronted her. The river had turned into fast running rapids as she expected. She followed the river with her eye as it rose sharply into the mountains. Under different circumstances, she could have sat for hours marveling at the power of nature as the rushing water fought its way around and over jagged rocks in its quest to find the ocean. But today was different and Bridgette ignored the spectacle of nature and focused on something manmade in front of her.

She had only seen one other rope bridge in her life and that was at a holiday camp in junior high school. Bridgette remembered how her aunt had forbidden her from going anywhere near the apparatus, claiming it was too dangerous. She knew her aunt wouldn't have approved of this structure either as she hurried forward to take a closer look. The bridge comprised four main ropes slung from one side of the river to the other to support a single walking plank. The top ropes on each side were joined to the bottom ropes at regular intervals by short suspender cables also made of rope. The layer of snow covering everything made it difficult for Bridgette to tell its condition, but she thought it looked flimsy. She grabbed the top left rope of the structure and pulled back on it. She frowned as the whole structure swayed from left to right. She wasn't afraid of heights, but as she looked down at the rushing river below, she knew crossing the sixty-foot span wouldn't be easy.

Bridgette stared down at Butler's footprints and followed the track they had left in the snow as she had crossed the bridge. She looked up at the snow-covered area of open ground on the other side of the river and followed the line of footprints until they disappeared up into the forest. Pocketing her Glock, Bridgette gripped both top ropes to steady herself and tried not to think about what might be waiting for her on the other side as she stepped onto the bridge.

Chapter 46

Bridgette took a few tentative steps forward on the bridge as she held on tight to the guide ropes. She found the swaying sensation disconcerting at first but soon got into a rhythm. She tried not to look down knowing if she fell, the rocks fifty feet below would bring an abrupt and grisly end to her life. Instead, she kept her eyes focused on the forest opposite looking for any sign that Butler was lying in wait for her. She estimated there were forty yards of open country between the end of the bridge and the forest. She knew she was vulnerable while she was on the bridge but consoled herself that Butler would need to be an excellent marksman to shoot accurately with a pistol from that distance.

As the snow continued to fall, she wondered how long ago Butler had crossed the bridge? The footprints looked fresh, but it was hard to tell. As she approached the halfway point, she felt the bridge sway as a gust of wind came up. Bridgette bent forward to shield herself from the cold and braced with both hands until the worst of the gust passed by. Keeping a firm grip on the guy ropes, Bridgette frowned as she studied Butler's footprints again. She noticed they were slightly larger on the bridge and not as pronounced as they had been on the trail leading up to the crossing. At first, she thought it was because of the unsteady bridge platform but then she realized something was wrong. Bridgette looked up and studied the footprints Butler had left as she made her way off the bridge and up into the forest and realized she had made a grave mistake. She pictured Butler walking backward from the forest edge, carefully and patiently retracing her steps as she backtracked across the bridge and quietly cursed herself for not realizing sooner.

Bridgette knew Butler could now be anywhere behind her but decided her best option was to continue forward as if she hadn't noticed.

She only managed one more step before a voice behind her said in a casual tone, "Trying to escape in heavy snow is such a bitch. You leave a trail that even a blind man can follow..."

Bridgette bit down on her bottom lip as she realized she'd been played.

Butler demanded, "Turn around."

Bridgette thought about the Glock in her coat pocket but realized Butler could fire two or three rounds before she got a hand to the weapon. With no other choice, Bridgette obeyed the command and turned around to face Butler and a gun pointed at her chest.

Butler moved forward and put her left foot up on the bridge plank. With a smug grin, she said, "I didn't think I could outrun you, but I thought maybe I could outsmart you. When I got to the bridge, I knew I had an opportunity. The ruse only needed to work long enough to get you out in the middle—"

Butler paused as Bridgette stole a glance at the river below and then laughed. "Go ahead, you'll save me a bullet."

Bridgette tried to remain calm as she felt adrenaline pumping through her body. She had never felt more vulnerable in her life but tried not to show fear as she held Butler's stare. "Was it all worth it?"

With an amused look, Butler pulled the hammer back to cock her pistol but said nothing.

Bridgette continued, "Killing and stealing from honest people in a small community?"

With a smug smile, Butler replied, "I'm nine million dollars richer than I was yesterday. Of course it was worth it."

Bridgette knew she was only delaying the inevitable but continued the conversation anyway. "Why did you kill Quinn?"

"I'm not interested in your questions."

"I know Quinn brought you in when the deal with the Chinese went south. You were his partner — that much I've figured out from Amorand."

Butler ignored her and put her right foot up on the bridge as well to move closer. Now less than fifteen feet away from the barrel of the gun, Bridgette held her nerve as she continued. "Wasn't your cut big enough?"

Butler laughed again. "I got in before he did and turned two million into nine million in the process."

They stared at each other for several seconds before Butler asked, "How did you get onto us?"

"Tyson had a hidden file. There were some geological reports and a lot of photographs, including one of Snowbridge. It took me a couple of days to figure out he was investigating more than just Olivia Hodder's disappearance."

Butler nodded. "You're smart, but as it turns out, too smart for your own good."

"I'm not sure when he discovered Snowbridge wasn't viable, but I know either you or Quinn had him killed."

Butler held the gun steady as she responded, "Tyson's big mistake was poking around Snowbridge. We weren't sure if he knew it was being built on a fault line, but we weren't prepared to take the risk of him going public. So, Quinn had him taken care of."

"So it was Quinn's idea to scam all the locals then?"

Butler shook her head. "He was in a full-scale panic when the Chinese found out about the fault line and pulled out. He was afraid of lawsuits from the local investors. It was me who told him not to tell anyone and keep going as if nothing was wrong."

"So this was all your masquerade?"

"We kept the surveys quiet, poured a few concrete blocks and had some steel delivered. We even hired two Chinese actors towards the end to make it look like it was all business as usual."

Butler took another step forward and said, "The money kept rolling in, but that wasn't going to continue forever. Now it's time to disappear..."

Bridgette could sense Butler was ready to pull the trigger. Desperate to delay it as long as possible, she said, "It was you in the forest wasn't it?"

Butler gave a barely perceptible nod. "How did you know?"

"You don't have a man's height or build. Even in snow gear that was obvious. I was fairly sure whoever it was that tried to shoot me was either a teenage boy or a woman."

"I thought you were as good as dead when you fell into that gorge... I underestimated you."

"I was lucky I had friends looking out for me."

Butler's features hardened as she said, "It looks like your luck ran out," and pulled the trigger.

Chapter 47

Bridgette closed her eyes as Butler pulled the trigger. It was an automatic response — the body recoiling as it attempted to block out the pain and horror of death as it took place. The sound of the gun discharging and the sensation of a bullet ripping through her chest didn't follow as she expected. Instead, all she heard was the soft click of Butler's weapon as it misfired. She understood enough about guns from her police training to know they weren't one hundred percent reliable. Most were mechanical failures brought on by a lack of cleaning, but every so often it was something else. If she'd had time to think about it, she would have guessed Butler's fall in the snow had clogged the firing mechanism. But as the soft click registered in her brain, Bridgette didn't have time to think and instinctively rushed towards Butler as she dared hope of survival.

The unstable platform and snow made it impossible for her to cover the distance before her adversary pulled the trigger a second time. This time the gun discharged, but the shot flew high as Butler had to grab the rope with one hand to stop herself from falling.

Bridgette closed the gap before Butler could fire a third time and grabbed at the weapon. As they became locked in a struggle, Butler pushed back and Bridgette found herself falling backward on the slippery bridge surface. She understood her survival depended on keeping Butler close and grabbed at her coat. The two crashed onto the bridge deck, with Butler landing on top. Bridgette felt the bridge tremor as they wrestled for control of the gun. Desperate to keep the upper hand, Butler fired a third round, but her hand got caught in a rope suspender as she drew the weapon around toward Bridgette's face and the shot went wide.

Bridgette kept her focus on the gun as she reached up and grabbed Butler's wrist. In response, Butler bit down hard on her hand and drew blood. Ignoring the pain through gritted teeth, Bridgette hung on as the two writhed on the platform looking to gain control. Butler was stronger than Bridgette expected but the long hours she'd spent in the gym had helped develop her muscle strength. Bridgette started to gain control and gradually forced the gun further away from her body. Butler wasn't ready to give in and brought her knee up hard into Bridgette's groin as the gun fired a fourth time.

The pain from the blow to her lower body barely registered as Bridgette felt the bridge drop. At first, it was just a couple of inches, but then she heard one of the top guide ropes snap somewhere behind her head. The bridge instantly lost its form and Bridgette scrambled to grab a hold of one of the remaining suspension ropes as the planks around her began sliding out of their rope harnesses and crashing to the rocks below. Bridgette lost sight of Butler as she focused on hooking her right arm around one of the suspension cables. She detected movement to her right and turned to see Butler struggling to grip the top rope with both hands. Bridgette couldn't see any sign of the gun and presumed Butler had chosen survival over shooting her. She looked back towards the edge of the bridge. She figured it was only fifteen feet, but it may as well have been a mile as she realized the remaining bridge ropes were sagging further. Butler locked eyes with her and said, "This isn't over," and began crab-walking out across the knotted ropes towards the middle of what was left of the bridge.

Bridgette looked beyond Butler at the ropes in the middle section of the platform. No longer covered in snow, Bridgette stared in horror as they unraveled before her eyes.

She screamed, "It's not going to hold — you're going to kill us both," but Butler ignored her and kept moving.

Time seemed to slow for Bridgette as the ropes continue to unravel before they snapped and separated. She doubled her grip on the rope as the remnants of the bridge swung back towards the western face of the river bank. She had time to brace and groaned in agony as her body slammed into the rock wall. Winded and unable to breathe, she willed herself to hang on as she swayed forty feet above the river. Bridgette felt her hands slipping again and blindly searched for a foothold. She moved her foot to the left and right and whispered a quick prayer of thanks as she found a solid suspension link she could use as a foothold. Still barely able to comprehend she was alive; Bridgette threw her head back and groaned as her body was racked by a new source of pain. Looking down, she saw a knife embedded deep into her right thigh and Butler inching her way up the remains of the bridge towards her.

She stared in disbelief as Butler continued her climb. Doing her best to block out the pain, Bridgette tried to scramble further up the rock face, but she had trouble finding footholds. Realizing she couldn't get away, Bridgette looked down again and let out a cry of anguish as Butler removed the knife from her thigh to stab her again. She lashed out at Butler with her left leg but only managed a glancing blow. With her right leg rapidly turning red, she knew she would soon be too weak to fight and needed to finish it now.

Bridgette braced for Butler to swing the knife again. She waited until Butler began her thrust and swung her left foot across her body with all the strength she could muster. Her kick was far from precise, but her heavy snow boot connected with Butler's temple. She watched as Butler's eyes rolled into the back of her head. Bridgette had been concussed several times and knew the blackout that followed often only lasted a few seconds. She watched as Butler's body went limp before she let go of the rope. Bridgette knew Butler would never wake up — at least not in this life as she fell towards the river below. Bridgette chose not to look and closed her eyes as she heard Butler's life come to an end as her body smashed onto the rocks below. Keeping a firm grip on the rope, she breathed again, thankful to still be alive. She had no remorse over what had happened to Butler — the world was now a better place. The water continued to roar below her as if what had happened had just been a brief interruption to the natural order. Bridgette kept her eyes closed as the pain in her leg returned — sharp and all consuming. As she clung to the rope, with the cold of the rock wall pressed up against her face, she wondered how long she could hold on for.

Chapter 48

Bridgette spent twenty minutes inching her way back up the remnants of the rope bridge towards the top of the rock face. The freezing conditions had numbed her body to a point where she barely felt the stab wound in her thigh anymore. She shivered as she stared up at the remaining two and a half feet that separated her from freedom. Now overcome by fatigue, it took all her energy just to hold on. She was agonizingly close, but with no footholds any higher up the slippery rock face, she knew she couldn't go any further.

Bridgette noticed the snow had started falling again — light, soft and peaceful. There was no point in calling out — she knew no one would come. She wondered why she wasn't angrier or more disappointed by her predicament as she waited to die? Perhaps it was the freezing conditions and exhaustion that had robbed her body, not just of her energy, but her will to live as well? She closed her eyes and allowed her mind to drift as she waited for her body to give in and let go.

She thought about her week in Sanbury. It had only been her second case, but at least she had discovered who was behind John Tyson's disappearance. She hoped they would recover the money and wondered if Jack had gotten Hughey to the hospital yet?

She wondered what they would think when they found her near

Butler's body. There would be no evidence she had come so close to surviving.

As her mind drifted, she was seven years old again. Her body floated and soon began to soar. She was no longer cold and pleased to see her mother and father again. She tried to call out to her mother, but she didn't seem to hear her. A male voice called her name, but it wasn't her father. Puzzled, she stared at her father as she heard her name again.

"Bridgette."

Bridgette opened her eyes. It took her a moment to realize she was still clinging to the rope.

As the cold overwhelmed her, she heard the voice again, "Bridgette."

Bridgette looked up and blinked snow from her eyes as the concerned face of Hughey Warren stared down at her from the top of the river bank.

Confused and weak, she wondered if she was still dreaming? "Hughey?"

"Yeah, it's me."

"Why aren't you in the hospital?"

"Jack's truck broke down when he came to pick me up... so I followed the tracks and came looking for you. Jack wasn't very happy."

"But your shoulder."

"I still got one good arm."

"But your collarbone is shattered. You should be going to the hospital."

"You're my friend Bridgette. I was never going to leave you behind."

Bridgette thought for a moment. It was nice that Hughey had come to find her, but she didn't want him to see her die.

As she pondered ways she could get him to leave, Hughey lay down on his stomach. Despite the cold, Bridgette noticed his forehead beaded with sweat. His face contorted in pain as he shuffled towards the edge and she knew he must be in agony.

"What are you doing Hughey?"

Hughey reached his good arm over the side and said, "I'm going to haul you up."

"No, Hughey. I could drag you over the edge."

Hughey shook his head. "I weigh more than twice what you do Bridgette. You won't pull me off, I promise."

"Shouldn't we wait for Jack?"

"He can't move too good in the cold. He's called the police and is waiting with the truck."

Hughey reached down his hand as far as he could and said, "You take my hand and I'll haul you up."

In a voice barely above a whisper, Bridgette responded, "I don't have the strength, Hughey. I've been stabbed in the thigh... I've lost a lot of blood."

"Just let me grab your hand and I'll do the rest, Bridgette."

"But Hughey, you've been shot."

Hughey held Bridgette's stare and said, "The police won't be here for hours. You gotta trust me."

Bridgette sighed as she looked down at the river again. It wasn't the way she wanted to die. She admired Hughey's courage but didn't think he would be strong enough to pull her up with his injuries. She looked up again and decided it was better to die trying rather than just give in. She whispered, "Thank you, Hughey," as she reached up her right hand.

Hughey gripped her firmly by the wrist and said, "Grab my arm with your other hand as well and then I'll pull you up, okay?"

Bridgette took a deep breath and wondered what she would

feel when she fell.

As if he was reading her mind, he said in a soft voice, "I can do this Bridgette."

Bridgette nodded once. "I trust you, Hughey," and reached up her left hand.

She grabbed hold of Hughey's arm and focused all her attention on him. She nodded once as if to say she was ready and held on tight as Hughey began to lift her. Hughey's grip remained strong as his face contorted in pain. She felt herself moving, just a couple of inches at first. Hughey maintained eye contact with her and continued to lift her until her upper body rested on the snow-covered embankment. Bridgette marveled at his strength despite the seriousness of his injuries. Without releasing his grip or taking his eyes off her, Hughey rested for a moment as sweat poured off his face. Easing back from the edge, Hughey got up on his knees and pulled again until Bridgette was clear of the rock face. Bridgette could barely believe what was happening as Hughey got to his feet and dragged her backward until she was safely away from the edge.

Still shivering with cold, Bridgette rolled onto her back and whispered, "Thank you, Hughey. You saved my life," as he collapsed beside her.

As she tried to make sense of how Hughey had managed to rescue her, she heard his labored breathing and asked, "Are you okay?"

Hughey managed, "I'll be fine when the pain settles."

Bridgette reached out and took hold of Hughey's hand as she gazed up into the gray sky. His grip felt warm and reassuring. Too exhausted to move any further, she lay still and listened to the sound of the river as the snow continued to fall lightly on her face.

Epilogue

Almost six weeks on from the incident on the rope bridge, Bridgette still walked with a limp. The knife wound had required surgery to repair and even though the doctors were pleased with her progress, they cautioned her to be patient with her recovery. As she gingerly climbed the steps to the Sanbury Courthouse, she knew her leg was getting stronger and longed for the day she could return to full workouts in the gym.

Pushing through the front doors, Bridgette noticed a free-standing sign that read 'Court in Session' in the middle of the foyer. After stopping for a moment to get her bearings, she moved towards a large, heavy wooden door that had the words 'Courtroom 1' stenciled in large gold letters across its upper panel. She gently opened the door expecting the court proceedings to be in full swing. To her surprise, the judge was not sitting at the bench, and the gathering turned as one to see who had just entered. Bridgette stood at the back of the courtroom for a moment, ignoring the stares as she debated where to sit. She was surprised at how many people had come to the hearing and was relieved when she saw Jack Sutton wave at her to come and join him.

Relieved to see a familiar face, Bridgette moved to her left and joined Sutton in the pew-like bench at the end of the second last row in the gallery.

Bridgette whispered, "Sorry I'm late Jack. There was a pileup on the Western Freeway."

Sutton whispered back, "No problem Bridgette, you haven't missed much."

Bridgette looked through the crowd of observers and was able to make out the large figure of Hughey Warren, sitting alone at the defense table. With his back to her, Bridgette couldn't see his face and whispered to Sutton, "How's Hughey holding up?"

"He's nervous, but that's to be expected I guess."

They sat in silence for a moment before Bridgette asked, "So, where's the judge?"

"He's out back with Hughey's lawyer and the lawyer representing the state."

"So why are they meeting out back? I thought this hearing was just a formality?"

Before Sutton could answer, the bailiff called them all to rise as the judge, followed by Dan Strickland and the state's lawyer emerged from the judges' chambers.

While they waited for the judge to settle in, Sutton nudged Bridgette and whispered, "Your friend Corey Payne seems pleased to see you back here."

Bridgette glanced across the aisle at Chief Payne who was seated two rows in front of her. He glared at her for several seconds, but Bridgette refused to make eye contact.

She whispered to Sutton as they were asked to resume their seats, "Does the man ever smile?"

Sutton replied under his breath, "Not recently."

They all watched as the elderly gray-haired judge put on a pair of reading glasses and picked up a document. He cleared his throat and said, "Ladies and gentlemen, as you are aware, today's hearing was called to hear final submissions in an appeal lodged by lawyers for the defendant, Mister Hughey Warren, in relation to his conviction for the murder of Olivia Hodder. I have received submissions from the defense and the state and make the following judgement."

Bridgette held her breath as the judge paused to make several notes. She knew the evidence supporting Hughey's innocence was now overwhelming, but it never paid to second-guess what a court or a judge would do.

The judge cleared his throat again and continued. "Firstly, based on compelling new evidence provided by the defense team, which has not been challenged by the state, the court rules the charge of murder in the first degree against Mister Warren be dismissed."

The judge paused a moment as a series of hushed exchanges took place in the gallery.

When the noise had died down, the judge fixed his gaze on Hughey and continued. "Mister Warren, the court apologizes to you on behalf of the state for your incarceration. I have spoken at length with your legal representative and in addition to the expunging of your criminal record, a further hearing will be established to determine appropriate compensation."

Bridgette let out a long breath and relaxed a little as she watched Dan Strickland whisper in Hughey's ear. She smiled as she saw Hughey nod his head vigorously. He may not have understood what the judge was saying, but she had no doubt, Strickland had just told him he was now a free man.

Bridgette returned her concentration to the judge's remarks as he said, "Secondly, and as I'm sure you are all aware from recent media coverage, Sanbury Police have discovered crucial DNA evidence in the home of Mister Roman Quinn linking him to Miss Hodder's murder. This evidence will be presented at a formal hearing to be held in several weeks in relation to the recovery of Miss Hodder's remains."

As the judge began to explain this in more detail, Sutton whispered, "What does he mean by 'charges in absentia?', Bridgette?"

Bridgette responded, "They normally don't prosecute people for murder if they die before the case can be brought to trial. If none of Quinn's family object, the Hodder hearing may record Quinn as the likely perpetrator and close the case."

"After what Quinn tried to do to this town, I can't see anyone objecting."

They politely listened for another five minutes until the judge closed his summation and rapped his gavel to declare the hearing closed.

The gallery broke into a series of low and muffled conversations as people began to huddle to discuss the outcome. Bridgette smiled as she saw people coming forward to congratulate Strickland and Hughey on the win. Sutton leaned across and said to Bridgette, "Let's get out of here. I told Hughey we'd meet him out front."

Bridgette answered, "Good idea," and followed Sutton outside.

When they had walked a few feet clear of the front door, they stopped to wait. To Bridgette's surprise, Sutton gave her a bear hug and said, "It's good to see you again Bridgette. How are you doing?"

She smiled as she responded, "I'm doing okay Jack. I'm back at work and my leg is healing, so I don't have much to complain about."

Sutton nodded and with a contented smile responded, "I'm pleased for you Bridgette. This whole town owes you a huge debt of gratitude for what you did."

Bridgette responded, "I was just doing my job, Jack," as she buttoned up her coat to keep out the cold.

Sutton shook his head. "What you did was way more than your job Bridgette. You helped us get all our money back, and without you, Hughey would be back in jail."

Bridgette played down the compliment as she responded, "Finding some of Olivia's bones and Quinn's watch in that box certainly helped us, Jack."

"That and the rifle they found in the roof space of his garage. It makes you wonder why someone as sharp as Quinn would hold onto a weapon that he'd used to kill people with?"

"Quinn was planning on leaving the country on the day he was murdered. When you plan on starting a whole new life with a new identity, the evidence you leave behind becomes less important."

They were silent for a moment as they watched Payne and several of his staff walk out of the courthouse. Payne ignored Bridgette and Sutton and continued talking to his officers as they walked down the courthouse steps.

Sutton shook his head in disgust at the slight and asked Bridgette, "Is Payne going to interview you again?"

"No. Ballistics confirmed Quinn's rifle as the murder weapon used to kill Mitch Conden as well as John Tyson, so I'm not required anymore."

Sutton responded, "That rifle was Hughey's lifeline too."

Bridgette nodded as she thought back to the night she had spent in the cave with Olivia Hodder's body. The recovery team found a bullet amongst her remains that matched Quinn's weapon. It had given Strickland all the evidence he needed to seek a full acquittal.

Sutton continued, "What I want to know is, how did you know where John was buried?"

Bridgette smiled. "It was an educated guess, Jack."

Sutton scratched his chin, "That was some guess."

"The night of the storm, when I was staying at your house, I got to thinking about the Snowbridge construction site. When I visited the site, the security guard told me one of the concrete slabs, a small one, had only been recently poured. I wondered why they would send a team back for such a small job when everything was closing down until spring. It made sense when I wondered if Quinn had buried a body there that he wanted to make sure was never discovered."

With a bemused look, Sutton replied, "Well, it was a good guess, if that's what it was."

Bridgette asked, "What will become of the Snowbridge site now?"

"I'm not sure. The site has been resurveyed and most of it can't be built on. I guess they'll remove everything once they figure out who's going to pay for it."

Bridgette nodded. "It makes you wonder how the construction ever got that far in the first place."

"Quinn owned this town and a lot of the people in it. Bribes and well-placed threats meant he could do pretty much whatever he wanted. We're certainly better off without him."

Bridgette was about to respond but paused as Dan Strickland appeared at the front door with his client. Hughey looked apprehensive as a throng of reporters rushed forward and stayed behind Strickland with his head down.

Sutton and Bridgette watched as Strickland gave a brief statement about justice finally being served and that he would be seeking compensation from the state for his client. He closed by thanking a few of his support team for all their help and made special mention of a 'Detective Cash' from Hartbourne Metro for breaking the case open. Bridgette was relieved that Strickland didn't point her out in the crowd — the last thing she wanted today was to be hounded by TV crews for an interview.

They watched on as Strickland and Hughey accepted a few congratulations from well-wishers. Bridgette asked, "So how did the town respond when they heard Hughey was going free Jack?"

"They've all got right behind him when they realized he was innocent. He's even going to get his old job back at the feed store when he gets his arm out of the sling."

Bridgette smiled as she watched Hughey receiving handshakes of congratulation from some of the locals and said, "It's nice to know he's being accepted back into his community." She thought for a moment and then added, "He probably won't need to worry about working once his payout from the state comes through."

"Probably not, but I'm sure he will. Hughey likes to fit in and the job will give him a purpose."

Bridgette nodded and said, "It's a shame about his mother."

"Yeah, Della was a wonderful lady. She lived long enough to hear her son was going to walk free — so that's something I guess."

"And I hear Olivia's mother has made a full apology to Hughey?"

"More than that, she sat with Hughey during his mother's funeral service."

They were silent again as Strickland and his client walked their way.

Hughey couldn't contain himself and rushed forward. "Hello Bridgette, I'm free."

Bridgette reached her arms around Hughey and gave him a

gentle hug. "Congratulations Hughey."

Hughey laughed and said, "Thanks."

Bridgette pointed to the sling around his neck that was supporting his arm and said, "How's the shoulder doing?"

"I got metal and screws in there now. The doctor says I'll be as good as new in a few more weeks."

Sutton stepped forward and said, "Congratulations Hughey, congratulations Dan," as he shook hands with both men.

Strickland left Sutton and Hughey to talk and idled around to Bridgette and said, "I was hoping you would be here today."

"I wouldn't have missed it, Dan. It's a great day to see Hughey finally go free."

Strickland pointed to the front door of the courthouse and said, "I've got a meeting with the judge. Are you going to be around later?"

Bridgette nodded, "I'm staying at Jack's house tonight. He's got a small celebration planned for Hughey."

Strickland smiled. "Great, I got an invitation too, so I'll see you there."

Bridgette watched as Strickland walked back into the courthouse. She was still not sure what to make of the smooth lawyer but found herself liking him.

Her thoughts were interrupted as Sutton said to her, "Can you wait here for a minute with Hughey, Bridgette?" Pointing to the courthouse he said, "I've just got to go around back and get something."

Bridgette had no idea what he was talking about and said, "Sure, Jack," as she watched him walk away.

Pleased to have some alone time with Hughey, she turned to Hughey and said, "I want to thank you again for saving my life, Hughey. I don't know how you managed it with a shattered collarbone, but I'm forever grateful."

Hughey shook his head. "If it wasn't for you coming to town, I'd still be in jail Bridgette. So it's me who should be saying thanks."

"That's what friends do Hughey, they help each other."

Hughey's eyes started to glisten. He managed to choke out, "You'll always be my friend Bridgette. I'll never forget what you done for me."

Bridgette smiled. She'd learned a lot about the true meaning of friendship since first arriving in Sanbury and had added the word 'friendship' to a small concentric ring tattoo on her inner left forearm that already bore the word family. She decided now wasn't the time or the place to show Hughey how much he'd taught her about friendship and simply responded, "Friends for life, Hughey."

Bridgette heard a car start up in the distance. Hughey began to snicker as the car revved its engine.

Bridgette frowned. "What's so funny, Hughey?"

As his face spread into a knowing grin, Hughey answered, "You'll see," as he looked toward the driveway that led from the courthouse's rear parking lot to the street.

Bridgette raised her eyebrows and half smiled as she wondered what on earth Hughey was finding so amusing.

A moment later she watched as Jack Sutton emerged from the rear car park driving a fully restored mid-blue Mustang.

Bridgette said to Hughey, "That's the car Jack had in his workshop."

Hughey nodded, "Yep. It's all fully restored and ready to go."

Bridgette mumbled "I hope he lets me have a drive of it," as she watched Sutton park the car in front of the courthouse.

Sutton got out of the car and whistled as he walked back up the steps to where they were waiting.

As he approached, he said, "What do you think of her, Bridgette?"

Bridgette smiled and nodded. "You've done a great job, Jack. It looks perfect."

Sutton grinned and held up the car's keys and said, "Well, I'm glad you like it, because it's all yours."

Bridgette raised her eyebrows and said, "What do you mean?"

Sutton pressed the keys into her hand and replied, "Just what I said — it's all yours."

Bridgette frowned. "I don't understand."

Sutton replied, "A lot of people in this town are very grateful to you Bridgette. If you hadn't come along, some people would have lost their life savings in that Snowbridge scam, me included. When people here heard I was planning on restoring the car for you, a lot of them chipped in. I had mechanics help as well and it hasn't cost me a cent, just my time."

Bridgette shook her head. "No Jack. This is too much. It was your dream to—"

Sutton cut her off. "I'm too old to be driving around in something like this and you'll look a whole lot better in it than I ever will."

Bridgette went to hand the keys back. "Thank you, Jack, but I really can't accept it — it's too much."

Sutton held his hands up and refused to take the keys. "It's too late. I've already had it registered and insured in your name, so you're stuck with it."

Hughey asked, "Can you take me for a drive in it Bridgette? Jack wouldn't let anyone else get in it before he gave it to you."

Too stunned to say anything coherent, Bridgette mumbled, "Sure," as she stared back at the car.

Sutton said to Hughey, "Let's leave Bridgette to get acquainted with her new toy. You can come with me to buy some groceries before we head back to my house for your party."

Turning to Bridgette, Sutton said, "You can drive a manual, can't you?"

Bridgette let out a short laugh and then responded, "Yes, Jack, I can drive a manual car."

She moved forward and gave Sutton a huge hug and said, "Thanks Jack. This means a lot to me."

Sutton grinned and said, "You're welcome," and then asked, "And can you drive in snow?"

Bridgette nodded, "Yes, but slowly."

Sutton and Hughey said their goodbyes to Bridgette and left her standing on the steps of the courthouse staring at her new car. She looked around and noticed a few people were looking at her with some amusement.

She decided it was time to leave and walked down the steps as casually as she could manage. Bridgette found it hard to hide her grin as she opened the door of the Mustang and sat in the driver's seat.

She sat for a moment admiring the perfect restoration Sutton and his team had done on the interior. She whispered to herself, "Bridgette, you're such a petrol head..." as she adjusted the seat and rear-view mirror.

She put the keys in the ignition and started the engine. She smiled again as the engine responded with a deep roar as she put her foot on the accelerator.

After putting the car in gear and checking in her rear-view mirror, Bridgette moved out into traffic. She hoped they wouldn't be starting Hughey's welcome home party too soon. She figured her first drive in her new car was going to take a while.

About the Author

Trevor Douglas lives in Brisbane, Australia. After a long and successful career as an IT Consultant, Trevor published his debut novel, The Catalin Code, in early 2014. Trevor is married with two adult sons and when he is not writing, enjoys bushwalking, watching AFL and discovering the best coffee shops in Brisbane with his wife. He is currently writing his sixth novel, The Cold Light of Day, the fourth book in the Bridgette Cash mystery thriller series.

You can connect with me on:

https://www.trevordouglasauthor.com

https://www.facebook.com/trevordouglasauthor

Subscribe to my newsletter:

https://www.trevordouglasauthor.com/contact

Also by Trevor Douglas

Trevor's books are available in both printed and ebook formats from all good online retailers. For further information, please visit:

https://www.trevordouglasauthor.com/books.

Cold Storm (Free Novella)

Was it murder? Suicide? Or something else?

Bridgette Cash is the main character in my 'Cold' series. Find out where it all began in this introductory novella which you can download for free in Kindle or iBooks format.

Bridgette gets more than she bargained for on her first journey to sea as a fellow Naval officer goes missing. Not satisfied with the explanation that the officer has been washed overboard, Bridgette searches for answers and quickly becomes the next target.

Cold Comfort (free eBook)

How do you catch a killer who never leaves a clue?

(Bridgette Cash Series - Book 1)

Bridgette Cash is a rookie detective working her first murder case. The circumstances surrounding the murder of a young woman lead her to believe it's the work of a serial killer, but nobody is listening. Convinced the killer will strike again shortly, can Bridgette find enough evidence to catch the killer before another young woman is murdered?

Cold Hard Cash

The bodies are just the beginning...

(Bridgette Cash Series - Book 3)

The gruesome discovery of a skeleton and a body in an underwater cave become Detective Bridgette Cash's greatest mystery when forensics reveal they have more in common than just fatal gunshot wounds to the head. As Bridgette seeks answers, she is drawn deep into an underworld from which she has little hope of escape. Alone and exposed, can she survive long enough to expose the truth and bring justice to the victims?

The Final Proposition

Three million dollars or someone's life... Which would you choose?

After being exonerated for a crime he did not commit, Adam Wells leaves prison as the only living person who knows the location of a hidden cash fortune. Desperate to help a young friend who will soon die without an expensive and risky operation, Adam must weigh up the risk as he learns the money belongs to a drug syndicate who will stop at nothing to get their money back.

The Catalin Code

What would you be prepared to risk for a friend?

Robbie Mayne returns from a business trip to Europe to find his best friend has been killed in a hit and run accident. Not convinced it was an accident, Robbie searches for the truth, triggering a deadly sequence of events that force him into hiding and a fight for his life as he pitted against a notorious organized crime figure. No longer sure who his friends are, Robbie races against the clock to find the truth before he becomes the next victim.

Made in the USA
Las Vegas, NV
02 September 2022